TILL DEATH

TILL DEATH

KELLAN McDANIEL

NEW YORK AMSTERDAM/ANTWERP LONDON

TORONTO SYDNEY/MELBOURNE NEW DELHI

An imprint of Simon & Schuster Children's Publishing Division
1230 Avenue of the Americas, New York, New York 10020
For more than 100 years, Simon & Schuster has championed authors and the stories they create. By respecting the copyright of an author's intellectual property, you enable Simon & Schuster and the author to continue publishing exceptional books for years to come. We thank you for supporting the author's copyright by purchasing an authorized edition of this book.
No amount of this book may be reproduced or stored in any format, nor may it be uploaded to any website, database, language-learning model, or other repository, retrieval, or artificial intelligence system without express permission. All rights reserved. Inquiries may be directed to Simon & Schuster, 1230 Avenue of the Americas, New York, NY 10020 or permissions@simonandschuster.com.
First MTV Books hardcover edition March 2025
© 2025 by Viacom International Inc.
Jacket illustration by Elena Masci
All rights reserved, including the right of reproduction in whole or in part in any form.
MTV Entertainment Studios, MTV Books, and all related titles, logos, and characters are trademarks of Viacom International Inc.
For information about special discounts for bulk purchases, please contact Simon & Schuster Special Sales at 1-866-506-1949 or business@simonandschuster.com.
Simon & Schuster strongly believes in freedom of expression and stands against censorship in all its forms. For more information, visit BooksBelong.com.
The Simon & Schuster Speakers Bureau can bring authors to your live event.
For more information or to book an event, contact the Simon & Schuster Speakers Bureau at 1-866-248-3049 or visit our website at www.simonspeakers.com.
Jacket design by Kerri Resnick and Heather Palisi
Interior design by Mike Rosamilia
The text of this book was set in Arno Pro.
Manufactured in the United States of America
2 4 6 8 10 9 7 5 3 1
Library of Congress Cataloging-in-Publication Data
Names: McDaniel, Kellan, author.
Title: Till death / by Kellan McDaniel.
Description: First Simon Pulse hardcover edition. | New York : MTV Books, 2025. |
Audience term: Teenagers | Audience: Ages 14 and Up. | Summary:
"Two gay men—one young, one ageless—sink their teeth into reclaiming their lives and identities from those who would silence them"—Provided by publisher.
Identifiers: LCCN 2024032559 (print) | LCCN 2024032560 (ebook) |
ISBN 9781665949071 (hardcover) | ISBN 9781665949095 (ebook)
Subjects: CYAC: Vampires—Fiction. | Gay men—Fiction. | LGBTQ+ people—Fiction. |
Romance stories. | LCGFT: Vampire fiction. | Romance fiction. | Queer fiction. | Novels.
Classification: LCC PZ7.1.M434324 Ti 2025 (print) | LCC PZ7.1.M434324 (ebook) |
DDC [Fic]—dc23
LC record available at https://lccn.loc.gov/2024032559
LC ebook record available at https://lccn.loc.gov/2024032560

To Christian

PART I

CHAPTER 1

HOWARD

In my nightmares, my locker is a fortress guarded by a lock with an impossible combination. Once I get it open—if I ever do—the inside is stuffed with books at odd angles, crushing loose papers, stained with spilled coffee. On the door, creased photos hang alongside my class schedule and a whiteboard marked with former attempts at organization.

In reality, my locker looks exactly like that. Not because I want it to, but because this hallway is an active war zone for queers, and if I spend more than five seconds trying to organize it . . . Oh, thank god. Here comes Sue. Two bodies are always better than one; plus maybe he'll remember where the hell I shoved my math homework this morning. We were literally talking about problem six together when—

"Looking for this, Howie?" A hand plunges into the depths of my locker and grabs exactly what I'm looking for. Of course.

My heart sinks as I turn to see not Sue, but the familiar blonde buzz cut and square jaw of the guy I'd call my archnemesis if I thought he considered me a rival at all. "It's—"

Christof Holley crumples my homework in his fist and shoves it against my sternum so hard, I stumble backward and bang my head on the shelf in my locker. His hand lingers, hot and meaty, against my floral shirt. Then, just as fast, it's gone and he's gone, and my math homework drops to the floor, soon to be trampled.

Sue stops beside me, scooping up my ruined homework, then hurls "Eat shit, Christof!" down the hall before offering me a less aggressive "Howard, I've told you a million times—you can't let these assholes push you around."

He offers me the wrinkled assignment, which I take before any worse can happen to it. Knowing my luck, Christof will loop back around and dump his red sports drink on it or whatever. Shouldn't have lost focus. After twelve years at this school, I should know better.

"Howard." Sue says my name loudly as he tries to get me to agree with him. In the hall. Where other people can hear.

"You're right," I mutter, and it's not like I don't agree with him, but also it wouldn't have happened if I'd stayed on task rather than let myself grow complacent with Sue's impending arrival. I should just keep everything in my backpack from now on and carry it to class. Except that bags were banned from classrooms during school hours for safety. Not my safety, that's for damn sure. I rub the back of my head, trying to fix my hair. "I should be better about it."

"You're literally the secretary of the QSA."

"Sorry, Mister President," I say, managing a smile.

I almost earn one in response, but his mouth shifts into a serious line. "I know I just told you to be confident and all," he says, "but I'm nervous about the upcoming board meeting."

"Don't be. We've built a solid list of demands, and Gray and Tiana have both emailed me, like, a dozen relevant articles and statistics to support them. I've got the raw information in a doc—I shared that with you, right?"

"All three of you shared it with me."

"Oh, sorry."

"No, it's fine. I mean, when is Tiana *not* sharing something she read? And when is Gray *not* online?"

"And when have you *not* pulled together a great speech?"

"Fair . . ." His voice hangs on indecision, which is wild, because Sue's nothing if not sure of himself.

Sue's always seemed to have that quality, even back in freshman year when we first met at the Spring Fling. Christof was making this big, public show of asking me to dance, and I, like an idiot, thought he was serious—no, I *wanted* him to be serious, because he was taller and had muscular arms and didn't have acne but did have a lacrosse haircut. He's since buzzed that off, and I've since realized he's a complete ass, but that doesn't stop either of us from remembering how he humiliated me in front of the whole school. Laughing and scoffing. Throwing a "Gross, dude!" at me as he crossed the school gym, only to call me a fag a half dozen times to his friends. My favorite way to be reminded that Wyndhurst Preparatory School is really only preparing me for how queerphobic the world is.

Sue had appeared as Christof slinked off to high-five the other kids. Literally slid up beside me, dressed in a vintage suit he'd tailored himself. I was also wearing a vintage (read: thrifted) suit, but my oma had done most of the tailoring. He was totally at home under that tacky gym mirror ball, while I was ready to disappear. Without saying a word, Sue offered me his hand, twirled me beneath the glittering lights with a smile, and then led me out to the school courtyard, where we talked until Oma came to pick me up. Almost three years later, we're doing about the same, except everyone thinks we're a couple because he transitioned and most straight people cannot conceive of queerplatonic relationships.

"What—what's that tone?" I ask, still staring in the direction Christof has disappeared to. In case. "Wait, did you not—"

"Tell my mom I'll be reading our queer agenda? No. She's going to shit herself when she sees me up there, but I don't want to start a whole thing about it ahead of time—like, it's already hard enough living with her. And I don't want her having any advance notice. Not that she'll research our issues anyway . . ." He sighs. "I can already hear her ranting about how 'we can't just alter construction plans for the new gym to make the bathrooms and lockers gender neutral,' as if it's more than sticking an 'All Gender' sign on the door. I love her, but it's like she doesn't see me at all sometimes. Like she doesn't have a whole trans kid living under her roof."

Sometimes I don't get Sue. It wasn't hard leaving my parents—they were awful to me, so I left. Life got way better when I started living with Oma. Sue's situation's a little different, though. His dad moved to West Virginia when his parents separated, and I can't blame Sue for not wanting to move somewhere with *fewer* protections—but at least his dad was cool. At least he helped Sue get HRT and stuff. His mom fully sucks.

"Yeah, I remember when we asked about pronouns in school emails," I say, "and she gave you a whole speech about how much work it would be and how we didn't understand the cost or something."

"'Can't you just type it in yourself?' she said." Sue growls in frustration and kicks the locker next to mine, prompting the stack of books balanced on my shelf to teeter. I slam it shut before disaster can strike. And then in a scathing falsetto Sue adds, "'Why do you even need pronouns?' As if she doesn't use them daily."

"I'm sorry cis people are terrible," I say, scouring the hallway. Just need to drop off this math homework, and then we can go. Sue to his house. Me to volunteer at my favorite place in the world. "And I'm sorry your mom is among the most terrible."

"Same."

Sue walks with confidence alongside me, like he's my escort or bodyguard, as we head toward my math classroom. He waits outside as I slip my homework into Mr. Redd's inbox. I like to think of it as him keeping watch, but really I know he's just enjoying himself—a prince surveying his . . . "kingdom" isn't the right word, mostly because he doesn't believe in that kind of thing, but there is a power to the way he holds himself. Shoulders back, hands in his pockets, meeting the eyes of everyone who walks by him.

"Okay, let's get out of here," I say, rejoining my sentry, keeping a close eye on some lacrosse players down the hall. *Please don't notice me. Don't notice*—oh dammit. I feel their eyes on me before I can avert mine. This is why I usually keep my head down. "Sue, can we—"

"Sure," he says, reassuring me with a glance. Already his attention makes me feel safer. "You've got, uh . . ." He snaps his fingers three times, searching for the words. "Tonight," he finally concludes, knowing I can fill in the blank on my own.

"Yup." If I walk behind him, no one bumps into me and almost no one sees me. Ideal. "But let me know if you want help working some of those studies into your speech. I think we have some really strong examples in support of more rigorous and inclusive sex education classes."

"God, remember that video they showed us freshman year?"

"I've tried to forget it." I breathe in fresh air as we push our way into the courtyard and through a dozen small social groups neither of us belongs to. Almost there . . .

"There's my guy!" I barely dodge Kenna as she launches herself at Sue. He and Kenna aren't together like that, but they're also not *not*. She's had a crush on him for the last two years—ever since it became clear to her that he and I weren't going to hook up, actually. But Sue gets so much attention from the other queers, I sometimes wonder if hers doesn't go over his head. To my point, three other

QSA members drift our way: Tiana, who actually looks up from her book; Phoenix, who is bouncing alongside her, still dressed in her dance tights and tank; and Gray, who seems to be typing out a novel of a text message. We all watch Gray for a minute before he hits send and looks up like a gopher poking its head out of a hole.

"What essay were you finishing?" Tiana asks, voice dry as she adjusts her round black glasses.

Gray scrunches his face before smiling at me. We had a thing for a minute during sophomore year. Or, it's less we had a thing, and more we *tried* to have a thing. He was a cute transfer and also the only other queer guy I knew besides Sue. We even went out a few times, but it was . . . well, let's just say we weren't compatible. Our nights were better spent with him painting our nails while we discussed the men on that year's Olympics gymnastics team.

Sue's phone dings.

Gray looks over as if it's his—he's always looking at a screen—then says, "Oh," when he realizes the obvious.

"I was texting Sue a few more references for his speech," Gray says in response to Tiana's question. "Specifically, some local orgs that train teachers on how to work with queer kids and be more inclusive, and also examples of other Maryland schools that have implemented their methods with good results."

"Can you put them in that doc Howard's compiling?" Sue asks with a smile as he hugs Kenna closer.

"Of course." And Gray's back on his phone.

Tiana glances back down at her book. Phoenix is suddenly as tall as I am as she rolls up onto the toes of her sneakers, one arm outstretched as she balances with the other on Gray's shoulder. She's regularly cast as the lead in performances but has never been brave enough to audition for the parts she really wants. Instead of getting to wear tutus, she's costumed in black tights and a coat. Instead of being lifted, she lifts. Like, just because she has great arms doesn't mean she doesn't deserve to soar. The dance department might be more liberal than the athletics department, but it's still stupidly gendered.

Christof bangs through the doors with a few of his friends, and I tense. Sue glances between me and him. "I should go," I say. Read: I should run to my car before I can attract any more attention.

Sue sighs before nodding me off. "Go, then." He watches Christof whack someone on the helmet with a lacrosse stick. "But I will bother you about my speech tomorrow."

With a "Please do," I slink out the interior courtyard and back inside, trying not to glance over my shoulder. Sue's superpower is commanding attention, and mine is hiding from it. Often that means he's the only one who sees me. Even within what is ostensibly *our* friend group, everyone's eyes and ears are almost always on him, unless he calls on me at a QSA meeting or something. Which is fine with me, really. I have quiet moments with them, like when it's just me and Tiana reading silently beside each other or Gray trying some new nail art on me while I watch an old movie. Phoenix and Kenna, outside of meetings, I only really ever see on the stage or the field, but we're all so busy with extracurriculars. And besides, what's the point of drawing positive attention to myself when it's only ever been joined by negative?

I hurry as the lacrosse team hoots and hollers behind me, their voices growing louder. But I'm through the school's front doors before I can attract another ounce of attention.

"Oh, these are so beautiful, Howard. I just love pansies!" Despite her gloves and apron, Barbara has dirt all over herself. To think I'd suggested potting flowers as an indoor craft series. Last week, while painting her ceramic, she almost glazed Walter's wheelchair.

"You keep your dirty hands away from me, Barb," Walter says, giving her a sly look.

Those two have been flirting since I started volunteering at Spring Meadows my freshman year. I'm kind of hoping they'll get together before I graduate this spring. Depending on how my college applications go, I might be off living my best gay life at Ithaca, Columbia, or hell, even Princeton. And then who will hang out with the local over-eighty crowd on Wednesday evenings?

Barb presses one of her dirty fingers against Walter's cheek, and I just roll my eyes, giving them space. To be honest, the two of them finding each other after a lifetime of love and loss gives me hope. Like, maybe I'll find a boyfriend by the time I'm eighty. Maybe by then some of them will finally share some of my current hobbies, like horticulture. Then who will be cool for having been president of his high school gardening club? Yours truly. Assuming we haven't totally destroyed the planet by then.

"—and so late! When I moved in, I was told no movers after sunset, but I guess men don't have to follow the rules." I cock my head at the words. Rosalie is a retired journalist and certified gossip, and I love her. When she realized I was gay, she pulled out all her old articles about Stonewall, the removal of homosexuality as a psychiatric disorder, and the evolution of cross-dressing laws. "I even kissed a woman or two in my time!" she'd added, as if to her résumé.

"Oh, I saw him," says Gladys, Rosalie's partner in crime—I mean, in journalism. She presses soil around the roots of her purple pansies, of which she has managed to cram three into her small pot.

"Um, Gladys . . ." I reach over and rescue them before she can smash the roots. Just because pansies are hardy doesn't mean they're immortal.

"He's very handsome." Gladys pulls off her gloves to reveal a perfect set of pink nails. She reaches out to me, and I feel the press of her delicate skin against my hand, think of the day when my hands will become stiffer and bonier like hers. Hope I'll also have a great manicure. I bet Gray will. "I wonder if the new gentleman might like to join us for evening crafts." By which she means: *Howard, would you go ask the new guy to join us? I want to flirt with him.* Also hope my libido is still going this strong when I'm their age.

"I'll go ask." I make a show of standing so they know I'm cooperating. Rosalie fishes a small notepad out of her purse while Gladys winks at me. "Please, no one kill your pansies while I'm gone. Maybe just . . ." I airlift Barb's and Walter's pots from between them before they can knock them over. It's a wonder those two ever pay attention to anything besides each other.

I can still hear Rosalie flipping through flimsy pieces of paper as I wash my hands and dry them on a towel that's as soft as construction paper. I toss it toward the bin and miss, of course. I swear I'm coordinated—more in the direction of cultural dance than basketball, though. If Kenna were here, she'd have showed me the proper form. Instead, I place the crumpled towel into the bin directly, then head to the front desk.

Spring Meadows isn't one of those fancy new retirement communities with multiple buildings and sprawling grounds. It's "cost-efficient," according to my parents, which is why they moved my dziadzi here when he needed more support than he could get at home. That's why I started volunteering here. But even after Dziadzi passed, I stayed because the residents had grown on me, as had the building: a big mansion built in the sixties that was previously occupied by a hippie commune with a green thumb before being turned into a retirement home in the eighties. Their gardens are where Dziadzi and I spent much of our time and where I befriended Walter and Barb, and then a bunch more folks. It's impossible not to bump into Rosalie and Gladys when they're always hanging on open doors, Gladys cranking up her hearing aid. Got to scoop the hot goss.

"Hey, Ada." I lean onto the wooden counter and make eye contact with the overworked woman. She needs a real office.

"Oh." She straightens her glasses, tucking their beaded chain behind her ears. "Hi, Howard. You need something, hon?"

"I've been instructed to ask the new resident if he wants to join us for crafts." I glance down the hall, where Rosalie pretends to enthusiastically admire a painting that's been hanging on the wall since before she moved in.

Ada looks between her and me, then shrugs with the energy of someone who has a thousand more important things to care about. "Why not? He's in suite 217, west tower. Name's . . ." She clicks through a database that looks like it was created in the nineties. Actually, the computer also looks like it was created in the nineties. "James Bedford."

"Thanks." I make a point to smile, since I distracted her from the pile of papers on her desk, and head west. Don't have to look behind me to know Rosalie and Gladys are watching—maybe even following.

The west tower used to house the main bedrooms in Spring Meadows during its commune days. Now, of course, there are bedrooms everywhere, some even with little kitchenettes and vintage appliances that make my heart sing. Barb once joked that I'd be the facility's youngest resident if I could. She wasn't wrong.

I run my hand along the thick wooden banister that leads to the tower. There are elevators that are somehow both new and rickety, but I prefer the stairs. The big spiraling stairway is lined with photographs of the commune members who lived here until the state kicked them out over a scary number of housing violations, which have since been mostly remedied. Rosalie swears it's haunted, but I find it cozy.

I pause on the second-story landing. At the opposite end of the hall, a neat stack of broken-down boxes rests against the wall. That must be it. Down at the end of the wallpapered hallway, a door is ajar.

I'm good at approaching residents. Part of my volunteer work is literally recruiting them, getting them out of their suites to spend time with one another, keeping their bodies moving in healthy ways and their brains active and creative. And they like me here! Usually all it takes is a glimpse of my vintage aesthetic to spark their interest, but if it's not my fashion, it's my excitement for movie night—always something black-and-white and romantic—or needlepoint or gardening.

But for some reason, tonight I can't move. My beeswax leather boots stick to the floor as if they aren't well worn by my feet and the feet of those who owned them before me. Wood creaks behind me, and I turn quickly, hoping to catch Gladys or Rosalie sneaking up on me.

Nothing. No one. Didn't I just remind myself how cozy this place is? How unhaunted? I'm not scared. Don't know why I'm still standing here. *Get on with it, Howard. Before the folks downstairs destroy their pansies.*

I put on my best smile, check the collar of my shirt, and walk. The hardwood creaks with every step as I draw closer. I catch the eye of a photographed hippie before stepping in front of the open doorway.

Huh. The overhead lights are off; the collapsed boxes all say "Bedford 217," so James must be in here. I rest my hands on the sides of the doorway and peek in, not daring to step a foot over the threshold. This is someone's home, after all. I can't just walk—

A click sounds from the darkness before a soft light shows two silhouettes. Two. I flatten my back to the wall beside James' door, hiding myself as whispers sound from inside the suite. Snippets of a conversation I shouldn't be listening to. A deep, breathy, "I'm sorry, I . . ."

And a brighter, younger, "Don't." Before their voices hush again. ". . . to be okay." Shoes squeak over old, creaky floorboards.

I let out the breath I've been holding. Time to go. Tell Rosalie and Gladys—*ping!*

Oh no.

Ping! Ping, ping!

I fumble for my phone—the freaking sound is on. I glance at the screen; the ladies are blowing up my texts asking me to . . . "Sneak a pic?" I whisper incredulously to myself, before realizing I've said that out loud and that I'm holding my phone like a creep beside James' open doorway.

I peer around the edge of the door, into the suite, freezing as a figure steps into the light. A boy who looks my age, with silver eyes like a predator's at night. I face him fully, entranced as if I'm his prey. Can't help but stare as a wave of black hair falls across his pale, unblemished skin.

And then he's walking toward me slowly—slower than I think is even possible for someone to move—and we're only twenty feet apart. Fifteen feet. Ten.

I realize then that I'm gripping the doorjamb, holding myself in place so I won't—I don't know, trip over my own feet? He is beautiful and more so the closer he comes, and I cannot move. Cannot speak.

The boy reaches out and closes his hand over mine—over the edge of the open door. His touch sends fractals like lightning through my arm. No one's touched me—I mean, I haven't been touched—like this ever. And by "like this," I mean gently and with purpose.

Even though his purpose is prying my hand from the frame and slamming the door in my face.

CHAPTER 2

I never learned how to drive. My parents didn't have the money for me to learn—or for a car, for that matter—and I was saving every dime for college. So here I am, roughly sixty years later, riding the bus to visit James in the county. Technically two buses, and—I glance at my watch—almost an hour and a half so far. How much time that we could have spent together will I instead spend making this trip?

Too much.

It's hard thinking of time in days when we've gotten used to spending nights together. It's hard thinking like a mortal. A day ago, James and I could still pretend our lives were normal. That we shared a house and a life and a bed.

Our bed. Before leaving for the bus tonight, I went upstairs and lay down on it—on my side, on strange sheets because I insisted he take ours. Warm flannel for the winter, though we used them year-round. Curling up with a vampire tends to lower the temperature beneath the covers.

Last night—the last we would spend together in our home—it was like we were back in high school. But instead of beer, James drank coffee, and I drank his blood. Not as much as I used to, now that his body has grown delicate and his mind has begun to fade. But honestly, all I wanted to do was talk, hold him, stay awake until sunrise.

James almost made it. Been harder for him to stay up as late as he did even five years ago with his health deteriorating, regardless of our lifestyle changes. When I felt his body settle into sleep—pulse slowing, breath steadying—I fit myself against him, pretending it was like every night before, rather than our last.

I make myself smaller on the plastic bus seat as a woman slides in beside me with four shopping bags, their boxy paper scraping against my knees. Only one more stop until I get off, but I don't tell her that. I sit quietly, watching out the window as the houses thin and the road narrows from two lanes into one. Until I see it: a big old mansion at the end of a long driveway, surrounded by grass and gardens. The brochure made it seem like a nice retirement community, but from where I sit, it reminds me of a crypt. The place where James has gone to die alongside a bunch of strangers. Without me. Quickly I reach up and pull the cord to signal my stop, then shuffle over the woman who just sat down.

"Sorry." I squeeze between people who don't bother to move

out of my way as the bus pulls over. When the doors finally open, I step onto the cracked sidewalk and into the moonlight carrying nothing but a pillow, which feels a little ridiculous but also comforting. Even though it's mine, it still smells like James—how could it not? Our lives were infused, and now . . . they're going to make James live by the sun now, aren't they? Change his whole schedule, and then we'll have even less time together. I check my watch again as the bus pulls away, just to be sure. Six thirty. I left as soon as I could. I had to stop for a bite, though; I really didn't want to mess up my first visit to James' new place by showing up hungry and distracted. Of course, now it's *six thirty*.

Early this morning, before the movers arrived, I got out of bed. I didn't wake James up. Debated it. Waking up with the man I love has been one of the simplest and most perfect joys of the last twenty years. Lingering in bed, pressing kisses down his neck to its pulse point. My evening drink before his evening caffeine. But I wanted him to sleep—he needed the sleep given how much energy moving was going to take. So instead I shut off the alarm before it went off and slipped away.

Most couples don't have a secret blackout cubby in the basement, but most couples don't have a vampire in them. I lay awake down there, listening as the door above swung open and our life was carried away in boxes. James lingered on the stoop above me—I'm not psychic, but after living alongside his heartbeat for two decades, I can pick it out from a crowd.

As I approach the gates of Spring Meadows, I close my eyes and listen for it, as if I might hear it through the thick stone walls amid a hundred other heartbeats. Up close, the mansion looks like the kind of place where Dracula might live. But he doesn't and neither do I, so I sneak around the side.

The grounds are dark and quiet, the evening air crisp. November is my favorite month. That Baltimore humidity is gone. It's cool but not too cold. The clocks are set back, and the sun sets earlier. It's darker and cozier. Really makes me miss hot coffee. I wonder if James can brew it in his room—though I don't remember packing the coffeepot. There's no reason I would've kept it for myself. Was it on the list of prohibited items?

I try to picture our kitchen counter as I slip around the back of Spring Meadows, but everything blurs together: stand mixer, coffeemaker, stovetop, knife block, cooking utensils. Dammit, I can't remember. Doesn't matter. What does matter is getting into James' room undetected. At some point very soon James will add me to his approved visitors list, and I'll be able to enter through the front door. But for now I climb, searching for footholds along the stone outer wall, my ascent made slightly challenging by the pillow. But only slightly. Two stories isn't that high, and what's the worst that can happen—I fall? I've survived worse.

I tumble forward through the only open window I can find and land in a hallway with a decades-worn carpet; the air boils with radiator heat. I follow the path to suite 217 and stand in front of the nondescript wooden door. I don't knock or close the door behind me—nowadays the sound startles him, and after so long James is used to my quiet comings and goings. Besides, he knows I'm coming to visit.

The scent of peppermint hits me as I slip inside. James looks up from his little dining table, a mug steaming between his hands. He smiles and nods to the chair across from him.

"Took your time," he says, a smile tugging at the corner of his mouth.

I kiss the top of his head through his thin white hair and take the offered seat.

"It's been dark out for a while, George. I was starting to worry." His smile widens.

"Sorry, did I miss curfew? I got hungry." I lick my lips exaggeratedly, biting the bottom one to show off the point of my fang. It digs into the soft skin, and I taste my own blood.

"Guess we're both full now, then."

"Guess so. Plus, public transportation in this town isn't what it used to be."

The moment hangs somewhere between flirtation and hesitation. We let it as James takes a long sip of tea. I wonder how long he's going to be able to stay up with me while a light breeze billows the floral curtains he brought from home. *Home.*

"Let me put that into a travel mug so we can try out your new bed. Did you get the flannel sheets on okay?" I steal the mug before he can even think about stopping me and don't look back for his reaction. Probably one of protest. Probably put-on.

His chair scrapes across the floor. "Oh—well, they didn't fit," he says with unusual sheepishness. "Our bed back home is a queen, but this one . . ."

I screw the lid on the fancy warming travel mug I bought

James for his birthday last year, despite having insisted we stop celebrating mine. (Felt kind of rude, me being immortal and all.) But when I turn to join him, I see what he means. It's one of those hospital-style beds. Twin-sized. I don't comment, though. Don't want him to worry about what I think. And besides, after so long we can make anything work, right?

Framed photos already hang on the walls of his room—pictures I recognize but which I have little personal connection with. His daughter, Jacqueline, when she was a child, wearing a paper crown and blowing out birthday candles. Him and his wife, Theresa, kissing on their wedding day. Her dress was beautiful. Makes me wonder what James and I would have worn if we'd ever been able to get married. (Of course I survived long enough to see marriage equality laws but didn't actually *live* long enough to be able to legally marry. Can't submit a death certificate to the courthouse as identification.)

But we made our own life exactly as we wanted it. Those decades with Theresa and Jackie belong to him. And if I'm being honest, they still hurt a bit to think about. We never got to graduate from college together. Never got to go out to the gay bars in New York, never marched hand in hand at a Pride parade.

The two of us certainly never had any children. When we first reunited and I learned about Jacqueline, I remember wishing more than anything that I could be part of her life. Not as a parental figure—she was in her twenties by then—but as *someone*. But James more than implied she wouldn't understand me, much less the immortality, so I only ever saw her in pictures or occasionally from a distance.

"Come here, you."

I realize that James has beaten me to the bed. He's arranged my pillow on it alongside his. In the dark, if I squint, I can pretend we're home. With determined steps, I walk around to the other side of the bed as he sits on "his side" and I on mine. The mattress crinkles as I rest my weight on it—a plastic cover. Right. Because this is a place where people go at the end of their lives, while their bodies are deteriorating.

I climb in, reaching over to set his mug on the nightstand, and then scoot until the sides of our bodies align as if they were joined. James takes a sip of his tea, then offers it to me. We both know I rarely indulge in human food or drink anymore, but a little tea, lightly steeped, without milk or sugar? Mostly flavor to my body. And warm—warm where I am always cold.

He takes the mug back and cuddles against me.

But I've come for more than a cuddle. Might as well get out with it. "Didn't know you were planning to sell the house."

"What?" James turns his head toward mine, but I can't quite meet his eyes. Not with the fresh flush of embarrassment on my cheeks. "No."

"There's a sign out front. I saw it as I was leaving."

"I might be losing my mind, but I think I'd remember—"

I click my tongue, furrow my brow. "We're not joking about that. Not right now, please."

"I'm not joking." His hand covers mine. Fingers wrap around mine delicately. If I were to squeeze too hard, I could snap his bones. "I didn't put the house up for . . ."

He's quiet a second too long. My dinner flops in my stomach.

"I'm sorry, I—" he whispers, as if afraid I might overhear. "I didn't think she would—Jacqueline. She insisted on ownership when I was diagnosed, you know, to make things easier."

"Right." I'd be lying if I said I found that comforting, but it's more comforting than James entirely forgetting that he'd put his own house up for sale. "Well, it was just a surprise, is all. Almost fell down the stoop doing a double take at the realtor's sign. New neighbor across the street gave me a look." Our neighborhood has changed a lot in the time I've lived there, and I know it's old-guy stereotypical of me to not like change, but the new construction has brought the kind of people to Locust Point who file complaints with the city if your little garden or façade isn't *just so*. The same kind who call in noise complaints on the college kids who're home partying during summer break. I miss the early years when we mostly knew everyone.

"No, it's my fault." James shakes his head, presses his lips into a hard line. His dark blue eyes look away from mine and up to the ceiling. "The way you've taken care of me lately, and I couldn't even—I should have done better by you." He presses the heels of his hands into his forehead.

"Hey, don't." Gently I take them in my own and bare his face to mine. I refuse to let James leave this world scared for me. The dementia's given him plenty to be scared of on its own. "I took care of myself for forty years, and I can do it for another forty." *Thousand,* I think. "And I'm sure your daughter was just looking out for you. Spring Meadows is . . ." Nothing comes naturally to mind. I don't like it here. Don't like *James* here. Don't like my house sold out from under me. That I can't even stand up for myself without tearing the remainder of his life apart.

Immortal. Invisible.

"Well." I try for confidence. "They've got medical professionals here and staff around the clock—you know, who don't spend daylight hours locked in a dark room."

James winks. "You mean your coffin?"

Our little joke—what I used to call the blackout room in the basement. I recently stopped using that word, since James is so close to his own.

"I'll be locked in a coffin before you ever are," he adds with a wry laugh.

The death jokes have been harder on me lately, but I let this one slide for his sake. He's all that matters now. "Scoot over. You know I like to spread out." And I do, spreading my limbs like I can make a snow angel in his sheets.

That earns me a chuckle. James picks his tea back up. He kisses my cheek. "Whichever lucky bastard lands you next is going to have a handful in bed—between your energy and literally how much space you take up," he says, giving me the hardest shove he can manage. "I'll make sure to mention in my references that you're a kicker."

"Oh, please. That's the *least* of my strange bed mannerisms." I nudge his toes playfully with mine. "And who says it'll only be *one* bastard? Some of us messed around during the sixties. And seventies. And eighties and—" I stop suddenly as the avalanche of memories hits me. Fucking around wasn't quite the same in the eighties and nineties. Not for mortals, anyway. And how could it be for me when I held so many of the dying in my arms? Those no one else would touch? But I suppose no one else was immortal. I never knew for sure whether I could catch or, worse, *spread* HIV, but I knew I could hold people. So I did.

Beside me, James' soft, familiar voice. "I wish things were different."

"So do I." Barely a whisper now. I'm afraid if I admit that, he'll feel bad, and there's nothing I want less. I glance at the clock, keenly aware that Maryland is no New York. That I can't catch a bus home anytime I want before sunrise. "But it's going to be okay. *I'm* going to be okay." An electronic *ping* highlights my final word. Confusion crosses James' face. Concern creases mine.

I'm on my feet faster than I intend—faster than should be possible. *Slow.* Slowly I step toward the figure peering through the doorway. The light reveals him to me: a boy not unlike me, except in every way. Tanned skin where mine is pale white. Golden brown hair combed back where mine hangs in dark curls. Young and alive where I am old and dead. When I say he stands like a deer, I do not mean one in headlights, but one alert to danger. To the threat of me.

With my cold fingers, I pry his from the wooden doorjamb. How dare he. I have half a mind to sink my teeth into his neck and make a mess of his blood on the hardwood floor.

But I don't. With immense control, I release the boy's hand and slam the door shut on him. The sound plays over and over in my head, so loud that I can barely—can barely hear James call me back to bed or the boy's footsteps as he leaves us.

CHAPTER 3

HOWARD

The following week, James is not at craft night. I'm not even the first to notice; Gladys and Rosalie have been on the case since he arrived. Apparently a young man has been visiting him. And I'd be lying if I said the mention of him didn't warm me. Literally. A full-body flush and tingle as I recall the feeling of his hand on mine—imagine the same certain touch on my waist and sliding down my—

"If you ask me, he should get out more. See some sun." Rosalie flicks a lighter in the general direction of her cigarette.

Even though the image of a retired feminist journalist balancing a six-inch vintage cigarette holder between her fingers is the stuff of my gay dreams (minus the likely lung cancer), I shake my head at her affectionately. "You know you can't smoke on Spring Meadows' grounds, Rosalie."

"We're outside!" She gestures as if I hadn't noticed the fresh air, hadn't smelled the remnants of the earlier rainstorm. "And you're not my father, no matter how much you dress like him."

"Yeah," Gladys says, though she steals Rosalie's cigarette, snuffs it out, and tucks it into her breast pocket. "Respect your elders, Howie."

I flinch when they call me Howie. Christof's the only other person who does. But one of their remaining joys, besides gossiping and flirting with each other, is teasing me, their willing victim. So I breathe out the tension in my chest and relax. I'm safe here. At home.

"I do," I say, "which is why I don't want any of you to get lung cancer and die."

The two of them smirk at each other. Then at me. Then at the west tower, second floor.

"What?" I ask, even though I know. *Je refuse* to give them a lead for their next story. Is no one interested in Barb and Walter? She wheeled him off down the walking path five minutes ago, and they haven't reemerged. I don't even want to go after them for fear of what I might find.

"Second week in a row the new guy isn't at craft night." Rosalie slips her fingers into Gladys' pocket like she's picked it before and replaces the cigarette in its holder. "Better go check on him, or we'll have to tell Ada you're slacking on the job."

I stand defiant for a long thirty seconds before sighing. "I will, but not because you two have made it your mission to harass James."

"You know his name, I see," Gladys says.

I ignore her. "Because I would encourage *all* residents to join extracurricular activities like craft night. Because I'm good at my job. Which is a volunteer position, by the way. It's not like I get an annual review or a raise."

Rosalie flicks her lighter. "And what's his young visitor's name, hm?" I'm already halfway to the door when she shouts, "Come back when you figure *that* out!"

The last thing I see as I step inside is a puff of smoke. The first thing I feel, as the silence settles in, is butterflies in my stomach. I could easily have ignored Gladys and Rosalie's bait, but deep down I didn't want to, and they knew it.

My phone vibrates, and I open it to a text from Gladys.

Gladys: Found Walter and Barb . . . . turned around immediately. Yikes !!! Take your time in there Howie.

That's followed by three winking emojis. I spent a whole craft night earlier this year teaching them how to text and what the various emojis meant. Ever since then I've been regularly receiving messages from multiple residents. I wish I could say I regret it, but besides Sue, no one really texts me. Not outside of QSA business.

I slide my phone into my pocket and stride down the hallway with as much confidence as I can muster past Ada, who doesn't even look up from her ancient computer, and—into *him*.

Standing in front of a vending machine in an oversized cardigan and high-waisted pants, he's trying to flatten a dollar bill between his palms. (It's not working.) In the mundanity of the hallway, I could almost mistake him for a resident. But there's no mistaking the pang of pleasure that pierces me when he bites his lip. A white canine almost breaks the rosy skin. I wonder what they would feel like biting mine.

"You again." His gaze startles me even more than his implication.

"Every Wednesday," I say.

I watch as he straightens up, not quite my height but somehow as imposing as someone with a few inches on me. He licks his lips, his glossy eyes trailing over my body, and again I feel like he might eat me. I wouldn't say no.

When he doesn't reply, I step forward and pluck the worn bill from his fingers, absorbing the spark of contact as if it's static electricity. His brow furrows, but he doesn't stop me from pocketing the dollar and producing a crisp flat one from my wallet, which used to be my dziadzi's.

"These things are finicky," I offer, stepping into his space.

Like Ada's computer, the vending machines haven't been updated since the nineties. When I say I'm into vintage, what I mean is fifties, sixties, seventies, and eighties fashion, art, and culture. That and the history, of course. I can—and have—spent hours poring over images of the queer and civil rights movements, inspired not only by their spirit but also by how everything looked. What I'm *not* into are thirty-year-old vending machines that absolutely won't accept money that a person has dared to touch.

I'm in this now. I want to know more about this guy who dresses like a hot grandpa—*why* is that doing it for me?—and who stares into my fucking soul every time he looks at me. Even if it's only to learn that he's not interested. But from the way he lingers behind me, giving neither of us the space we'd give a resident, I'd wager he is.

CHAPTER 4

I'm going to die soon, George."

I squeeze my eyes shut against the world—against the reality of James' words and the vending machine I've been fighting for the last five minutes. I can't even eat this damn food, and here I am, feeding money into the machine over and over, hoping it will take pity on me.

It does not.

"But you don't have to! I've told you a thousand times that you never have to die."

The machine vomits my dollar out, and again I rub it between my palms. Maybe if they generated any heat . . . I slide it in yet again, and of course it's rejected back into my hand.

"I know, I know. But I've made my peace with death, love. I don't

want to live forever—which you know has nothing to do with you.
But I do worry about you. Being alone."

I scowl at the vending machine. At James' implication that I'll fall apart without him—I know it was in jest, but he's the only one who knows the real me. Everyone else just assumes I'm some troubled teenager running around after curfew, parents wondering where he is. They have no idea that my parents died decades ago or that I didn't speak to them for decades before that. I've been the only one looking out for me since 1960. Or, well. James and I looked after each other once we reconnected. Maybe I should have been looking after *him* more. Maybe then we wouldn't be here.

"I'll be fine. I've done it before."

Was I too snippy with him? James knows I don't blame him for those years I spent by myself. And I wasn't completely alone. I had friends, people I'd met in bars in Manhattan in the seventies, fellow queers I was proud to walk beside during protests in the eighties and nineties. But those relationships were short-lived; they had to be. I couldn't tell them what I was, and after a few years I'd have to disappear or face questions I couldn't answer. In far worse situations, I would lose them—to violence, disease, suicide—before our time was up.

But I know what James means. He wants me to find something that lasts, and he's not wrong—I hunger for intimacy and partnership. It was my fault for not seeking him out after that monster attacked me and turned me into what I am. My fault for thinking he wouldn't be able to love me for what I'd become. I tear the bill from the machine and curse it as his words knead themselves into my brain.

"I know, but I don't want you to have to do it again. And I don't think you want that either. There's got to be others like you out there, who are destined to live forever or who want to. And just because I wasn't meant to become a vampire doesn't mean no one else is. That you won't find someone else who—"

Footsteps. As they slow, I feel eyes roaming over my body. I tilt my head to find what's becoming a familiar interruption. "You again."

"Every Wednesday," he offers.

I feel my spine line up, my instincts hone in, as I examine him in this new setting—which is to say, on my own. Without the defensive instinct to protect what little James and I have left. The vampire who's come down from his tower to walk among the mortals.

And then he's lifting the wrinkled dollar bill from my hand and trading it for one from an old leather wallet that I swear is the same as the one I got James for our high school graduation back in 1960. It certainly looks as old.

"These things are finicky," he says, stepping forward—nearly on top of me—and I . . .

I don't move. I let him take what little space lies between my body and the machine, and I feel the heat radiating from him. The curve of his neck is so close to my face. I breathe in deep, and I can smell how he would taste clenched between my jaws. But I've tried to make a point of eating before visiting Spring Meadows because

I don't want my hunger to take over while I'm with James. Because I've promised not to turn him. Thousands of times, apparently.

"There." The boy steps aside—not *too* aside—and gestures at the waiting machine. "Know what you want?" He swallows, his Adam's apple bobbing beneath the tanned skin of his throat. A small constellation of freckles marks where I would sink my teeth into him. If I were thirsty.

"Um, no." I blink the thought away. "I've been fighting this thing for so long, I forgot, to be honest. I mean, it's not for me, it's for . . ." Feels strange naming him in front of this mortal. Like doing so would break the spell that's bound us for all these years.

"James?"

My beloved's name spoken by this—who is he? He can't be staff; he's too young. My age, or the age I was when I died. It doesn't feel as bad as I thought it would, hearing someone else speak it with such care. There's a warmth to his voice that matches the warmth of his body. When I breathe this time, I hold the air in my lungs. Let his scent marinate and linger on the back of my tongue.

I breathe him out with a "Yeah. He really likes Raisinets." I reach past him and type in the number. We both watch as they fall in their sunny cardboard box. The boy retrieves them, and as he offers them to me, our fingers brush. He leans against the display and looks down at me with dark brown eyes. Looks down like he could be on top of me.

"And what do you like?"

I almost say, *You.*

But then he's feeding his own money into the machine and

eyeing its candy insides. "I could use a snack too before I head back out there with the journalists."

"The journalists?"

"That's what I call a couple of the residents. Rosalie and Gladys. Rosalie actually did use to be a journalist. She got her start writing sex columns in women's magazines back in the seventies but then went on to cover a lot of the social movements, especially the queer one, until she . . ." He tilts his head. "I don't think she'd call it 'burning out'—more that she wrote about death for so long that eventually she couldn't take it anymore."

"Death?" I ask, fishing.

"Yeah, she—sorry, is this too grim?"

"No, not at all." I'm pretty sure I know what he's alluding to, and even though he's talking about one of the worst periods of my life, I actually can't believe someone his age knows anything about that era or that he brought it up.

"Okay, just checking. She wrote a bunch of articles about the AIDS crisis, way more than ever got published. Had a lot of trouble with mainstream outlets, no surprise there."

"Yeah, they preferred we die alone and unnamed rather than spread information or call out—" I cut myself off. This *mortal boy* can't possibly know me or what I've lived through, so why am I talking to him as if he does? As if he lived through it too, when he obviously has not. He wasn't even born yet, looking the way he does. Striped button-down tucked into brown slacks. His sleeves cuffed over taut biceps I'm sure he usually hides. Coiffed hair falling artfully from its hold. He looks like so many of the men I used to see on Christopher Street back in the day. We could be meeting at a gay bar in the seventies as much as meeting at a retirement home in the 2020s.

I dare to smile at him, to give him a peek at my teeth. "What's your name?"

"Howard." He extends a hand, and I'm instantly charmed. I didn't think modern-day teenagers still shook people's hands.

I take it and say, "George." I imagine he can feel the coolness of my skin, despite the blood from my breakfast in my veins, but I don't let it bother me. Because the fact of the matter is, I'll probably never see him again. At least not after James dies.

"Well, George, you never told me what you like." His fingers graze the vending machine's buttons. "We can share something."

"I, uh . . ." I scour my options, pretending I actually eat human food. "I can't eat sugar. Health thing," I offer as a consolation prize. "But I do like feminist journalists who wrote about queer people when that kind of thing was nearly impossible."

"Oh?" For the first time Howard looks off-balance. In a good way. Like he didn't expect my interest. And I am. *Interested.*

"Do you want to come down to craft night and meet Rosalie and some of the others?" he asks, hope in his eyes. This young man is attracted to me.

"Sure."

"Would James want to come?"

"Not tonight. When I left him, he was napping." James is still clearly getting used to his new sleep schedule.

Howard punches in a code, and I watch as another box of

Raisinets falls. He tears open the box and pours the contents into his mouth, much the way I did when I was still alive. I try to remember the last candy I ate. Maybe Peanut M&M'S? The year I died was the same year they made them different colors; before that they were just tan. We walk slowly alongside each other down the hall. Our shoulders bump a few times as he tells me about his volunteer work. How he's been coming to Spring Meadows almost every Wednesday since his dziadzi died. And he doesn't even ask about James, for which I'm grateful, because I don't think I have it in me to lie and call him my grandfather. Not after having denied our relationship to so many people for so long.

Howard pauses at the door to what I assume is the common space, his hand gripping the knob. He half turns and looks at me. "I'm sorry for seeming like a creep last week. The journalists—and Walter and Barb, the lovebirds—tasked me with bringing the new resident down to craft night. That's why I was standing there. I didn't want to interrupt when I realized he had a visitor."

"Oh." Seems like a silly grudge to hold now. Not like I behaved particularly admirably. "It's fine. I should probably also apologize for slamming the door in your face. That was kind of rude of me."

His chest slowly deflates as he breathes out; clearly he was worried. "I probably deserved it, but . . . I'm glad things are okay."

"Me too."

A familiar *ping* sounds from Howard's pocket. He rolls his eyes, reaches in, and pulls out his phone. "Rosalie." He glances at the message. "She'll be disappointed when I don't come bearing James, but you're a solid consolation prize." Then with a smile, he pushes through the door, and I follow.

Immediately about a dozen heads turn our way. "I had no idea our new resident was so young!" One woman snatches another's cigarette and snuffs it out in a flowerpot. She dumps a handful of dirt on top, which can't be good for whatever she intends to grow.

Howard coughs, waving his hand in front of his face for show, and the two others giggle at him. "George, this is Walter and Barbara." He nods at a man in a wheelchair sporting a newsboy cap, who's holding hands with a woman sitting beside him at the picnic table. Looking at them, I'm instantly reminded of Sidney Poitier and Katharine Hepburn in *Guess Who's Coming to Dinner*. "And those two are Rosalie and Gladys." These women, whom I assume are *the journalists*, look like iterations of Blanche Devereaux from *The Golden Girls*. And like they're up to almost as much mischief.

"Clearly *you're* not 217," Rosalie says.

"No."

"Though, the way you're dressed, you'd fit right in here," she says, throwing a smirk toward Gladys. "What is with you boys and old-man clothes?"

I look at myself and then at Howard. I mean, she's not wrong. We're definitely wearing clothes associated with a bygone era.

"Actually, Rosalie, grandpa fashion is very in right now," Howard says.

She rolls her eyes, then fishes out a new cigarette and fixes it to a silver cigarette holder that Howard probably considers vintage.

"What do you think of our boy Howard, George?" It's not really a question. But "He's kind of cute, isn't he?" sure is.

If there were more blood in my body, I'd flush the same color Howard turns at her words. His mouth opens like he's going to respond, but he comes up empty.

Walter saves him with an "Oh, stop your prying, Rose. If you scare Howard off, how will we finish Potted Plants Month? Aren't we crocheting plant hangers next or something?"

"I wouldn't scare him off," Rosalie says, clapping a hand on Howard's arm.

He plunks down onto the seat beside her. Gladys directs me to sit on the other side of the table, beside her. Where I have a perfect view of the blush that lingers on his cheeks, especially as he watches the journalist manhandle me. We make eye contact across the array of plants and pots and a stray cigarette butt, and his blush deepens.

"Howard knows he's the reason I care about crocheting and mosaic flowerpots or whatever." Rosalie winks at him.

"That, and he helps you find your favorite movies on the streaming websites," Barbara adds. She picks up her own crocheting—a long scarf already wrapped once around Walter's neck. I can't help but notice that the color complements his hazel eyes. They must be the lovebirds. They seem sweet.

In fact, the whole lot of them do. And watching Howard with them—his ease, his patience, his curiosity—creates this odd stirring in me. I watch him hold up his own phone and show Barb how to find her watch list and how to add shows to the queue. I gently reach out, grab his wrist—again with the deep blush—and tap the phone's screen. His own watch list is full of movies James and I went to see in high school, along with game shows I used to watch with Cassidy, a lesbian friend whose couch I slept on for a few months during the late seventies.

"That Paul Lynde was such a looker," Gladys says, poking at Howard's phone.

"You know he was probably gay, right?" he says.

"Oh, he was certainly gay. Doesn't mean I can't look."

"True," Howard says. "And he *was* a looker."

"That he was," I agree, but I'm looking at Howard, which earns me a shy smile—and a bunch of knowing glances from the residents.

"I know that's why you watch all those old game shows," Gladys says to Howard.

"Oh, please." A furrowed brow, a stifled smile.

Barb steals my attention to show off her scarf as Walter wiggles his shoulders with delight. And then she points with pride to the crocheted little flowers that Walter has fixed on his wheelchair for decoration.

". . . didn't know they made a movie out of that book. I remember our high school making such a big deal out of it. The principal swiped every copy of—"

"Did you ever get to read it?" Howard asks.

"No," Gladys says. "Just never got around to it."

Rosalie whacks her with one of the scattered magazines. It looks like the residents have been cutting pictures out of them and Mod Podge-ing the images onto the planters. "Well, get on it, woman! We don't have that many years left."

Gladys laughs. "Can't I just watch the movie? If I've only got so many minutes left on my clock, why should I spend a bunch of them on a book when the movie's—what, two hours long?"

"I know Howie's read it."

That's when I realize I have no idea what book or movie they're discussing. Not game shows, anymore; they don't make books out of those.

"Please, you know I hate it when you call me that," he says, glancing sideways at me. A silent ask that I not adopt their nickname for him. I wouldn't dare. "And yes, it's one of my favorite books, but the movie's good too. You should pick up whichever you have time for."

"Thank you!" Gladys relishes in his validation.

Rosalie rolls her eyes. They land on me. "What about you, Georgie?"

Walter snorts as she rolls out another nickname. I also hate mine, but . . . this is also the most relaxed I've felt in a while, and I *don't* hate the way Howard is looking at me.

"What is this book or movie you're talking about?"

"*A Single Man,*" Howard says.

"Oh, yeah. That book blew my mind when it came out."

Quiet settles across the table for a moment. Rosalie takes a long drag from her cigarette before blowing smoke over her shoulder. "Impressive, seeing as you weren't even born when it came out."

Oh. Right.

"I meant the movie," I say, doing a bit of mental math before adding, "When I watched it the first time." I shake my head like, *What a silly mistake,* and it was, but they don't need to know in what way. "One of the first queer books I ever read, though."

"Same." Howard's little smile might as well be the sun for how I almost combust looking at it.

But his attention is reclaimed by the journalists, and mine by the lovebirds, as we help them snip from magazines and arrange their designs. But every now and then I find myself distracted by the mortal boy sitting across from me. Dressed like I would have, crushing on *Hollywood Squares* panelists, and waxing on about formative fiction from my younger years.

And when he catches me looking, a blush reclaims his cheeks. A rosy pink beneath light brown freckles. A retirement home is the last place I expected to meet someone like Howard—James will be so tickled. I'm biting my lip before I can stop myself—a reflex when I'm hungry. For Howard's blood, but also his lips and the crush of his body against mine. Maybe against that vending machine in the empty hall. He's already had a snack. I wouldn't mind one, either.

CHAPTER 5

HOWARD

As I sit in the library reading room during our QSA meeting, my mind replays Wednesday. Our fingers brushing when I took George's dollar from him, the way I caught him staring at me throughout craft night, how he spoke about *A Single Man* meaning so much to him. How he kept finding reasons to touch me.

"Let's make sure those are all the demands we want to make. I have a feeling we won't get more than one shot at this," Sue says.

Kenna warily responds, "That's what we said last year, and yet here we are...."

She's not wrong. And as our VP, she's been working hard enough, long enough, to have earned some skepticism.

Sue sighs. "Sorry, I just meant... this is my senior year, and I'm really feeling the pressure. I want to leave this place better than I found it, you know?"

"I do," Kenna says. "It's just that nothing ever seems to get past the board, no matter how much work we put in. And I know this is your last chance before you graduate. Howard's, too."

If I close mine, I can see George's luminescent silver eyes capturing me in their gaze. Maybe, if I ever bump into him again—he now knows I volunteer on Wednesdays—I'll get to stare into them.

"Did you get all those down, Howard?"

I blink up at Sue, who's standing right in front of me beside the list of our demands, which are projected onto the reading room wall.

"Sorry," I say, glancing between the notes on the wall and the notes on my laptop. I type the rest of them up along with Gray's additional references and give Sue a nod. I swear I've been paying attention. Definitely not daydreaming about kissing boys—well, a particular boy. I feel like "Howard kissing a boy, finally" should be on our Queer Agenda.

"Can you read that final list back to us?" Kenna asks, and this time I'm paying enough attention to respond.

I nod and then read, "'One: pronouns embedded in school email signatures, no limitations, fully customizable.'"

"Yes, please. Not that I think it'll stop everyone from misgendering me, but it does help," Phoenix says, combing her fingers through her short black hair. I wish my hair was that thick and wavy, but we can't all have those Greek genes. "Most of the dumbasses at this school wouldn't know a demigirl if she grand battement-ed them in the face. Which I totally could."

"Hey, would you also ballet-kick the people who call me 'she' and tell me that Sue is a girl's name?"

"For you I would," Phoenix says, already on her feet to demonstrate. Tiana ducks out of the way, but Gray's staring at his phone and takes a pointed toe to the nose.

"Hey!" he says, looking up. Then looking right back down.

"It's like none of them have heard 'A Boy Named Sue.' I literally have a song," he says.

"A classic," I add.

Sue shakes his head. "Kids these days."

"'Two,'" I continue, smiling. "'Conversion of student restrooms to all-gender restrooms, changing rooms in the arts wing converted to all-gender with privacy stalls, locker rooms in the new gym constructed as all-gender with privacy stalls.'"

"Please," Kenna groans. "Like, I know I'm not the only queer woman who plays sports. Half the girls' field hockey team has hooked up with one another, but if I get called a dyke one more time by someone who isn't, I swear to—"

"God is not looking out for us," Phoenix says, who has been forced to change in the boys' area for every performance of every show she's ever done at this school. "We are on our own in those locker rooms."

"Sure are," Sue agrees. He does use the boys', but he had to fight to be able to do so. He reached out to a local queer legal organization that contacted the school and, citing Maryland law, threatened to file a claim on his behalf. Not like it's going great, though. He changes in a stall every gym class. It's the only time I ever see him nervous. And who can blame him? The boys' lacrosse team carts their sticks around like weapons.

"'Three: degender the dress code.'"

At this, Gray actually looks up from his phone. "I was literally given detention for my nails today. Tiana has her nails painted. What's the difference between us?"

Tiana puts her book down and nods in agreement. "Go on, Howard. Number four." She knows what it is; it's on the projector.

"'Four: establish a concrete anti-bullying policy, with specific consequences for acts that target gender identity and expression and sexual orientation.'"

And even though they're all also bullied, everyone looks at me.

"Look, I'd love to walk the halls at a normal pace without wondering whether I'll be sideswiped by some jock in shoulder pads," I say. "Like, why are they even wearing protective gear in history class?"

"I know it's scary, but you've got to start taking up space," Sue says. "We all get picked on, but you're the only one who has a permanent bruise from being pushed against your locker so often."

That stings a bit. "Tiana doesn't take up space."

"Because I'm busy reading," she says, tapping her book, *Kings of B'More* by R. Eric Thomas. "Which is code for 'don't notice me.' But I'm also Black, so it's hard for them not to when there's, like, a dozen of us total." She looks at Kenna, who is also Black, and who is snapping her fingers. Tiana adds in her usual matter-of-fact tone, "This is actually my fourth copy of this book because people keep ripping it out of my hands and throwing it in the trash can or toilet. So fingers crossed I'll actually get to finish copy number four. At least the author's getting royalties." She shrugs and picks it back up.

"Fair enough," I say, returning to my list to get the attention off me. "'Five: sensitivity training for all teachers annually.'"

Mrs. Sullivan, our club sponsor, doesn't usually participate in our meetings—she's adamant that this is our show. Plus, she's not queer. Not to our knowledge, at least. None of the teachers are publicly. Probably not allowed to be. But we all look at her, and she slowly lifts her gaze from the homework she's been diligently grading.

"I've brought it up at every faculty meeting since I started advising QSA," she says, as if she needs to justify her presence. (She doesn't.) "You kids have got this, but I'm here if you need me."

"Anyway." Sue shoots me a look.

"'Six,'" I say. "'More inclusive and comprehensive sex education.'" As the word "sex" crosses my lips, I imagine tearing off George's grandpa sweater, buttons flying everywhere as he angles that cutting chin of his up toward me for a kiss and a kiss and a—

Sue is still looking at me like he expects me to say something.

"What?" When did it get so warm in here? I glance at the thermostat. Not that they ever seem to work in this building.

"You've been half here the whole meeting," Gray says.

"You're only half here all the time." I grab his phone only long enough to illustrate my point and then hand it back.

"Yeah, but you're usually the one trawling us back through retro queer history, talking about how ridiculous a gendered dress code is when gendered fashion has flip-flopped and evolved so much since the nineteen-blah-blah-blahs," Gray says, putting his phone to sleep for the first time all meeting. He rests it upside down on the desk.

"What *is* going on?" Sue sits on the desk beside me, and Kenna takes her place beside him. "If you weren't typing, I'd swear you were doodling hearts in a notebook over here."

"Oh." I am so busted. "What happened to our anti-bullying stance?"

Sue cocks an eyebrow. "No, no, no. No avoiding the question. I saw what happened to you when you said 'sex education.'"

"Oh shiiiit." Phoenix smiles and climbs gracefully onto the desk in front of me, eager for the tell-all.

They all are. Even Tiana and Gray are looking up and at me. Yes, I've been well and truly busted.

"Okay, fine," I say breathily. "There's a boy."

"I knew it!" Phoenix says so loudly that several students glare at us through the library windows. This room is not soundproof—not against excited queers, at least.

Sue takes a seat in the chair beside me and presses my laptop closed. "Where the hell did *you* meet a boy?" He rubs at the little hairs on his chin as he smiles.

I usually *hate* attention . . . but this feels kind of good? I mean, these are my friends, but I don't think any of them has ever taken an active interest in my life besides Sue. "You're never going to believe it."

"Is it Marco from AP Calc?" Tiana asks.

"No." I pause. "Does he like guys?"

Tiana shrugs. "I always thought he kind of looked like a lesbian. Like, if I had to date a boy—"

"Uh, no, it's not Marco." I give Sue a knowing look. "I actually met him at Spring Meadows."

"Howard!" Sue's volume earns us another bothered look from others in the library. But notably not from Mrs. Sullivan, whose stacks of homework seem to have shifted. "Please tell me he's under the age of seventy-five," Sue says.

"Yes! Jesus, how is that even a question?" I punch his shoulder playfully. "Of course he is. Not that I asked how old he is, but he looks our age. He was visiting his grandfather, I think." Actually another thing I didn't ask. Just assumed.

"Okay, but what does he look like besides 'our age'?" Phoenix pries.

"Um." Actually, "our age" only barely applies. One of the reasons I'm attracted to him is because, like me, he doesn't carry himself like someone our age. "Don't laugh, or I swear I'll invoke the anti-bullying policy again."

This makes them all laugh, but they each hold up a Scout's honor in turn. None of them are Scouts, so I don't know why I trust that.

"Okay, he's a bit shorter than me—"

"Perfect standing-on-his-toes-to-kiss-you height." Kenna smiles sweetly at Sue, who returns it.

"Yeah, he is." Wonder where that might happen. In an empty hall, pressed up against the historic slate walls? Or maybe out in the garden where the journalists and lovebirds can't snoop on us? Finding each other's warm bodies in the cool of autumn . . .

"You're touching your lips," Sue says.

"I am not!" I am. I stop.

"You have it so bad for this guy."

"Look, he's really hot and likes all the same old books and movies I like."

"Whoa!"

"Which books?" Tiana interjects unsuccessfully.

Sue plows on. "Tell us his name already!"

"Why, so you can tease me about him?"

He deflates a little, his forehead creasing, as his shoulders slump. "Real talk: I'm happy for you. And I super hope this works out."

"And . . . ?" I prompt him.

"And I promise not to tease you about him." Sue gives me a solemn nod, and the others all follow.

"Okay. His name is George—and no, I don't know his last name. Yet. I don't even know if I'll see him again. Most guys our age don't hang out in retirement homes."

"Yeah, but that's why you're so into him."

It's true. "And his grandfather could die tomorrow, and then we'd never see each other again—or even worse, he wouldn't want to see me again because I remind him of his dead grandfather."

Gray picks up his phone. "That got dark." He sets it back down just as quickly, like he decided morbidity was more interesting than social media. He *is* wearing black nail polish with a skull design this week.

"That is not going to happen," Sue says.

Tiana looks like she's considering the possibility a bit too hard. "It could, though. Technically anything could happen."

"Thanks, Tiana," I say.

"You're welcome."

Kenna tries and fails to stifle her laughter, and Tiana's already reading *Kings of B'More* again. Then Mrs. Sullivan's chair scrapes loudly across the floor as she stands.

"Okay, everyone, great meeting," she says, looking at the clock.

Thank god. Phoenix rolls backward off the desk, landing perfectly on her feet, while the others gather their things. Mrs. Sullivan blinks several times as if waking from a trance. Looking at her pile of grading, I'd believe it.

After a kiss on the cheek from Kenna, Sue lingers, clearing our notes and the projector. He slides the chairs more neatly into place than they've ever been. Except for mine, because I'm still sitting in it. Watching him.

"What?" I know this show is for me. That he wants a moment alone.

We get it as Mrs. Sullivan shoves her things into her bag and waves on her way past, saying, "Really proud of you kids."

Sue leans against the desk and looks me in the eye. His signature undercut falls forward onto his face. It's really no wonder all the other queers are hot for him. He was always magnetic, and the testosterone has only improved that. Along with his shoulders. But we were never meant for each other like that. I'm hoping I'm meant for George *like that*.

"Howard, you've hyped me up plenty over the years, and I've tried to give you the same confidence. Never seems to stick, but I hope you take it this time."

"Oh?"

"You're stylish, smart, and *way* too well-rounded. But what I love most about you is your passion. Which only ever seems to come out when you're nerding out over black-and-white movies or queer history—not a tease!" He holds up a finger as if to silence my protest.

I only smile in return.

"Sincere," he says. "And I sincerely hope this hot grandpacore boy feels just as passionately about you as you seem to about him." Before I can demur, Sue claps a hand on my shoulder. "I promised Kenna a ride home, but I definitely want to hear more about George later." And then he walks off, same swagger as always, drawing eyes as he moves confidently across the library and toward the hall.

"Passionate," I say quietly to myself in the empty room. Never really thought of myself that way. But I like it. And I really, *really* like George.

CHAPTER 6

GEORGE

His skin is more fragile than it used to be twenty years ago—even five years ago. Which I know is a long time for him, but it's not like we reconnected when James was forty. He was sixty. And now he's in his eighties. Well, so am I, but my skin doesn't have a blemish on it, much less the fragility of age.

"We used to stand and do this," he says, lowering himself carefully onto the couch. I hold out a steadying arm behind him, just in case. But I know he wants to do it alone, so I settle beside him, wondering whether I should help him unfasten his collar. James' fingers quiver as they fumble with the small buttons.

I reach up and slip them free from their holes, parting the ironed cotton and exposing his throat. James had called me just as I was about to leave the house, asking if I would feed on him tonight.

When I bite someone, it can be a terrifying experience or a deeply intimate act. With James it has always been the latter, eventually becoming more ritual than necessity. I don't *need* to eat every night, but if I'm full, I'm more firmly in control of myself, less prone to temptation and carelessness. So when he called to make the request, I understood what he was asking for, and I was happy for it.

But it strikes me: Should I even bite him here anymore? With so much personal attention, won't the staff catch on? No. People never suspect *vampires*. They explain away everything that doesn't fit in their little boxes. Just like they don't know James is queer. Just like they don't know I'm his partner.

"Just relax," I tell him in my most soothing voice—a near whisper that has *that effect* on mortals. It's not unlike "glamouring" on *True Blood* (which I loved), but far less powerful. I always imagined honing the ability with a mentor or maker, but, as with Lestat, I was abandoned from the start. I only even realized I had this ability during those first few years as a vampire, in the alleyway behind a Baltimore bar that's long since been demolished, with a man who was much bigger than me and who tried to fight back. I never used to use it with James, but lately it seems a kindness.

(Is it kindness, though, to soften and smooth over the edges of James' emotions? Am I caring for the man I love or deceiving him?)

"You of all people relax me the most." He smiles as he closes his eyes and leans back on the couch, his neck exposed. Relaxed, yes, but not so much that his hands don't find my waist as I straddle him and run a hand through the waves of his white hair. As I trail my fingers down the side of his face and find the pulse point on his throat.

I don't announce myself; he knows what's coming. The press of razor-sharp fangs through layers of thinning skin. The dizziness of blood loss—not too much, never too much. At his age, James isn't my main course anymore; I don't want to drink him dry. He's dessert wine. A familiar and beloved sweet that is best enjoyed sparingly. Savored, not binged.

He rubs one hand slowly up and down my back, resting the other on my neck. When he said we used to stand for this, he means shoving each other against the wall like teenagers, mouths clamoring for each other, fingers tearing at buttons, blood smearing across lips and shirt collars.

Now, when I finish—when I've had enough and his heart is still beating within a healthy range—I leave only two small beads of blood in my wake. I kiss the spot gingerly, cleaning up with the swift flick of my tongue.

When James opens his eyes on me, they're wide. Startled, unknowing. I'm familiar with the flicker of terror that comes when someone realizes I'm the monster that's about to attack them, and that's how he's looking at me now. Like I've *done* something to him. Like he doesn't recognize me. Like—

"It's me," I say cautiously. "It's your George."

James tilts his head, searches my face, and then—"I know."

Relief hits me so hard, I almost teeter over. Was that my fault or the encroaching dementia's, or simply a reminder of his old age? He blinks, and his usual liveliness returns to those blue irises.

We slip into our usual patterns as I slide off his lap and he buttons his collar back up. "Want to play a game of chess?" he asks. "As you know, I need to keep my mind sharp."

I won't claim to know the science, but I'm almost positive one game of chess won't keep the James I know and love with me. "What if we got out of this room—out of the dark?" I say, relaxing sideways against the striped cushions. It won't ever *not* feel like hotel furniture to me. And I've spent nights in some incredibly seedy hotels. "It's Wednesday."

"Is it?" James almost winks, eye twitching like he's on to me.

"I know you know it is." I slap his knee playfully and curl myself up against the arm of the sofa to face him.

"Pray tell, what's so special about Wednesday?"

I bite my lip, enjoying the tease. To think I was considering avoiding Howard altogether, but he charmed me from the vending machine to the picnic tables, introducing me to the residents, his friends. Reminding me of books and television from my youth. Reminding me a bit of James when we were in high school with the way he dressed. And with the way it felt when he touched me.

"You remember that volunteer I mentioned? He hosts craft night. They've been learning about flowers and decorating planters."

"I see, I see." James thumbs the wispy hairs on his chin. "So it's definitely the crafts you're into, not this volunteer?"

I break. I smile and flop back against the couch and run my hands through my hair as his blood rises fresh to my pale cheeks. "Am I that obvious? You always know when I have a crush—and even let me sweat about whether they like me back." I nudge him with acknowledgment in my heart and a wink between us.

"If you can't experience the pitter-patter of a beating heart, you should at *least* get to sweat about it." James nudges me back. "You know I understand. Us mortals can be tricky for an undying vampire like you."

"That you can. Luckily, I can always rely on this one." I take his hand and kiss his knuckles.

There have been many things that have surprised me about my relationship with James, but near the top of the list was his openness to being in an open relationship. He was the one who brought it up within the first year of our reunion. He'd been monogamous with his wife for nearly forty years. *Forty.* During those same years, while I sometimes loved, I rarely lingered. Not only because it might betray my immortality, but because my norm was *free love* as opposed to marriage.

"So what's his name?" His smile is soft and interested. Curious.

"Howard," I say, taking James' hand and gliding the cool pads of my fingers over the thick lines of his fingernails. "He's . . ." Hesitation creases my forehead. "I'm about to say that stereotypical thing: he's not like other boys his age. But it's true. He actually sort of reminds me of you."

"Oh." Surprise alights on James' face. I watch as he thinks—as he slowly begins to nod and then smile. "A compliment I'll happily take."

"I think you'd like him."

"Well, I won't know unless you tell me more. Or we meet." James pauses. "Do you want to gush about him a little before we go down? So I can give you covert looks? Reminds me of when we used to go pick up men together."

My eyebrows shoot up as I lean forward. "You want me to help you pick up one of these retirees?"

He chuckles and swats at me. "No, no. I can't handle anyone on top of your energy nowadays. But I know you can handle more than mine." His lips settle into a soft, wistful smile. And I know he means it with love and care—we have been doing this for decades—but I can't help but think he's still trying to set me up so he knows I won't be alone when . . .

"Help me off this couch." James plants his feet firmly on the ground and offers me his hands, which I gladly take, leveraging his weight until he's standing solidly. I match his pace, grabbing both our sweaters off the hooks beside the door, and then hold it open for him. The press of a kiss against my forehead almost startles me. "I love you," he says.

"I love you too," I whisper, before following him into the hall and closing the door behind us.

Rosalie's "Well, well, well!" greets James and me as we find our way into the official craft room. "This must be the mysterious new resident," she says, cigarette holder dangling between her lips, empty of an actual cigarette. Which is good, because I imagine smoking in a facility with oxygen tanks would be bad. There's not much that can kill me, but I'm guessing an explosion would almost certainly do so.

I spot Howard, whose face lights up when he sees me, and guide James to the table Howard is sitting at. "In the flesh," I say, offering James the promised covert look before taking the seat opposite him. And beside Howard.

"You again," Howard says with a wink.

"Me again," I say, trying not to stare at his lips, at his hands, at his throat. I want to put my mouth on all of them. "I heard craft night is the place to be."

"You're not wrong." He gestures at a swath of glitter spilled across the table. And then I notice the gold metallic flecks that dot his cheeks and fingertips. Not on purpose, I'd wager. "I'm glad you brought James down. Looks like he'll fit right in."

The two of us watch as the journalists fawn over him, straightening his collar (my fault) and interrogating him. Walter kisses his offered hand rather than shaking it, and Barb fakes a gasp of shock. But James is smiling, so I smile too—and when I catch Howard's eye, he's also smiling. We burst out laughing like kids misbehaving in class.

"Yeah, I think it's good for him to get out—well, as out as *downstairs* is. Make some friends—" I almost say *his own age*, as if that's not me. I shift awkwardly in my striped chair instead. God, I hate the furniture in this place. "Make some friends and be active."

Howard offers a noncommittal "yeah" in response, and I see him turn inward.

I want to ask, but there's a reason I don't have any lasting friendships, and it's not because I'm bad with people. It's because people are bad with vampires. Because simple questions about how I spend my days and what I do for fun necessarily end in lies. That I might also be eighteen years old, a fundamental thing Howard thinks we have in common, is a lie. And yet I find myself not wanting to lie to him. So I risk it.

"You okay?"

He sits up straighter, eyes darting around as if unsure who asked him that. "Oh, um." This is not the Howard I met by the vending machines. Or it's a side of him I've yet to see. "Your comment about friends made me think of my own friends. At school. It's not a big deal."

It's obviously a big deal.

"What? You can tell me." I tap a finger against his knee. Tonight he's wearing green corduroys with a bright color-blocked shirt tucked into them and a watch that looks about my age. I imagine delicately removing it from his wrist before biting into him.

"I go to this private school called Wyndhurst—I am not rich," he qualifies quickly. "It's the only thing my parents will still pay for."

It sounds like he doesn't have their support. I know what that's like.

"Anyway," he continues, "we have this Queer Student Alliance. It was hanging on by a thread when I joined freshman year, but my friends have spent years bringing it back to life. And I just don't think . . ." Howard's gaze wanders. He shakes his head defeatedly.

"Don't think what?"

He sits up straighter and pushes his hair behind his ears, looking at me square on. "We've been crafting a list of demands—it's incredible. We have primary sources and testimonies and research to back up why everything we're asking for is not only reasonable but actually beneficial to the school. Beneficial to *us*," he adds.

"Well, that's great," I say. "It sounds like you and your friends have worked really hard on this. I'm sure there are other, less vocal students who really appreciate it too. Even if you don't know it."

"Maybe . . ." He glances at where my hand lingers by his knee, no longer touching, but—I want to. The urge to rest my hand on Howard's knee and comfort him is overwhelming. I wish we were curled up on one of those terrible sofas together. "I just don't think the school board is going to go for . . . any of it."

"What kind of demands are you making?"

"They don't give a shit about us" does not answer my question, but it does tell me something about Howard. That he feels defeated and has felt so for a long time—comparative to the length of his life. But even if it's only for a decade, I know what constant rejection can do to a person. I also know you have to fucking fight.

I lean forward and look him in the eyes. "What kinds of demands?"

He counts six extremely reasonable demands on his fingers, noting how his friend Phoenix is hassled in the arts wing and another friend, Kenna, is bullied in the gym. How his closest friend, Sue, has to correct people on his pronouns a dozen times a day. And that's not even the whole of it.

"But the board," he says, that defeat returning to his voice, "is made up of a bunch of rich white straight Christians who are just as happy to vote against the interests of queer kids at school as they are in the presidential election. The kind of people who think they know what's *best* for us, that we don't know ourselves or how to make our own decisions. That if they can just suppress our needs until we graduate, we'll see the light and turn straight and binary. Don't know what your school's like, but . . ."

My high school certainly didn't have a QSA. Like, things seem better for queers now in the 2020s than they were in the 1950s, but it's all the same cycle, isn't it? Conservatives accusing us of phases, of perversions, of devilry. I never came out to my parents, and I definitely never came out at school. It wasn't until I was armed with a set of lethal fangs that I started opening up.

"It sucked," I say—past tense. I'm aware that might raise questions, and that I should be careful how much I tell this mortal and when. That, more than liking him, I have to *trust* him. But this is a partial truth. A taste. "Yeah, I found other queer friends—love, even." I glance at James, who now also has glitter on *his* hands. His family won't be able to deny his bisexuality when they see *that*. "But I never told anyone—couldn't. Not my teachers, my straight friends, my parents."

"You're not out?" Howard asks, as if all this happened last year. Let him believe that. Or not. "Wait, are you in college?"

"No." My answer is stronger and more bitter than intended. Not Howard's fault. He doesn't know only James made it to Columbia. That I was attacked beneath a bridge that is now an overpass by a *thing* that dropped down on me with bone-white skin and fangs. "I didn't—haven't. I mean." I pause. Draw a deep breath. "I graduated high school but am . . . on a break."

This time I look directly at James. Howard follows my gaze. "Life isn't about hopping from one thing to the next as expected— that shit's for straight people," I say. "Being queer is about knowing what—and *who*—is important to you and seizing it." I clench my fist, drawing his attention. "You're graduating this year?"

"Yeah."

"Imagine the legacy you and your QSA will leave behind if you actually fight. That the two of us are sitting here now, having this conversation openly at a retirement home filled with people who know you and support you, didn't just *happen*. It's because of decades and decades of work. Of queers refusing to be erased and hidden away. Of punches and bricks thrown at Stonewall."

The shock and power of that night is forever seared into my brain—I wasn't there, but I sure heard about it the night after. "It's not about *who threw the first* . . . It's not about any specific one of you standing up for yourself—it's about all of you standing together. It's about the energy that rose around leaders like Marsha P. Johnson and Sylvia Rivera. About their founding STAR—that's the Street Transvestite Action Revolutionaries, if you don't—"

"Oh, I know." Howard's tone is breathy, his body literally on the edge of his seat. Like he might jump out of it and throw one of these glittery planters out the Spring Meadows craft room window as an act of protest.

"Do you know about the die-ins? About spreading the ashes of activists and loved ones the government isolated and killed?" I feel the heat return to my skin like I remember from my youth. The growing fury of shouting at a well-manicured White House lawn until I lost my voice, knowing not a damn person in there was listening. That none of them cared.

How many passages did I ease when few others wouldn't so much as look at AIDS patients, much less hold them? The *blessing* of immortality. I can't remember the last time I spoke freely about those times. In the early 2000s, when I reunited with James, queer deaths had finally begun to slow, and states were considering civil unions and equal marriage. The atmosphere was . . . improving, even if things weren't *fixed*. I told James some of what I'd seen and done during those decades apart, and though he listened intently to my stories, he didn't seem rooted in them the way I had been. How could he be, when he was pocketed away in domestic bliss? At the time I wasn't aware that he had never spoken about his sexuality with his wife, but she'd recently passed away, so I didn't want to pry.

We spoke about her, of course, and of our pasts. I couldn't imagine what it must have been like for James to live apart from the queer community all those years, unable to open up, though I didn't get the sense that James regretted his choices. Meanwhile, James couldn't quite wrap his head around my experiences: what it was like to march and protest, to be so desperate to be heard that I'd screamed myself hoarse on numerous occasions.

"They want to ignore us—always," I tell Howard. "We have to catch their attention. You want to be part of that; I know you do. Don't give up before you've even started. So what happens next? Is there some kind of town hall or student gathering?"

"A school board meeting." Confidence slips into his voice again. Howard's spark has returned. "There's only six of us, but we've all been working on our demands and presentation for years. Literally," he adds, reminding me that *years* is a long time for him. "I'm only the secretary, though. I won't be delivering the speech. That'll be my best friend, Sue. Actually, you guys are alike.

You both have that energy, that *fire*. I think he'd really like you."

"I'm, uh . . . I'm sure Sue's great and all, but I admit I'm more interested to know how *you* feel about me."

"Oh." He blushes again. I love it when he does that—when the blood warms his freckled face. It makes my mouth water and my pants feel a bit tighter. He pushes his hair back and lowers his voice. "I hate school." He looks down at his hands.

"It wasn't the best for me, either."

"It's not that I don't like learning. I'm graduating summa cum laude; I'm actually quite smart."

"I can tell," I say, and mean it. That confidence of his grips me like a fist.

I watch his pulse jump at the base of his throat. "It's just that no one gets me there? Like, I have Sue, and he's incredible—just like this bold, charismatic supernova that people are drawn to. Honestly, sometimes I don't know why he's friends with me."

He goes quiet. I give him the space to think, to finish.

"I hang out with Sue, and sometimes I'll go to parties or whatever if he invites me. But I always end up making friends with the house cat, watching everyone else laugh and drink like it's easy." Howard pauses, this time a question on his pursed lips. "Do you have a lot of friends?"

"I've been lucky in my life when it comes to friends," I reply. And it's the truth.

"Do you want to maybe introduce some of them to me?" he asks with a sad laugh.

If only. All the friends I lost to AIDS—Carlos, David, Missy K,

Shawn, Patty—and to violence and to suicide. And then all the friends I lost to time. "I've actually not made a lot of friends since I moved in with James."

He nods. "I get it. That's why I practically live at Spring Meadows."

I allow my lips to curl into a smile. "I can't blame you there. Old people are awesome."

Delight shines on Howard's face.

"Well," I amend. "Except the ones who have forgotten what it was like to be young. Them? Not so good."

Howard's smile fades—not into a frown, into *consideration*. His eyes drop to his own lap momentarily, like he's steeling himself for what he's about to say. I know I've barely told Howard anything about my life, that I've just hinted at my experiences, but I realize that I've opened up more to him than to anyone besides James in the past few decades. I have a feeling he might be about to do the same with me.

"Do you . . . ever get lonely?"

"I do."

"Me too." Those words from someone so young—so in his prime—break my heart. He glances at me, then quickly looks away, fixing a hair that wasn't out of place just to do something with his hands. "I have a hard time making friends, much less close friends." A pause. Another hair fixed before his eyes settle on mine. "Much, *much* less a boyfriend."

And then it's my turn to say, "Oh."

CHAPTER 7

It's not easy admitting you're lonely. Especially when it seems like everyone else has someone—or the possibility of someone. I have Sue, yes, but Sue also has Kenna, and there's nothing like a budding romance to pull your best friend away from you. Sure, I'm friends with the others in the QSA, but I just can't be totally open with them like I am with Sue. Like, if I expose my squishy insides to too many people, they'll become my outsides, and everyone will know I'm a lonely loser.

I know it's dramatic, but sometimes I wonder if I'll just continue to exist year after year, never finding the right person. Or finding them, only to discover that I'm not *their* right person. The older I get, the fewer single people I meet. Like, if I don't find a boyfriend in high school or college, that's it. Dying alone.

But I admitted it to George, and that . . . that means something. I know we've only even hung out a few times, but it feels like we're entirely in sync. Like he might understand. "Do you want to go for a walk?" I ask, before I can get too nervous about it.

George glances at James, who seems to be in good hands with Rosalie and Gladys. He smiles softly to himself—then at me. "Yeah. Let's get out of here." As we stand and pull on our sweaters, I swear Walter winks at me.

We hurry down the hallway like two thieves on the run: hands in our pockets, walking as fast as we can without running, glancing over our shoulders every few seconds to see if we're being followed. The journalists for sure know we're running off, so I make a mental note to text them my thanks for the privacy later. They love to tease, but I know they also want the best for me.

"Our grand escape," George says, pushing the door open. Cool night air seeps inside, and then we're outside, carrying our own warmth with us. Body heat.

We walk past the picnic tables, taking a path that leads toward the gardens, where the groundskeepers have already started hanging holiday lights on the evergreen trees. Luminous snowflakes decorate the path ahead instead of the normal solar lights. "It's only November," I say, nodding into the distance.

"I like it, though." George shrugs.

"I didn't say that I *don't* like it." I nudge his shoulder with mine.

We walk in pleasant silence for the few minutes it takes to reach the gardens. I've never gone on a walk with a boy, let alone a proper date. Wait. Is this a date? No. Just two guys walking alone beneath the stars. Though it's certainly more than I ever did with Gray. More than I did with that *nice boy* Oma tried to set me up with or that guy who gave me his number during the annual Polish caroling but who turned out to be more into sports than singing.

No, tonight feels different—it feels *right*. Like this is where our night truly begins. The white lights against the dark sky remind me of an old black-and-white movie. *Miracle on 34th Street* or *It's a Wonderful Life*, for sure, but . . . "Have you ever seen *The Shop Around the Corner*?"

"You've seen that?" His face simultaneously lights up and is illuminated as we reach the garden.

"Yeah, like every December with my oma—my grandmother," I add before he can ask. "I live with her." The reason *why*, I'll save for another day. "Which is perfect, because we like all the same things."

George chuckles. "You're an old soul, Howard."

"If I am, so are you."

"Guilty."

I pause a moment before saying, "I wish it was like this all the time—this easy."

"I admit, I have a hard time picturing you as the outcast you're framing yourself to be." He looks me over with a discerning eye, as if he can pinpoint my weak spot. He won't find it here, though. Not at Spring Meadows.

"That's because everyone here is seventy-five to a hundred years old."

"Just like you."

He says it kindly, as if he understands why I feel most at home here. "Just like me." I slow to a stop beneath a tall evergreen with twinkling lights. In the low light, we really could be in grayscale. "When I told you I have a hard time making friends, I meant it. Sue's the only one who really gets me, and that's only because he's spent a ton of time eating popcorn in my living room with me and Oma, forced to watch movies like *Maurice* on repeat."

"Oh, I love that one," George tosses in so casually, so naturally. Like we've known each other for years and are having this conversation for the dozenth time.

"You would," I say. "You're the only one I've ever met who dresses like me and knows all my favorite books and movies and shows. Well," I add with the tilt of my head and a bit of a squint, "the only one my age."

George laughs and tosses his hair back, running nimble fingers through black waves. I imagine threading my fingers through his, pressing his hands against the wall—pressing our bodies flush against each other. I realize that all my previous sexual fantasies involved people I'd never met before, and if I'm being honest, most of them were actors from a bygone era who are now dead. But here I am, having dirty thoughts about a boy walking *right next to me*. I've never had it so bad for a guy.

"Would you like to go out sometime?" The nerves only hit me once I've asked. Like I should've thought through whether he'd say yes, but I didn't, because he's going to, right? We're perfect for each other, and he's always flirting and finding a reason to touch me, and we're having a great time—just the two of us alone—in my favorite place. Still, doubt creeps in. If he says no, he'll probably stop coming by on Wednesdays, and I'll only hear about him from the journalists until James eventually passes—like they all do—and then that'll be it.

But George doesn't say no; he says, "Yeah, actually. I'd really like that."

"You would?" I guess I *was* expecting a *no*. Where's that confidence he was literally just telling you to have back inside? Believe in yourself, dammit. "I mean, that's—do you maybe want to see a movie at The Charles? I don't know if you're familiar . . . though you're familiar with almost everything I mention, so . . ."

George laughs and sits down on a bench beneath two snowflakes. It's not even winter yet, but I get a slight chill when I sit beside him. Like the mere presence of holiday decorations makes the air colder.

"I know it."

"Then you also know they have a revival series."

"I do."

"They're playing *My Beautiful Laundrette* on Friday."

"Are they? Haven't seen that one in years." He digs into his pocket and fishes out a worn leather wallet stuffed with wrinkled bills. No wonder he had trouble with the vending machines—who even carries cash anymore? (Okay, I do. But only because Oma hands me a five whenever I go out.) From the wallet's depths, George pulls out a scrap of paper and tears off a corner. And then he produces an old ballpoint pen, like a rabbit from a hat, and begins writing on it.

He slips it to me like a note in class. "My number."

I almost drop it—which would be a disaster because we're outside and it's dark—because he wrote his name—*George Culhane*—and number down on a slip of paper for me rather than typing it into my phone. I can't believe I'm the kind of person who finds this romantic.

"Thanks," I manage. "I'll text—" Wait, what if he doesn't have a cell phone? Though who doesn't have a cell phone? Landlines only exist in schools and offices now. Even Oma has a smartphone. "Or should I call?"

"You can text me."

Oh, so he has a cell, and he wrote his number down for me on paper. Okay then. I open my own wallet, pull out one of the QSA cards Sue had made up for all of us, and write my number on the back of it. Not as cute as a slip of paper, but it'll do.

I hand it to him. "Same."

"Ooh, am I invited to your club?"

"Only if you want to reenroll in high school."

"A tempting offer." He pockets the card, then pulls his feet up onto the bench.

I do the same such that we're looking directly at each other. I could take his hand right now. Lean forward. Kiss him . . .

"George, is that you?!"

Our feet are flat on the ground at the sound of Ada's voice. I'm supposed to be inside, helping.

"George!" Ada calls, rushing toward us.

"What does she want you for?" I ask, but he's already on his feet, worry lining his face, his eyes no longer on mine.

Ada slows to a stop, panting. Must be bad if she ran all the way out here looking for him. "It's James." I stand up, taking my place beside him as she explains, "He's having an episode. Seems to think you're in high school together? You know we can handle these on our own, but he's asking for you and it's always easier if someone familiar—"

"I'm coming," he says without hesitation.

"Hey, Howard." Ada gives me an apologetic look and mouths *sorry.*

"Don't worry about it," I say. "This is important."

"I don't know if I'll be back," is the last thing George says as he jogs back toward Spring Meadows, Ada following.

As soon as they disappear inside, I sit. I put my hand in my pocket and finger the flimsy piece of paper with George's number on it. I wish I could be there for him like he was for me tonight. But this is beyond me—a private part of his life I'll have to be invited into, if I am at all. I want to help him. I want *him.* Not only for his fashion and his taste in books, but also his passion. And the way he cares for his grandpa. Which is why I give him his space. Which is why I wait.

CHAPTER 8

GEORGE

James is in bed, and as Ada informed me when I arrived today, he has been in bed all day for the second day in a row. I don't try to squeeze into it beside him, because he just looks so fragile. This is what happens when mortals age. This is what caring for my dying partner looks like: sitting with him, talking to him, holding his hand. *Not* feeding on him.

I feel guilty for having done so two nights ago. As I rub my thumb over his, I can't help but wonder whether I make James' bad days worse. Ada says they're not my fault, but she doesn't know I'm a predator. Howard doesn't know I'm a predator either, but he might suspect something tonight on our date.

"You should eat," James says, releasing my hands to go for his collar—flannel pajamas I bought him for his birthday. The set reminds me of one I had as a child.

"No." I lace my fingers through his again and put his hand back onto his lap. I'm always stronger than him, but he feels especially weak now. He doesn't pretend to fight me. He doesn't play. "You need your strength." I don't tell him that I worry that my feeding on him affects his mind, not in the least because I have no evidence—only a bad feeling.

"And you need those rosy cheeks of yours for your date with Howard." James cracks a smile. "Yes, I remembered. And I remembered his name."

I smile in return. "You did."

"I'm still here."

"You are."

I've barely left James' side since I left Howard in the garden. I can't think of anything other than how much worse and more frequent his bad days are becoming. I did share with James that Howard had invited me to see *My Beautiful Laundrette*, a movie I saw by myself when it first came out in 1986 and one I shared with James when we first started "dating" again. James encouraged me to see the movie with Howard, but the idea of going out on a date while the love of my life lay ill in bed felt wrong. After we exchanged numbers, Howard sent me the showing information, but I didn't respond.

My phone vibrates on the nightstand: another text from Howard. I should write him back, tell him that I can't make it. "I'm not going out." I turn my phone over, muting its soft glow.

James leans forward. "Yes, you are."

"No! I'm not leaving you. This is where I belong."

"You belong where you're happy," he says.

"I'm happy here."

"I know," he says quietly, leaning back. As much as I dislike the hospital-style bed, it does allow him to relax in a sitting position. To easily get in and out. To look at me while he chides me. "I'll make you a deal."

"What's that?"

"You tell me a story about one of our dates, and then you go on yours. Make a new memory to share with me when you get back."

"You'll be asleep when I get back." I give him a smile, encouraged by this hint of his usual playfulness.

"And you'll be gone when daylight hits, but we always find time. Make a good memory. Save it for me."

"Fine," I relent. "But first a bedtime story for you, old man."

James makes a show of settling in and pulling the covers up. "I only regret never becoming your sugar daddy, as they say."

I burst out laughing as I climb onto the end of his bed, careful not to sit on his legs. "I've literally been living with you unemployed for twenty years. If you want me to call you Daddy, I will. Better than 'Grandfather.' Makes me want to walk into the sun."

James watches me roll my eyes, a smile fixed to his face. "I'm waiting."

"Hmm." Our time together has been separated by a sea of years. We didn't really *date* when we were teens. We couldn't be seen holding hands or seated at a table for two. Not that men didn't eat together back then, but we always shared an intimacy that drew looks. When we found each other again decades later, we did go on dates, but we still had to be mindful of our affections in public, both because of the apparent age difference and because we were two men. I regret—and resent—that James and I never had the chance to show the world the depth of our love, that we always felt compelled to hide parts of ourselves. It takes a toll.

A memory comes to me, one from a few years ago. "You know, Howard and I are going to The Charles."

"Oh, I love that theater—you know I do."

"I do."

"They don't make 'em like that anymore."

It's exactly what he said when I told him yesterday about possibly going there with Howard. But I press on.

"They don't. Last time I saw a movie in a theater was with you, you know." That's it. That's the one. "That old theater, the Parkway, where we used to go in high school. Where we saw *Ben-Hur* when it was first released—right before the theater closed. We saw it twice there, didn't we, just for the way Messala looked at Ben-Hur. When they opened back up—when was it? I can't remember the year. Not long ago. They'd remade the film not long ago, so there was a screening during some kind of film festival, and you insisted it would probably be even gayer than the original because, quote, 'Times have changed.' And then it was *less* gay, like disappointingly less gay."

I chuckle to myself and rest a hand on James' thigh, enjoying his warmth. I haven't fed since Wednesday, so I'll be extra cold tonight. I should make a point not to hold Howard's hand. That I have this thought as I sit on my lover's bed results in a pang of guilt.

"We got all dressed up, even though we were only going to sit in the dark. I think you said something like, 'One of us is nocturnal.' To which I relented. No complaints, obviously. You wore an old tie clip your mom gave you—it's still in the jewelry box back home. I can bring it if you'd like."

James doesn't answer. He's probably asleep; I'm probably talking to myself, but not for nothing. I want to hold on to as many of his memories for as long as I can. To keep him alive as long as I am.

"Anyway, how handsome you looked—*very* handsome— is beside the point. I accidentally bought tickets to the wrong screening—you know I'm still not very good at the internet. Just because I look like one of those kids walking down the sidewalk with their eyes glued to their phones doesn't mean I am one." I squeeze James' leg. His eyes are closed now. I watch to make sure that his chest is still rising and falling.

It is.

"I was too embarrassed to tell the ticket guy that I'd bought tickets to the wrong movie, so we snuck into that showing. I'm glad we did. And there was no reason to be nervous, since the theater was empty. Still, we sat all the way in the back. I spent the previews trying to toss popcorn into your mouth."

When I look at James, he's looking back at me. Then he's taking my hand between his, and we might as well be back on that date.

"And I held your hand in the back of that theater. And we kissed in the back row, like two horny teenagers." *Like we should have been able to when we were actually teenagers.*

James squeezes my hand.

"You know, I cleaned up all the popcorn off the floor when you went to the bathroom. I couldn't leave it for the custodian. And because you had the wrong ticket, they almost didn't let you back into the theater!" I burst out laughing. "I remember an usher coming over and asking me if my 'grandfather' was okay, and you know I normally hate that, but somehow you'd convinced them you were just a confused old man, and they sent you back to your seat with a complimentary bucket of popcorn." I sigh dreamily. "God, what a night."

"What a night," James repeats, rubbing his hands over mine. Repetition makes me nervous. It's a strategy he uses to engage in conversations when he doesn't remember and doesn't want me to worry.

I worry. "You bought me a rose from a street vendor on the way home." I still have it pressed into the pages of my journal. "And then we immediately hopped onto the couch and watched the original on DVD. Pretty sure you also ate popcorn for dinner that night," I add.

"Popcorn for dinner, huh," he says. "Sounds like me."

It does. Because it *was you*, James. I'm too nervous to ask outright if he remembers. Even more nervous that when he's gone, I'll be gone too in a way, as there will be no one left who really knows me. Whereas James and everyone else I've met will live on in my mind.

I glance at the clock and then at my overturned phone.

"Aren't you going out tonight?" James asks, following my gaze.

"With Howard," I answer, hoping the name will catch in his memory.

"That's right. We made a deal—you'd tell me a story and then you'd go on your date."

That he remembers gives me a sense of relief.

"I meant, shouldn't you be leaving soon?"

Right. "Yes, I should—I'll need to catch the bus shortly. Or maybe he'll pick me up here. I haven't really discussed it with him."

"And why the hell not?" James nudges me so hard, I almost lose my balance and topple off the bed. I look at him, and he has this mischievous smile on his face. Things feel almost normal.

"I've been busy."

"Didn't you just declare yourself a kept husband or some such?"

That gets another laugh from me. Even though the answer is that I've been busy worrying over him. What will happen when he's gone? After my visits to Spring Meadows, I've been rushing home to pack up our most personal belongings and hiding them so that his daughter doesn't throw them in the garbage. Every night when I come and go, the FOR SALE sign in the yard taunts me. "Could you do me a favor?" I ask.

"Anything, my love."

"Would you let me know as soon as the realtor schedules a visit at the house? Someone came by earlier, and I was caught off guard. Is your daughter giving you that information?" I ask. "Could you pass it along?"

"Oh." Worry lines his face. James pulls his hands away and begins fiddling with his collar. "I can—well, no." Embarrassment floods his cheeks. As if she isn't taking advantage of a dying man. As if it's his fault for not knowing everything. "I can ask her to tell me. Knowing Jackie, she keeps a calendar on her phone." He begins to reach for his own, but I close my hand over his gently.

"Ooh!" He exaggerates a shiver and pulls back. "Your hands are so cold." He brings them to his mouth and blows hot air onto them before rubbing them together.

And *again*, I am afraid to ask if he's forgotten I'm always cold. That it's because I'm an undead thing that feeds on blood—his, often. What if the last time I did so was our actual last? It has always been a consensual act, but as his dementia worsens, I need to be more mindful. I could never risk him forgetting while my jaws were clamped around his throat. Terror in his eyes, screaming about a monster sucking his blood. *Never.*

I force a smile and bring my own hands to my mouth like James did. Breathe on them and rub. They do not get warmer.

"As I was saying about the calendar . . ."

That he's well enough to bring that back up settles me a bit. But I don't want him to worry over me. "Oh, it's not a huge deal."

"No, no, it is." James shakes his head. "I'll ask Jackie if she'll share it with me so that I can share it with you. In case I . . ." We let the implication hang between us for a moment. "I assume you were safe since you're here?"

"Yes, I managed to stay out of sight."

He narrows his eyes at me. "What does that mean? Did you make it down to the basement bunk?"

"Not exactly."

We built the little hidden room not long after I moved in with James. The first thing we'd done was to make our bedroom lightproof, and that was where I'd spend the daylight hours. But there were always going to be people who needed access to the house during the day, like tradespeople for repairs, and sometimes our neighbor Shelly would bring her two little girls over after school—they loved James. On those days I'd move from our room down to the basement just before dawn.

In those early years, we were selective about who met me, how I was introduced, and for how many consecutive years they could see me before it became suspicious that I didn't look any older. James was constant, though, and beloved by those on our block. We had a neighbor then named Bart, a friendly young man who used to bring him home-cooked meals once per week. James' wife Theresa had passed, and that's what you did when a neighbor suffered a loss: cooked for them. Helped them keep going.

As the years pressed on, our favorite neighbors, like Shelly and Bart, moved away, for the county schools or because of a developer offer or wanting a lawn or . . . any number of perfectly valid reasons. As a result, the bulk of our neighbors are now strangers. And because of that we have far fewer visitors, so I've spent very little time in my secret basement bunk.

"George, don't—don't do this. We've always been open with each other. I don't want to hurt you or put you in danger if I can help it."

He's right. I just don't know that he *can* help it.

I sigh, and though I want to take his hands again, I don't. Not sure I can handle him pulling away or calling me cold a second time tonight. "I hid." I don't blush easily, especially when I haven't fed, but I feel the faintest warmth on my cheeks when I admit, "In our closet."

At that, James takes my hands himself and pulls me toward him. I leverage myself slowly into the small space beside him, lie on my side, and curl against his. He turns his head to kiss the top of mine. "I'm sorry," he whispers. "You deserve to feel safe in your own home."

Your own home.

It is. It's where I've lived—where *we've* lived—for the past two decades, our belongings enmeshed and embedded in every room. My dirty socks on the floor and his half-read books on the coffee table. Our toothbrushes by the sink, our bed neatly made. But my name isn't on the deed, not only because he keeps me secret from his family, but because I'm legally dead. I can't apply for a mortgage.

But I can lie in bed with the man I've loved for over sixty years. I can burn this moment into my brain so that it lives as long as I do. Even when our home is gone. Even when he's gone. I glance at my phone as it vibrates against the nightstand. Another text from Howard. Like I said: I've survived alone before, and I can do it again.

CHAPTER 9

Sue taps the side of his head, signaling for me to remove an earbud. When I do, he asks, "Are you listening to ABBA again?"

"Maybe." Like that's a bad thing. Like they don't have numerous songs for when I want to waste away emotionally in my bedroom because George hasn't texted me back and we were supposed to be going on a date tonight? Because they do.

"And are you listening to 'Chiquitita'?"

I narrow my eyes at him—"Maybe"—as I pop the earbud back in and try to care about my calculus homework. Just because I'm good at math doesn't mean I like it. And I get through one whole problem before Sue's tapping the side of his head for my attention again and I'm pausing my song, looking at him expectantly.

This time he grabs the earbud right out from my other ear—before also snatching the one in my hand, so I can clearly hear Sue say, "Stop—"

"Hey!"

"—worrying."

"I wasn't *worrying*, I was *moping*. Let me mope." I flop down onto my bed, the absolute worst position to do homework in, but sitting at my desk had felt less emotionally dramatic, so I'd let Sue sit there. Of course this is happening to me. Of course I find the perfect boy and then he stands me up. I'm allowed to be sad.

Sue crosses his arms and plants his feet, staring down at me from what he must feel like is a superior vantage point. "He'll text—"

"You don't know that."

"And if he doesn't," Sue plows on, "it's his loss."

I sigh and drop my head flat onto the sheets. Reach out and press play on my phone, unleashing "Chiquitita" on both of us. In Sue's defense, I did invite him over after school for emotional support, so I can't blame him for doing exactly that. I would definitely feel worse lying here alone, listening to an even mopier and more embarrassing ABBA song. Like, George and I haven't even been on one date yet—might not at this rate—so that does not qualify us for breakup songs.

"Is it?" I ask. "Or is it *my* loss, because we're perfect for each other and it'll be ages before I find anyone, assuming I ever do?"

"Look, I'm not going to call you dramatic because I know you're really into this guy."

"Thanks."

He smiles. "But also, I'm pretty sure 'Chiquitita' is about cheering up your bestie, soooo . . ."

I snort a laugh. It's undignified, but Sue's right. Really got myself with that one. "Okay, okay. Let's just pretend he's not going to text, and that way I won't be disappointed if he doesn't. And we can make cookies with Oma or something, and I can make you watch *Ben-Hur*—the original, not the remake—so we can point out all the homoerotic parts."

"Howard, isn't that movie, like, three hours long?"

"Three and a half. It's a classic. It won eleven Oscars. And I watched this documentary about how it *was* canonically queer—"

"Howard! Sue!" Oma's voice carries up the stairs and through my open bedroom door. "Dinner's ready!"

"Oh no," Sue says with enough sarcasm that I actually smile. "Time for dinner!" He's on his feet so fast, I find myself scrambling off the bed and down the stairs into the kitchen after him.

"Slow down, slow down!" Oma says as we careen into the room. "There's enough for all of us."

"Smells great, Oma," I say, lingering while Sue goes to set the table. And it's true—hachée is my favorite. It's warm and comforting. On a normal night, I'd love to make myself a plate and settle onto the couch with the two of them, but today it just reminds me that George hasn't texted back, and this is my night now.

"Then why do you sound so sad about it?"

I guess if anyone can tell when I'm sad, it's Sue and Oma, and tonight they're giving me the metaphorical one-two punch. I glance at Sue, who I can tell is purposefully giving me space to fill

Oma in, setting down spoons like he's setting afternoon tea for the queen of England.

I sigh. "I was supposed to have a date tonight."

"And why didn't you tell me about it?" she shoots back.

"You know I would have, but . . ." I tilt my head back and forth, wavering. "I wasn't sure it was going to happen. George—that's his name—"

"Good name, George is."

"Yeah, but—I mean . . ." I've lost my footing. "He agreed to go out when we were talking, but I texted him to confirm and he hasn't texted me back, so . . ."

"Well, maybe he's not on his phone all the time like *some of you* are," Oma says, loud enough that Sue looks up from his where he sits at the table, which is only half set. But then she rests her hand on my shoulder and squeezes. "Do you want to tell me about this boy—George?"

"Not really. I mean, if we're not going out, it's over. No use getting myself all excited about him for nothing, you know?"

"Well, then, if you'd like, I'd planned to put on a *Golden Girls* marathon that starts in . . ." She checks her watch. "Fifteen minutes. We can take our dinner over to the couch. I'll even make popcorn for dessert."

I tell her the same thing I'd told Sue when he'd asked whether I was being sad to ABBA: "Maybe."

Oma nudges my chin gently with her knuckles before shooing me off to join Sue. It's not long before she joins the two of us, dishing out comfort food with a smile that I try to match. I can tell they're trying to cheer me up or distract me—I've never seen Sue so hyped about a *Golden Girls* marathon. I'm trying to hype myself up for the same when my phone pings. All three of us look at it.

I slide it off the table and into my lap—consider excusing myself to my room so I can take the rejection in private if needed. But it's not needed. "It's him," I whisper, reading the text over and over to make sure I'm not hallucinating.

George: Sorry for the slow reply. See you at the theater shortly.

I grin. "I have a date tonight."

I shovel the rest of my dinner into my mouth while Sue spills the few details about George that I've shared with him already and Oma nods along, asking questions and being interested without embarrassing me too badly. I take it. The atmosphere is warm, and the old stained-glass lamplight is warm, and the hachée is warm. And when I finish, Oma doesn't even make us stay to do the dishes, waving me and Sue off with a smile on her face.

"Oh no," I say as we barrel into my bedroom.

"What?" Sue stops in his tracks.

I stare back at him. "Now I have to actually go on the date."

"Oh, shut up!" He whacks my shoulder before making space for himself amid the pages of calculus homework on my bed.

I scour my closet, pulling out several options. Knowing me, I'm going to stick my foot in my mouth at least once tonight, so I might as well look okay doing it. "I just haven't done this before, you know? And I definitely get the sense that he has. I don't want to embarrass myself."

"Don't overthink this, Howard. It's just a date."

"But I don't know how to go on a date! This isn't like one of the movies I've watched with Oma where the guy picks up the girl, holds all the doors, pays the check, and kisses her at the end of the night."

"No, it's not, and those scripts suck anyway."

"They do! But at least there *is* one."

Sue gives a plaid blazer a thumbs-down. "Look," he says. "I haven't been on any dates since before I came out, and they were fine, but you know what I would have loved?"

"Flowers? Chocolates?"

"Communication."

"Oh no."

"Oh yes. Sounds boring but—"

"Is actually terrifying? Like, are you suggesting that I should *ask* about splitting the check?"

"Is that . . . scary?"

"Yeah! Straight people get to just *know* what to do."

"Only if they want to conform to outdated gender role bull-shit," Sue says.

"Fair." I pause, letting the notion sink in. I've got to stop watching so many old romances. "So, does this mean I should, like, ask to kiss him rather than just go for it during whatever moment feels most romantic? Always seems to be at the end of the night on the other person's stoop."

"I mean, that's certainly your last opportunity of the night, but yes. You could ask."

"Oh god, what if he says no?"

"Then he says no!" Sue leans forward, smiling as I pull together another outfit. "Which might mean 'never' but also might mean 'not right now,' and in that case, he *knows* you want to kiss him, which is very hot."

"Still sounds terrifying, but if you say so."

"I do. And I'm the only one of us who's kissed a boy, so that makes me the expert." Sue hops to his feet and fixes my collar like he's my dad sending me off to prom, but his validation relaxes me. Even if everything goes to shit, I still have one friend who cares. "Listen, you're going to be great. You don't have to be Clark Gable or Cary Grant or one of those old-timey leading men. Just talk to him and have fun—the whole point of a date is getting to know someone better. And if you want to plant a big smooch on his mouth, say so. Who knows, maybe he'll kiss you. But you're taller, so it would be easier for—"

"Oh, look at the time," I say, not looking at the time at all.

"Well, if you two kiss, you've got to tell me about it."

I pull Sue into a hug and hold him for a moment before pulling back and looking him in the eye. "I will. And thanks. Seriously."

"Of course. Now get out of here so I can marathon *Golden Girls* with Oma while I finish my homework."

"You don't want to go home to your mom, do you?"

"Not at all."

I don't blame him one bit. His terrible mom and my terrible parents are one of my least favorite things we have in common. But at least we each have someone who understands. Oma has warned him before that she's known for taking in strays. (It's me. I'm the stray.)

"Well, enjoy," I say, finally cracking a smile. Makes Sue smile too. "I have a date."

I arrive fifteen minutes before the time we agreed to meet and sit in my car, praying George doesn't see me on his way in. Did I park a block away just so I could watch for him to arrive and then hop out at that exact moment and walk up looking cool and casual?

Yup.

My plan backfires when the city bus pulls up and drops off a handful of passengers, including George. Now *he's* early and just standing around looking cute and alone. I can't make him wait, right? Sue wouldn't.

I slide out from the car and start down the sidewalk toward the theater, looking both at him and everywhere but. That is, I can't let him catch me looking too soon, or I'll have to maintain eye contact the rest of the way, and I'm not strong enough for that yet.

George has the grace to lean against the brick building and stare at his shoes: tan leather loafers, well-worn with fresh soles. Rest of him looks damn good too. Black high-rise jeans with a striped button-down tucked in, chunky grandpa sweater over the top. I wonder what it would feel like to walk up and slide my hand around his waist—between the cool silky texture of his shirt and the warm wool of his sweater.

Instead, I stop awkwardly a few feet away and shove my hands in my pockets. Clear my throat and say, "Hey."

He looks up at me with an intensity that reminds me of James Dean. "Hey," he replies, pushing himself slightly off the wall.

"You're early." I say it like he should apologize for it, which I don't mean to—don't mean to say it at all.

"Oh yeah." He glances from his watch to me. "I was worried if I caught a later bus, I'd miss the movie. Baltimore isn't known for its public transportation."

"True." I'm lucky Oma lets me drive her car pretty much whenever I want, even though it's old enough to have a cassette player. I've decided that means it's vintage. "Well then, we have more time for popcorn."

George's smile is . . . an attempt. A line he struggles to hold. "I guess."

I wilt. Haven't even made it inside, and it seems like I've already messed up *communicating*. Don't even know how. Oma and Sue were wrong. I'm not going to be great.

"Okay," I say, mustering as much optimism as possible. My smile is also an attempt. "Well, let's get our tickets, yeah?"

George nods and follows me to the window, where I offer to buy his ticket—it's the gentlemanly thing to do. I invited him, and I want to pay. Not that I have a ton of cash to spare, but I have been saving the fives that Oma gives me. And she slipped me a fifty and a wink on the way out because she knew I'd do something like this.

"Thanks," George says as I hand him his ticket. He studies it intently as I lead us toward the inside.

This theater makes me feel things. We're literally standing inside a piece of Baltimore history, one that upholds historic film traditions. Its brick interior, lights, balconies, bold-striped concession stand, and high ceilings make you feel like you've stepped into a different era. Even when I've come alone it's always felt romantic, and with George here even more so. Or at least it should. Like we should be sitting across from each other at a little table, passing the time over popcorn, our hands accidentally touching inside the bucket.

"Did you still want to get popcorn?" His voice pulls me to a present where he seems to be going through the motions of a date rather than *being on one* with me. George gestures to the concession stand as if I should go up and order on my own.

"Oh, don't you want any? Or a drink?" I step up and survey our options. "My favorite is Tab, actually, but they only sell Coke here."

Part of me expects him to smile and agree—it's what he might have done the last time we were at Spring Meadows. Seemed like we had everything in common then. Now?

"No, thanks."

Maybe he's sick—I don't *want* him to be sick, but I might want it more than *he hates me.*

"I'll get a medium drink and popcorn, and you can have some if you'd like." Another stab at optimism, and another miss as George lingers a few feet away from me, disinterested. I sneak a glance as the cashier rings me up. Does he look paler than usual? I can't believe how much I hope he's not feeling well. Horrible of me.

"Ready?" he asks as I walk up to him with my snacks.

"Yeah," is all I can manage.

We walk silently to the ticket-taker and down a long dim hall toward the theater. *My Beautiful Laundrette* is playing on the smallest screen they have, and it's empty when we arrive. I stare at the sea of empty red seats. "Guess we can sit wherever we want."

"Guess so," he says.

It would have been better if there were fewer choices. If I were here with Sue, we'd aim for center middle for the best view. With Oma, closer to the front so she could see and hear better. But I have this impression that people on dates sit in the back so they have privacy. So they can make out. Which is something I would have liked to do with George, if he were showing me any of the interest he did when we were talking in the gardens in Spring Meadows. Maybe we should just sit in the middle.

He brushes past me. "Let's sit in the back."

Oh.

I follow him to the center of the back row, where we sit in silence. I hold the popcorn bucket on my lap, afraid the sound of my chewing will make whatever awkward spell has settled over our date even worse.

Ten minutes pass in silence as we stare at the various preshow ads playing on the screen. My mouth starts to feel like the Sahara, so I risk leaning forward for a sip of my Coke. I can't believe he didn't show even a hint of recognition at Tab. Guess it doesn't matter. I close my eyes and take a long drink before eating some more popcorn. Once the lights go down and the sound of previews add their own distraction, I find it easier to relax a little, since you're supposed to be silent during a movie anyway. In the dark I glance sideways at George. He's not even looking at the screen; he's looking at his phone. If he isn't sick, maybe something else is wrong. Something that's not me.

I glance around and see we're still alone in the theater.

"Is everything okay?" I ask, following his eyes up from the device. Before he has a chance to answer, I add, "Sorry, I'm not trying to pry—it's just . . ."

George sighs. He turns off his phone and slides it between his thighs. Away, but not *away*. "I'm sorry. I'm not usually this distracted."

I feel guilty about the relief that slides through me. Maybe it's not me. "Do you want to talk about it?"

He looks around the theater, and even though it's empty, he still speaks in a soft voice. "James isn't having a good week, and he's . . . well, he's really important to me. And I'm scared. I'm losing him, Howard. Not all at once, either. Parts of himself and his past—our past—or more frequently, our present. Sometimes he looks at me like I'm a stranger, and that terrifies me. It's like he's dying in slow motion. His body and mind unraveling. And he's all I have."

"Hey." I place a hand tentatively over George's on the armrest. His skin is cold—no wonder he's wearing such a warm sweater. For a moment the theater is pitch black, and I'm staring into the reflective silver of his eyes. "It's—I won't tell you it's going to be okay because people die. That's life, and none of us can stop it. Just like my dziadzi and . . ." My voice wavers. "I know Oma won't be around much longer, either. She's getting old, finding it harder to get around. But it sounds different for James."

George nods. "Yeah, he still gets around just fine. But he's forgotten entire summers we spent together, or he thinks we're in high school. And that hurts, but I can handle it. What I can't handle is scaring him because he thinks I'm a stranger in his room. I miss him already." At that he twines his fingers with mine, allowing himself to be held.

"Have you . . ." I always hesitate before bringing up another queer person's parents, because I know how complicated—or outright traumatizing—that can be.

As the actual movie starts to roll, the screen lighting up George's face, he asks, "What?"

"Are your parents cool? I mean, do you have support?"

"Oh. No, my parents passed away. But I never came out to them when they were alive."

Well, damn. "I'm sorry to hear that—I think? I mean." This could be going better. "I know families can be complicated for people like us. That sometimes they're gone and you don't miss them."

"What about yours?" He sounds sincere. Interested in my parents, even though his are gone.

"It's a bit of a story."

He glances around the theater as if proving we're not interrupting anyone. "I don't mind."

I've never shared this with anyone besides Sue, and definitely not in public. But George just opened up to me, and we're alone. "Well, I live with my grandma, so you can probably guess that I'm not close with them." I try to laugh, even though I know it's not funny. "I came out to my parents the summer after eighth grade."

"Wow. That's so young," George says.

"Yeah, but I just knew, you know? And so did all the kids at school. I mean, I started getting bullied in kindergarten. Middle school was especially bad. . . ." I pause, remembering how kids used to pull at my long hair, now cut short. How they called me a girl any time we were split up by gender. How I heard the word "fag" long before I knew what it meant, except that it was clearly bad and not a thing I wanted to be. "My mom used to comfort me after I'd had a particularly rough day. So I honestly thought they'd be okay with me being gay; I felt like they already knew.

"But when I told them, they acted like the idea had never crossed their minds. It baffled me. It was like, *Can you see me? Can you hear me?* I wasn't fooling anybody, and I wasn't trying to."

The expressions on my mom and dad's faces are seared into my mind—shock, disgust, disappointment—and I feel my heart pound as my cheeks burn.

"My mom said some awful things, like 'Don't go and die of AIDS,' and 'If you're going to choose this life, please don't be like those men we see in the parades.' My dad just sat there silently, ignoring me, the child he used to ride bikes with and make grilled cheese sandwiches for after school."

I glance at George to gauge his reaction. He's watching my face with understanding and anger in his eyes. I can tell he's really listening. So I continue.

"After Dziadzi moved to Spring Meadows, which was right around when I started high school, we started doing Sunday dinners at Oma's. On the drive to one of those dinners, I decided I was going to tell Oma that evening—I just needed to tell a family member who I was sure would accept me. I knew my parents wouldn't want me to, so I was a stressed-out wreck the whole time. At one point, Oma went into the kitchen to make tea for stroopwafels, and I fled to the bathroom because I just couldn't be alone with my parents another minute. I heard her calling my name when she returned and my parents telling her I wasn't feeling well. Not a total lie. She must've known, though—some grandmotherly instinct."

"That's real," George interrupts. "The older you get, the more you just *know*. At least James does."

That softens my smile. "She found me crying in the bathroom and asked what was wrong. When I told her—both that I was gay and how Mom and Dad had reacted—she just said, 'This is your home. You live with me now.' And I have ever since. I didn't even go home that night. I honestly don't know what Oma and my parents said to one another, and I kind of don't want to. Like, it hurt that they were all, 'Sure, you take him,' even though it was also such a *relief* to be away from them. Like I'd shed a weight I didn't even know I was carrying."

"Do you ever see them? Your parents?"

"Less and less." That they were fine with getting rid of me hurts less and less, too. "After I moved in with Oma, they still came over for Sunday dinners." I think back to those first few meals. "God, it was *so* awkward. Just, like, tense and silent; any time I spoke up, they found a way to knock me down, like I'd gained too much confidence without them. And a small part of me kept expecting them to apologize or hug me . . . something!" I shake the memories away. "Oma would tell me some people just need time. But I got sick of waiting—they had enough time." I take a deep breath as my eyes start to burn. "I started finding reasons not to be home for Sunday dinner. The last time I saw them was maybe four months ago?" It's the most I've said about my mom and dad in years.

"I'm sorry your parents didn't accept you," he says. "But your oma sounds amazing."

"She is. Honestly . . ." I hesitate. Easier to say this to someone whose parents are still alive.

But George nudges me. "You can say it."

So I do. "I wouldn't miss them if they were dead. But I also feel a bit weird wishing death on them."

"It's okay," George says to my relief. "You're right. Family *is* complicated for people like us. And the more you talk about your oma, the more I want to meet her."

"Guess I'm spoiled for having met James already."

"Yeah, you are." He squeezes my hand before trading it for his armrest. Letting go now that he no longer needs the comfort, I hope. Already I miss the cool length of his fingers between mine.

We actually watch the movie for about fifteen minutes before George bumps the side of his head gently against mine and says, "Thank you. For being patient with me. I don't really have anyone besides James and . . . it feels really special having found someone I can open up to after all these years."

I risk a glance at him and—oh fuck, our eyes meet, and how I wouldn't love to kiss him right here in the back row of this historic theater. Make some history of our own.

"I feel the same way," I whisper, even though we've been alone this whole time. "Like, I'm sort of embarrassed how terrible I am with people my own age. No one wants to hang out with me and my grandmother or hear about embroidery night at Spring Meadows. Sue falls asleep almost every time I put on movies like this."

"Well, I'm wide awake, and I love this movie," George says, smiling. His gaze shifts from my eyes to my lips and for a moment I—

"So do you want to actually watch it?" He laughs.

"Yeah," I say, grinning as we relax into our seats, leaning our shoulders against each other. Can't do that in those fancy new theaters with their recliners. "I do."

CHAPTER 10

GEORGE

When we spill out into the night, I feel like a time traveler. It takes me a minute to readjust to modern-day Baltimore, despite how different now is from then. I first saw *My Beautiful Laundrette* in this little independent theater in the Village that the straights had all but given up on. I went by myself, but I wasn't alone; the theater was packed with queer people, all eager to see a version of their lives depicted on the big screen—a rarity then. The energy was palpable; it felt like I had a heartbeat again.

Tonight could not have been more different, and yet I swear there's a pitter-patter in my dead chest. Back in Baltimore, in an empty theater this time, save for me and my date. *My date.* As memorable tonight as it was the first time, but for all its own reasons. Howard's with me now, and that conversation inside meant everything. To be able to open up to someone again, even a little, and for them to trust me in return . . . it's powerful. If I'm being honest with myself, it makes me want to kiss him. The heat of him pulses beside me as we almost glide across the sidewalk. I turn, taking a few steps backward just so I can watch him come toward me, so alive and buoyant as he catches my eye and blushes, smiles.

"What?" Howard asks as if he can't see his own spark. I see it, though.

"Nothing," I say as he catches up. "Just you, looking radiant."

He laughs nervously but doesn't demur. If I wanted to take a drink from his gorgeous neck, it'd be so easy; I wouldn't even have to *try* if I wanted a bite. Just like Johnny did to Omar in the movie, I could pull Howard close. Lick the side of his neck. Mark where I'm going to bite him . . .

"I can only imagine what it would've been like, watching that in the eighties," he says, face flushed with blood. "Especially the end, when they literally had sex in the back of the laundrette . . ." Howard's eyes gloss over as he looks away. It's not that he doesn't *want* to look at me; it's that he can't because he's shy. I can hear his pulse picking up speed, feel the warmth radiating from his body.

"I can imagine it, all right." I am not going to bite him—I can't.

But I *want* to. I like to think, after all that popcorn, he'd taste of butter and salt on my tongue—both his blood and his lips. I steal the empty popcorn bucket, toss it into a city trash can, and take his hand firmly in mine.

He grins and leans his body against mine, our hips and shoulders touching. I guide our clasped hands behind us, letting them come to rest on my lower back. Showing Howard where I want him to touch me, hold me.

I haven't been on a real date like this in so long. Evenings curled up on James' lap, pressing kisses to each other's skin between stories and laughter. Nights in dark rooms with men who are into biting—who love *that thing you do with your teeth, George,* as they would tell me. But not a *date,* like meeting at the theater and getting to know each other in the dark while the two men on screen do the same. I'm thinking about how I'd like Howard to take me in the projection room the way Johnny took Omar in the back room. I could kiss him. Right here on the street. In front of everyone. Pull him into my cool arms in the cool night air—so smoothly, he wouldn't even notice until my lips were on his . . .

"Obviously, I want to feel safe and open and accepted," Howard says, cheeks still tinged pink. "But I also love feeling like I've got this incredible secret." He looks around the street at, if I were to guess, what are mostly straight people. "Like no one else knows how meaningful and hot that movie was—we were literally the only people in the theater! I feel like . . . anything is possible. Like if those two can find love despite prejudice and violence and family bullshit, then I can too."

Howard presses his hand flat against mine on my back and looks me in the eyes. What if . . . what if I held this young man's joy in my bare hands, pressed my lips to it, sank my fangs into it? Drank it—drank *him*? He's so hot in his green corduroys with his old leather watch, I could—

"Fucking fags all over the city." Angry words prickle through the hairs on the back of my neck.

Howard looks up like a prey animal, like he's not sure whether that was a gunshot or fireworks. His hand jerks in mine, but I hold tight.

"Yeah, I'm talking to you, faggots."

I hold his hand tighter. Because I am not a prey animal—I am a predator. "No," I say to him, threading our fingers together. Sharing his warmth, sharing my strength. "Don't let go; it's our right."

I steer him forward, ignoring this man but also not wanting to lead him to my bus or Howard's car.

We walk. Howard's palm becomes slick against mine, and I can sense that he wants to move faster. We pass straight people on dates and out with friends. A woman walking her dog. Three students jog by, and not even their pulses match Howard's as it races with fear.

"It's okay," I tell Howard. "We're okay."

He looks at me with scared eyes but nods.

The man's footsteps sound uneven against the pavement as he slurs, ". . . Gay shit . . ." It's clear that he's not giving up on us. After the night we just had. I can smell Howard's fear racing through his veins—a fear I usually only taste—and now I'm pissed.

Is this what things are like still? Admittedly, I've spent the last twenty years secluded. When I returned to Baltimore and learned James was alone, when I went back to him, I was happy to live together in peace. After decades spent hiding in basements and in the shadows of glittering gay bars, time alone with my lover was all I wanted. A bed in which to curl up together. A table at which to play chess. A couch to feed and make out on by the light of a muted television.

"Coupla perverts . . ." His footsteps quicken.

I tune out the rest of our stalker's words, having been called them all before—and worse. I flinch, though, remembering the *thwack* of a police baton, the knuckles of an angry fist. The heat of testosterone angling for a fight, spitting slurs. I'm hard to kill and have been for decades; I could easily drain this man of life, and an overwhelming part of me wants to. But I refrain, because even though I might be dead, I still feel pain.

I think about the knife that once slipped between my ribs the time a group of straight men cornered me in an alley. I was on . . . not a *date*, but the two of us had slipped between buildings for a good time with each other's bodies after a good time at the bar. I didn't need to breathe, but Pierce did, so I threw myself between him and their slurs and their knife. It still took my breath away and sliced through any confidence becoming a vampire had given me that I could thrive as a queer in the open.

They'd left Pierce with a black eye and a bloody nose, and me propped up against the wall we'd just been groping each other against minutes before. They'd left me clutching my wound while the blood I'd drunk earlier that night leaked from my side. They'd left laughing.

Howard deserves more—deserves to take a boy on a date and hold his hand and walk him home and not worry about bleeding out in an alley. "Go into that diner over there," I mutter, the words like sandpaper in my throat.

"What?" He can't help but look over his shoulder, and I squeeze his hand, drawing his attention back to me. *Don't look at the threat behind us; don't let him get to you,* I think.

"Go," I repeat firmly, picking up speed to encourage him. "I'll meet you there. I've handled assholes like this before. I know what I'm doing."

"But—"

"Go," I growl, fangs bared to the dark.

I breathe Howard in as he goes ahead. Remember the scent of vintage leather and pine, salt and buttered popcorn. But I slow down. I'm not trying to outrun this piece of shit; I'm trying to bait him. When I glance over my shoulder, I catch him trying to decide whether to follow me or Howard. Then he catches my eye, and the decision is made. The animal at the edge of the herd, the easiest to attack, most vulnerable.

With a deep breath—with the scent of Howard on my tongue and in the back of my throat—I turn down a nearby alley between a closed barber shop and a bustling restaurant, feigning fear. Men like this guy love feeling like they've made someone else feel small.

His footsteps follow, staggering and heavy. His scent over- whelms me—there's cheap whiskey flooding his veins. Booze always gives the blood an *off* taste; I don't even like feeding on James after he's had a glass of wine. But tonight I'll make an exception.

I feel his "Where do you think you're going?" on the back of my neck and turn to face him.

No one taught me this vampiric power—I can't even always

get it to work—but it's *there*, lurking beneath the surface when I've really needed it. I lock eyes with the stranger and feel a shift in the weight of my words. "What seems to be the problem?" I say. My glamour confuses him, and he shakes his head, trying to clear it. It's all the time I need to sink my fangs into his neck. A gargled gasp escapes the man as I break the walls of his arteries. Blood floods his throat and my mouth as I tear his taut flesh. His whiskers tickle my lips.

Once the initial shock of having me latch onto his neck subsides, he begins to struggle. I'm not like the vampires in stories. Yes, blood invigorates me, but I can't rip people's heads off bare-handed. This guy is bigger than I am, and he lifts me off the ground and rushes forward. My bones crack against brick as he slams me into the wall, trying to throw me off, and I feel a gash open on the back of my head. Unfortunately for him, I've never felt stronger or more determined. I am *latched*. Predator, parasite. I gulp him down.

Out the corner of my eye, I see a figure pause in front of the alley—our tussle has seemingly caught their attention. I'm not bothered, though. No one ever stops to help those in need. As expected, once their curiosity is satisfied, they move on. And when they do, I let go. I stumble backward, heady with blood and rail whiskey. I've drunk too much, I know instinctively. If he doesn't get help soon, he will bleed out in this alleyway. At this point I would typically disappear into the shadows, and my victim would call for help or crawl to safety, forever wondering what attacked them. But tonight I don't retreat.

The man fumbles with his cell phone, no longer dexterous enough to even call 911. I take it easily from his hands and drop it to the ground before him. Then stomp the heel of my boot through its fragile glass screen. He slumps against the wall, clutching his neck, where blood seeps between his knuckles and soaks his clothes. He looks half dead, but I have never felt more alive.

CHAPTER 11

What am I doing? What have I done? I peer out the window of the diner, looking for George. I should never have let him stay behind. Maybe I should go back—I should go back. But what would I even do? Small groups stream past, friends going to house parties and straight couples on dates. Dog walkers and rideshares. People whose hearts aren't about to beat out of their throats, who aren't sweating and terrified that their date is dead in an alley, who aren't filled with regret for not helping.

I step out of the diner and back onto the street. I can't fight that man—was George planning to fight him? He's even smaller than I am. I wish I could say I felt safe calling the police or knew a community hotline or *anything*. Neither of us is equipped to handle—

"Oh, thank god," I breathe as I spot familiar black curls. His silver eyes catch the light of a streetlamp from a block away. I walk toward him, a smile plastered on my face, and I'm relieved to see a matching one on his. He looks . . . whole. Good, actually. George jogs toward me as if he's the romantic lead in a movie, running through a field to be reunited with his lover. Sure, this is a crowded block packed with row houses and a pockmarked sidewalk, and there are two random college students shouting at each other on opposite sides of the street, but it's still giving romance vibes.

I couldn't care less because he's okay. I'm okay, *we're* okay. My heart is still beating out of my chest, but at least it's no longer in my throat. Am I glowing? I feel like I'm glowing. George literally does as he passes beneath another streetlight, and then he slows.

I can't help but rest my hands on his waist, if only to make sure he's still in one piece. I search his face for cuts or bruises or blood before I realize I should just ask. *Find your words, Howard. Find yourself.* "Are you o—"

Suddenly George's body is flush against mine, his hand sliding warm against my cheek, cupping my face down toward his, pressing our mouths together, and I am . . . kissing him. Oh god, am I *kissing him.* Nothing prepared me for this—not watching a hundred kisses on screen in black and white. Not lying in bed at night, hand beneath my boxers, imagining *the moment.* No.

I rest my hands on his waist and lower back and pull his hips against mine. My hips almost can't help but thrust as I whimper against his lips. For two whole seconds we pause, foreheads against each other, open mouths hovering not an inch apart. I can't believe I'm holding him like this, holding him so close to me—and *in public.*

What do we look like to them? The middle-aged man walking his golden retriever, still wearing a suit. The two women sitting on their porch, having a cigarette and drinking wine. People waiting outside an upscale bar for a seat. Beneath their gazes, the hairs on the back of my neck stand to attention, almost as much as the rest of me is. I let out a slow, jagged breath before meeting the *want* in George's eyes. Before taking his mouth with mine again and again. We are tongues and teeth and—I want him in ways I can't have him on the sidewalk.

George breaks away and looks up at me through fluttering lashes. He stumbles a little as he comes down off his toes. I stare at his beautiful face as he bites his bottom lip and considers mine. As his hands slide to rest on my neck. As a slow thumb traces my clavicle. He says, "I've never been better."

I want him so bad, I kiss him again, curling my trembling fingers against his sides to steady them. He's hot now, and I feel like the damn sun where we collide. Just minutes ago I was scared to hold his hand, and now I'm making out with him on Charles Street, oblivious to the passersby. When I pull his body closer, I can feel we're both hard—both wild with desire. I could do this all night. I *want* to do this all night—don't ever want to stop.

"Let me drive you home," I say finally, breathlessly. If only so we can be alone in my car and then, perhaps, alone in his bedroom if he'll let me. . . .

"Are you sure?" He hesitates, glancing toward the bus stop.

With a sureness I haven't felt in years, I grab George's hand and lead him toward my car. My nerves light up like fairy lights as I lace my fingers between his intentionally. Now we're *really* holding hands. In public. Fearlessly, on a bustling street, where anyone might see us. It's thrilling. "Oma always said to be a gentleman, so now that I actually have the chance, I'm taking it. Come on. Let me drive you home."

George looks down at our hands—bites his bottom lip again as his eyes graze my crotch, I swear—then back up at my eyes. "Okay. Yeah." He grins too. "I'd like that."

I've always wanted to open the car door for someone. Well, not for *someone*—for a boy, a date. When I do for George, he smiles before kissing me again, quicker and softer this time, like people do when they're just *in a relationship*. When they're comfortable with each other. No one has ever made me feel more comfortable.

"Thanks," he says, before licking his lips and sliding into the passenger seat.

I shut the door gently, then make my way to the other side, get in beside him, and pause, seat belt halfway to *click*. "That was my first kiss," I blurt out.

George looks down at my lips as if he can't help but *not* at the mention. "Well, it was a good one."

I turn away, blushing as I fasten my seat belt. If I look at him, I might never drive us home. Might be tempted to climb into the back seat and drag him with me. Which I absolutely cannot do, with all these people around and Oma expecting me home.

When I feel George's hand rest on my leg, I start the car. At least driving gives me an excuse to focus on something other than how much I want to keep making out. "So, uh, where am I taking you?"

"Locust Point."

"Oh." The smile sticks to my face. "We're all on the peninsula. I live in Riverside, and Sue lives in Otterbein. You'll have to meet. I really think you'll like him."

"Given he's your best friend, I'm sure I will." George squeezes my knee before letting go. "But not as much as I like you."

That does it. I stare at the curl of his lips for much longer than someone who should be paying attention to traffic *should*. I feel George's hand suddenly on mine, steering the wheel back to, well, *steering* as an oncoming horn blares its horn.

"Are you trying to kill us?!" A laugh bubbles out of him.

I return my eyes to the road and laugh with him, still unable to believe he's sitting in my car. That we kissed and kissed and kissed. That we escaped that homophobic piece of shit. "Hey, what did you do to that guy?" I ask, glancing over at him.

His face gets serious, and he just stares straight ahead.

"I immediately regretted letting you send me ahead," I admit. I should've been there. Not that I would have been much help, though it doesn't look like you needed any—you don't have a scratch on you."

"Oh, I, um . . ."

I try not to look at him again while I'm driving, but the silence stretches on until we're stopped at a light.

Finally he says, "I have a history with men like that. I've learned how to handle them, but it's not . . ." George hesitates. "I was going to say that I'm not proud of that part of me, but you know what? They deserve it. He would have done worse to us—I've had worse done to me. But that's a story for a time when I'm not sitting beside the hottest guy in Baltimore."

I feel his hand rest on my upper thigh and squeeze. It takes me by surprise, and I gasp. My foot comes off the brake, and the car lurches forward. Again cars honk at us.

"Sorry! Sorry," he says. "My fault that time."

"Your fault *every* time," I tell him. "And I'm not mad about it one bit. Going to get me *killed*." I wink.

I switch on Classic 101.5, rolling down the windows as we drive down St. Paul, as St. Paul becomes Light Street, as Light leads us into Federal Hill. Through the throngs of cars blocking the road and drunk people wandering around Cross Street Market.

By some miracle I make it to Locust Point without running over any bros. It's quieter here. Neat lines of row houses—some over a century old, some just a few decades—line the street. The newer ones don't have the same heart, in my opinion. I love the old houses. When I think of Baltimore charm, that's it. Exposed brick and colorful doors. Narrow houses with original hardwood floors and twinkling lights strewn across streets. I wonder which one George lives in.

He points down a street of mismatched façades dotted with trees and with lamps shining over painted doors. "This is my block. I can just get out here."

"No, no," I say as I make the turn. "After what happened earlier, I'd rather drop you off at your door. Even though you can clearly handle yourself."

"You don't have—" And then, "Okay. It's that one there, the blue one with the yellow door."

The house is pretty, definitely one of the older homes on the block but beautifully maintained. As I pull in front of it, I notice the sign: FOR SALE.

"We just put it on the market." George shifts in the passenger seat but doesn't unbuckle his seat belt.

I guess it makes sense—why keep the house James is no longer living in? Well, because George is living in it. Alone.

Even though I've only hung out with him a few times, the idea of George leaving fills me with dread. "Where will you go?" I ask, trying and failing to sound casual. Maybe to college? He said he was taking a break before he went, I assumed to spend time with James before he passed.

But he doesn't answer my question. With glossy eyes, George says, "It figures, you know? His daughter is selling the house, never mind that I've lived here for years. It's my . . ." He hesitates. "It's my home, too."

I take his hand and squeeze. George turns to me, and I look fully into the depths of his eyes. It's just us again, like it was on the sidewalk. Two queers taking up space in the world. "You deserve better—and I don't mean in some cheesy, *it gets better* way. I mean, like . . ." I clench my fists, feeling anger flood my body on his behalf.

"Like, fuck those who don't understand how fragile *home* is for people like us," he finishes. "How our claims to home and family have been denied for ages."

"How they kick us out when we're not what they expected." I imagine my parents would have done just that if Oma hadn't rescued me from them.

"How . . ." George's voice softens. His grip on me tightens. "I'm scared, Howard."

"That's okay," I whisper, because I want him to know but also want to give him space to continue. To feel.

"James doesn't have much longer. And I don't have anywhere to go. It feels selfish worrying about where I'll live when James is dead, almost like I'm . . . planning for his death."

"I mean . . ." I haven't told anyone besides George this, not even Sue. "Oma is healthy for her age, but she's in her seventies. I told you in the theater—I worry about the same thing." I pause, trying to put into words this fear that I carry around. "I'll never go back to my parents, no matter what. But if something were to happen to Oma, like, what would I do about college? Where would I go for holiday breaks or whatever? I just . . . I have a hard time picturing my life without her." I don't even want to consider it.

"It's too much," he says, and I nod in agreement. "I should be figuring out the next stage of my life, not ignoring it."

He brings my hand to his lips and presses a gentle kiss to my knuckles, closing his eyes. It's the sort of thing people do in old movies, but this isn't some romantic gesture. It's closeness. He rests our hands on his leg and says, "It's a little easier when I'm with you."

I hold on to him, because I don't know what else to say or do. How do I tell George it's going to be okay when James is dying? When I'd be terrified if the same were happening to Oma? It's not only losing someone you love; it's losing your future.

This offer isn't mine to make, but I can't *not* make it. "Look, I can't keep James alive, but I can keep a roof over your head. There's no way Oma would let you live on the street."

A smile slowly warms George's face. "As wonderful as she sounds, your oma doesn't even know me."

"Well, we could change that." I lean forward and kiss his cheek.

George stares at my lips. When he kisses them again, my whole body heats up, and his fingers pulse with electricity where they come to rest at the base of my throat. Is it going to be like this every time? Because they're still giving me butterflies. I hope they do forever.

I don't want the night to end, but I know Oma is expecting me. I pull away from his gorgeous mouth and whisper, "I should probably walk you to your door."

"Don't," he says, breath warm against my lips. "I'd rather remember the end of our date right here. Like this."

George kisses me one last time and gets out of the car. I lean forward so I can watch him walk inside. He glances both ways before opening the yellow door and disappearing. I hear it close behind him, but no voices welcome him home. No lights turn on.

CHAPTER 12

GEORGE

". . . Really need to get one of those number-pad locks." A woman's voice swims in my head—in reality or in a dream? In a dream. I roll over and drag the down comforter with me, drifting back to sleep in its warmth. It's not a body curled around mine, but it still smells like James. I breathe deep, relax.

"Yeah, I'm at the house now."

I bolt upright. Definitely *not* in a dream. I'm in my bed in my house and . . . there's someone else also in my house—*again*. Exhaustion hits me as I roll over and pour off the mattress and onto the floor, my body not cooperating. Thanks to the blackout shades James installed, the bedroom is pitch dark, but a glance at the clock confirms my fear: the sun is still out. I am not my best during the day.

Quietly I rest my feet on the ground, leaning my weight onto them. Our house is over a hundred years old; its hardwood floors are a minefield of creaks. I manage to pull on a pair of discarded flannels without a sound—thank goodness I hadn't tossed them in the hamper.

I tiptoe toward the door, weighing each step before committing to it. Even though I don't need to breathe, I still hold my lungs full of air as if that helps. Palm sweaty around the old brass doorknob, I release the breath slowly and I turn it. Not a single squeak from the metal—I sprayed both it and the hinges with WD-40 after the last realtor interruption. Can't do anything about the floors, but the door glides smoothly open, and I peek through the crack. Though I can't see the intruder, my ears prick to attention. With nothing between us and my vampiric instincts on high alert, I can easily hear the woman wandering downstairs—and recognize more than her words this time. I recognize her voice: It's James' daughter. It's Jacqueline.

"Mm-hmm. I had multiple cash offers," she says. "Yeah, the housing market is great for sellers right now—especially with the new construction in Locust Point. I mean, I know it's only a few neighborhoods from our place in Otterbein, but you know how the city is. Always just a few blocks away from trash or gunshots or both."

I roll my eyes and lean against the doorjamb. How the apple managed to roll this far away from the tree—because I've never heard James say a bad thing about his former wife. How I wouldn't love to storm down the steps and confront Jacqueline. Not only am I her elder, but I went through more during my short human lifespan than she's experienced during all of hers.

"No, I put my father in a home. A cheap one; I'm not shelling out for somewhere with a spa or whatever when he's just going to die soon. Besides, maybe he wouldn't be in such decline if he'd given himself to God, you know?"

I could end it early. Just the thought has saliva gathering in my mouth, coating my fangs. Can't sell a house if you aren't alive to sign the paperwork. Maybe with my help, James could figure out how to will the place to . . .

"I know I'm preaching to the choir, but sin kills. Honestly, just being in his house gives me the heebie-jeebies. Probably should have contacted Pastor Patrick and asked him to pray in here with me before putting it on the market, but almost everyone moving to the city is a heathen, so what does it matter? I'll be rid of this place soon enough."

The brass dents in my grip as I squeeze the doorknob. I won't run downstairs and commit a murder James would never forgive me for. That I would, vicariously, never forgive myself for. And forever is a long time to carry guilt.

"No, I decided not to put in cameras."

The mention of cameras—even their absence—has the hair on my neck standing straight out.

"The woman who moved in across the street not long ago—yeah, she's nice. A Republican. Don't know why she'd want to live here. Anyway, she asked if there was supposed to be a teenage boy hanging around the property, and I said absolutely not, so I wanted to check on the place. Luckily, nothing's broken and there's no vandalism, but you can never be too careful."

A teenage boy hanging around the property? I think I would know if—"Oh." That's me.

A familiar creak sounds from below, one I know by heart—the first step leading upstairs. "Hang on, I think I heard something upstairs. No, I'm fine; I always carry pepper spray." She's coming. And though pepper spray, I assume, would have no effect on me, if she happens to open the shades, I'm in major trouble.

". . . Stay on the line." *Creak, creak.*

Fuck, fuck, fuck.

I don't even close the door—can't risk the sound or time it would take. I rush to tuck in the duvet and fluff the pillows before scanning the floor or nightstand for anything I might have left out. Anything that might betray—

"Hmm." A flick sounds from the hallway, and light spills into the bedroom through the crack I left between the door and its frame.

As I did before, I open the closet doors and slip inside. It's not ideal in here, with its slatted doors. Should have replaced them with something more solid—but when did I ever think I'd have to hide in my own closet?

The irony strikes me as I flatten myself against the wall, behind a row of James' old suits. The worst hiding place. The last hiding place. And though I remembered that creak on the stairs, I do not remember the one in the closet. Why would I? I haven't been in one for sixty years.

"Dammit," I whisper, before clamping a hand over my own

mouth and nose. No more speaking—no more breathing. No moving, no nothing, except waiting and hoping.

"Hello? Is someone there? Tamara, is that you?" Her voice sounds closer—as do her footsteps.

Despite my oiling its hinges, I can hear the bedroom door swing open as it displaces air. Usually my preternatural instincts kick in only when I'm hungry and hunting, but they light up now. Fight or flight. But I have nowhere to fly, and the hardwood creaks beneath Jacqueline's feet as she enters the room.

"No, it's not her," Jacqueline says to whomever she's talking to on the phone. "Which is good, because she knows I'll go with another realtor if she surprises me again, regardless of whether she's also on the school board. Like, I don't hire people just because we're sort of friends; I have standards." A sigh. A purse tossed onto the bed. My bed. Through the slats in the closet door, I watch as Jacqueline brushes her fingers through her long, graying hair. She wanders over to the windows. "And why does she keep closing the curtains? There're only six windows in this old row house; it needs all the light it can get."

She walks past me, and I realize what she's going to do only seconds before—sunlight floods the room, seeping through these damned slatted doors toward me. I feel its burning heat on my skin. I draw in a breath and hold it, hold myself still and away from the bright line of death.

Silently I clench my jaw, squeezing my eyes shut as pain sears my fingertips. With unbearable care, I release the suit I was holding on to and flatten my blistering fingers against the closet wall.

How long can my body stand it before I go up in flames? Before Jacqueline smells the smoke and opens the doors and screams as she watches me burn?

"No, it was nothing. I just had to check, you know. If a buyer backs out, I'll be stuck with this hellhole even longer, and I don't want to sink another cent into repairs. My dad never did squat with this place—still looks the same as when I was a kid but somehow . . . darker and gloomier."

As Jacqueline moves toward the dresser she casts a shadow, blocking the sunlight that threatens me. For a moment I allow myself to relax, to release the tension in my limbs. I watch Jacqueline open the dresser and pull out one of my wool sweaters, but she can't know that. She has no reason to believe anyone else has been living here; vandals don't keep their clothes folded in drawers. Phone pressed between her ear and shoulder, Jacqueline unfolds my sweater, holding it out before her.

"I've got to go, but I'll see you soon. Okay, bye." She slides her phone into her pocket and when she moves, so does her shadow. As sunlight seeps back into the closet, I bite down on my own tongue to keep from crying out in pain—taste my own blood.

Please just go. Get your hands off my stuff, your business out of my bedroom, and go.

But she doesn't. Jacqueline rummages around in the dresser again before pulling out one of James' sweaters, one he left to keep me company. His clothes don't fit me, but they're nice to sleep in, especially during winter. Cozy and warm and smelling of sandalwood and bergamot. Like him.

She lays it out beside mine on the bed, and as she looks between them, I silently dip down, crouching behind well-worn suits and patched jackets, out of the sunlight's reach. Hiding in the closet again—the parallel isn't lost on me. Coming out wasn't really a thing my friends and I did when we were in high school, not like Howard and his peers do nowadays. I never told my parents. None of my aunts or uncles or cousins, and certainly not my grammy and pop. I never *really* told anyone, which isn't to say people didn't know I was gay. Us few queers at school found one another through what felt like a secret code back then, and in my undead years following, I simply slipped into queer spaces, where we all just *knew*.

But to my family, I died straight. Died so young, when I'd had such a bright future ahead of me: a college education during which I would meet my future wife, whom I would provide for with a high-earning job while she stayed home and raised our three children. That never happened, though, and I suppose I have the monster who turned me into a vampire to thank for the easy out, despite how it shattered the rest of my life.

"Is this old?" Jacqueline's voice breaks the silence. She's thinking. Deducing. "Doesn't look old." I dare to rise up a little, to peek through the slats and see her rummaging around—through more of my clothes, I assume. Comparing. Wondering.

And then, "Huh." She picks up something from the floor. Something small that fits in her hand. I crane my neck, trying to see what it is—my watch. She slips it into her purse before replacing the sweaters, sliding the dresser drawers closed, and flattening the duvet . . . and walking toward the closet, toward me. She's going to open the doors, and sunlight will flood the space. I'm going to burn alive in my own—

Her phone rings. She stops. I look away as she answers, as if she won't be able to see me if I can't see her. "This is Jackie. Oh, hi, Tamara. Yes, I'm at the property now. Nothing *too* worrying, but I've asked that new neighbor to call me if she sees anything else suspicious." She straightens the alarm clock before heading toward the hall. "Of course, I'm more worried about the house than the board meeting. You have everything you need for that tonight?" There's a slight pause before, "Yes, the gay student club, or whatever they call themselves. You're clear on which way to vote on all their proposed initiatives? Don't let their woke terms confuse you." The walls muffle her voice as she goes back downstairs, and I hear the telltale *creak* as she makes it to the bottom. Hear the front door slam behind her and the deadbolt slide home.

I remain in the closet—I can't leave, not while the sun is out and the curtains are wide open. I would try to go back to sleep, but I'm afraid of drifting and sliding into the sunlight, of waking to the scent of my own flesh burning.

As soon as the glow of daylight fades from around the curtains, I stumble out of the closet, limbs numb and aching and colder than usual. Veins screaming with thirst. I have to feed. I dress quickly, pulling on clothes Jacqueline didn't have a chance to examine just in case she starts coming to conclusions. It's too early to hit up any of my usual late-night spots where the men like teeth as much as tongue, but right now my hunger is veering toward animalistic in a way I wouldn't inflict on my own people.

That said, I would happily eat a whole homophobe, but am I strong enough?

I draw a shuddering breath as I make my way to the top of the stairs. I grab onto the banister, use it to right myself. No, I need to be around my people—around James or George or both. At Spring Meadows, minimum.

I grab my keys and wallet and look for my watch before remembering that Jacqueline stole it. It's fine. It's only a thing I've owned my entire life. It can be replaced. But James can't be, Howard can't be, and I can't be.

I slip out the back door like a burglar making his escape. In the dark, I survey the little balconies and rooftop decks that overlook the alley for signs of life. When I'm sure no one's looking, I sneak out into the cool of night. The street is quiet except for the distant sound of cars and my own boots on the pavement. As I leave the alleyway and loop down to the street, I catch sight of a swinging sign. Bright red, with stark white lettering and a cheery exclamation point. I slide my fingers along the edge of the corrugated plastic and read the word to myself—because it can't be real. If I speak it aloud, it will be. TAMARA WILLIAMS REALTY: SOLD!

CHAPTER 13

HOWARD

I always hate these things—the board meetings.

"... custom pronouns in all email signatures ..."

Not because they aren't important; they are. They're literally the only place where anything gets done around this school. Sue fought hard for our right even to appear tonight, as he and the QSA's previous presidents have done many times before. But they always have my heart racing; they make me feel like a kid in the presence of so many adults.

"... In no school within the state of Maryland where all-gender restrooms have been implemented have there been any reports of trans, nonbinary, or gender non-conforming students disciplined for assault or harassment...."

It doesn't help that it feels like a courtroom in here: rows of neat plastic chairs, a geometric carpet, neon lights overhead, a plastic plant in the corner, a podium for speakers, and of course, the board members sitting at a long table in the front of the room.

". . . High heels were once the height of men's fashion. Blue a feminine color. There's no such thing as gendered clothing, and we should not be bound by . . ."

Murmurs of assent fill the room alongside the occasional clink of water glasses, the shuffling of papers, and the occasional *ping* from someone who hasn't silenced their cell phone. When I glance around the room, I'm surprised by the number of people who are rapt—as they should be. It's not only a good speech; it's *right*. But I've trained myself not to expect a positive response.

". . . By putting together anti-bullying policies that specifically address gender identity and sexual orientation, Wyndhurst is telling its students it cares. That we're welcome and safe . . ."

His words remind me of George's that day in the craft room. *"Being queer is about knowing what—and* who—*is important to you and seizing it."* That's what Sue's doing, what *we're* doing, I remind myself. I sit up a bit taller beside the other members of the QSA in support. I haven't always been good at that, writing myself off as the odd, quiet one whom no one wants to get close to. Not letting myself get close to them in return. But we're here together. We're a team.

". . . With sensitivity training, teachers can reinforce . . ."

Kenna is wearing her lacrosse uniform to show the athletics department's solidarity. Tiana's actually not reading a book for once. Phoenix is sitting with a dancer's poise despite the worry on her face. Gray picks at a hangnail, his usually perfect polish chipped. And we're not the only ones on *our side*, so to say. Almost all of Phoenix's dance friends showed up, along with half of Tiana's book club (they are reading on their phones, though). Gray's parents, whom I've met twice, were cool enough to show up and support him, as was Phoenix's mom. I look behind me and catch Oma's eye. She gives me an encouraging, determined look. And of course Mrs. Sullivan is here with us.

". . . Studies show that comprehensive and inclusive sexual education taught at the high school level prevents . . ."

Like a wedding, there are two obvious sides—but we are not coming together. No union is being formed tonight. Only one side actually believes in love. And on the *other* side, Sue's mom, whose face cracked with anger/shame/disdain when he took the podium. Now, she's barely paying attention, as if what her son is saying is of zero importance to her. Imagine going home with that woman after this. Imagine sitting down at the dinner table after she's rallied against her own son. Imagine doing that on repeat every day until college.

"They want to ignore us—always. We have to catch their attention." We are, George. The whole QSA poured ourselves into this speech. Sue is speaking our words with his fervor. And that feels . . . good. When I look around the room now, I don't *only* see his mom and the rest of the board or just hear the snicker of the boys' lacrosse team in the back. Today I also see the people who've worked hard, who care, and who want change.

"You want to be part of that; I know you do."

And it *does* feel good to be part of that.

We're all on our feet when Sue finishes—and not only the

QSA, a good half of the room. We're *all* a part of it. Sue beams as he returns to sit with us. Kenna kisses him right there and then. His mom's eyes flare, then contract, an obvious failed attempt at self-composedness. Good. She should feel threatened. Her and all the piece-of-shit conservatives who try to control our lives.

Sue returns our pats on the back, clasped shoulders, and *hell yeahs*. But then his mom taps her microphone, and the rumble of voices quiets. The board straightens up in their seats, glancing down their long table at one another. They have to have understood what Sue said, right? We included personal testimonials and studies; we laid out clear, manageable, low-cost plans. They have to . . .

"For the vote," she says.

I feel Sue's hand in mine, Kenna holding the other, and I take Phoenix's, who takes Tiana's, who takes Gray's. *Look at us*—see *us,* I think/pray. *We deserve to thrive like the rest of the students at Wyndhurst.*

"Those in favor of passing the so-titled . . ." She puts on a pair of reading glasses and squints dramatically at the paper, then reads from it as if it's in a foreign language. "'Proposal for the Support of Queer Students at Wyndhurst Preparatory School,' raise your hands."

There is a moment before they vote during which the board members all glance back and forth at one another, like their votes depend on the others'. One hand shoots straight up, the board member smiling at us. I smile back. Then another goes up, and I squeeze Sue's hand. That's two of nine. We only need five.

Phoenix's palm slides away from mine and flattens on my left knee, stilling it. "Sorry," I whisper. I hadn't even noticed I was bouncing it. But then a third hand raises, and we're grabbing one another's hands again. *Only two more—just two more, please.*

I perch on the edge of my plastic chair while the remaining board members stare down at their legal pads and click their pens. Who needs to think this long? What else do they need handed to them? Sue's speech was perfect. Our plan was complete.

"Final call for votes in favor of the proposed." Sue's mom is the only one who looks up, looks around for votes. But she refuses to look at us.

I stand. Not for any other reason than, I wish I had a brick. *Look at us.*

And then she does, startled. "The time for student input is over, Howard."

Her dismissal strengthens my resolve. I don't speak, but I don't sit, either. And then, suddenly, I'm not alone. Sue stands beside me, and Kenna beside him. Phoenix and Tiana and Gray. All the members of the QSA. We're a small group, but we stand together. I want them to look at us while they vote against us. Look at the pedestrians just trying to cross the road before you ram your car willfully into them.

They can't, and she doesn't. The coward looks back down at her notes and flips the page. We remain standing as she says, "Votes opposed?"

I narrow my eyes at each of the remaining board members as they raise their hands. Six of them, including Sue's mom. Six grown-ass adults who don't care for the safety and success of other children, despite having their own. And the ones who don't, like Mr. Percy, are almost more infuriating. Why is he even on the school board? Nothing better to do than micromanage kids? Get a hobby that isn't being cruel for no good reason. Absolutely enraging.

"Three for," she says, still refusing to—

"Mom!" Sue shouts. "What the hell?"

She neither looks at her son nor responds. "Six against."

"I hate her," Sue mutters, ripping his hands free from ours. He takes two long strides toward the table where our judges sit. They finally look up when he approaches, eyes widening as if Sue is going to attack them. They'd deserve it. "Queer kids die without support," he says, catching each of their attention in turn. "You're killing us. And you're doing it willfully."

His mother's mouth drops open as if to reply, but Sue doesn't give her time. He turns his back on her and walks away, loudly throwing the doors open before disappearing. Kenna snaps up his things and runs after him, her own eyes red and ready to spill over. To my left, I hear a soft sniffle and look to see tears coursing down Phoenix's face. It's good to be strong and determined, for the board to see that we won't back down. But I also want them to see us as people who feel pain—something they often get to look away from.

I pull Phoenix to my chest, holding her as her tears soak my shirt. Over her shoulder, I watch as Gray stares straight ahead in stunned silence. Tiana brings her knees up onto her chair and buries her head in her hands.

I watch as Mrs. Sullivan walks over to the three board members who voted in our favor and shakes their hands, thanking them. Behind me, I hear someone high-five someone else and say something about "gay shit."

And then one of the board members who voted against us catches my eye: a middle-aged man with thick blonde hair combed neatly back. He folds his arms across the Wyndhurst Boys' Lacrosse vest he wears over a blue button-down shirt, stiff collar open as if to convey he's well-off but relaxed about it. He quickly looks past, at someone behind me. I follow his gaze. It's Christof. The resemblance is uncanny, down to the vest and open collar—and disdain. When Christof catches me looking, I don't look away. I stare into his cold, uncaring eyes until they light up. Until he smiles. Until he puts on a fake sad face and offers a mimed *boo-hoo!*

What I wouldn't give for a brick right now.

I hate him. I hate him and his dad and the board and Sue's mom. I hate the adults who are killing their kids. As tears prickle at my eyes, I leave Phoenix with Tiana and Gray and walk as swiftly as I can toward the door with my head held high. I race right past Oma, who reaches for me, but I don't stop because I know I'll break down if I do. It's only when I emerge into the hall that I collapse into myself.

Stand—stay standing, I instruct myself. But I can't stand *here*, not when Christof could come up behind me, and—I could kill him. I would enjoy it.

I race down the hall and out through the front doors, flinging them both open before me as the security guard shouts for me to *have a nice night.* I let the cool, dark evening embrace me as I run to my car, one foot, then the next, over and over, a repetitive meditation. Because if I stop, I don't know if I'll be able to start again.

Not until I hit the driver's side door. Not until I slide in, panting, and lock the door behind me. Alone, I let the tears spill down my cheeks. Oma will just tell me everything's going to be fine, but it won't. Even though I love her more than anyone, she's not who I need right now.

Me: I need you

I text George while I wait in the car—he's about as slow to reply as Oma is to walk. I should go back and help her, but I can't show my face in there again, just like I can't bring myself to type the words, "We lost." The truth hurts too much right now. I fit my cell phone into its holder as Oma arrives.

"I'm so sorry, Howard," she says. "Do you want to go home and watch a movie? We can get ice cream. Try to take your mind off things tonight."

"No," I say, wiping my face dry. "Thanks, though. And I'm sorry I ran out on you."

"It's okay, sweetie." Oma kisses my cheek.

I'm about to give up on a response from George, when two texts come through.

George: Come to Spring Meadows.

George: I'm here for you.

His words hit me harder than he knows. I'm not used to that—to being someone's person, the one they think of first, even when we're apart.

Oma smiles softly, her eyes moving between my phone and me. She nods. I reply.

Me: <3

Me: Omw

CHAPTER 14

The night is cold, but I'm colder. Hungrier. Wrung out. I'm sitting on a bench outside an old folks' home at which, in another life, I would be a resident. *Should* be a resident. Wish I were a resident. If I were, my home wouldn't be *sold*.

After eighty years, I deserve to be in a warm room with James, maybe drinking tea on the couch, snuggled up beside each other, stealing kisses while we watch movies from our youth. Instead, I'm paralyzed with anger and fear and regret. That last one's the worst. I've had decades to plan a life on my own, with James, and thereafter, and what do I have to show for it? All the vampires in books and shows have decades of savings—accountants and lawyers and a secure place to sleep. But not me.

I've got no income or bank accounts to speak of, my dying partner has been put in a home without my input, and soon I'm going to be *homeless*. Again. I should have planned better, shouldn't I have? Instead, I got comfortable, which was stupid because I've learned that queers aren't allowed to get comfortable. It's always taken from us, isn't it? I should just sit here until sunrise, let the dawn take me, rather than storm in there and remind James I'm a monster. At least then I wouldn't have to worry about my future.

Something vibrates in my pocket several times before I remember I have a phone and that really only two people have my number. One of them has too much trouble with the buttons to text me, so that must mean it's . . .

Howard: I need you

My thumbs hover over the keypad while I consider whether I should even respond. Howard's club had its board meeting today. This message can't be a good sign. If I can't give myself strength, maybe I can at least lend some to him.

Me: Come to Spring Meadows.

Me: I'm here for you.

Howard: <3

Howard: Omw

I stare at those last three letters, which he obviously thinks I understand, and eventually deduce he's on his way.

For thirty minutes I stare at my phone. I wait while a few residents step out with a caregiver for a walk over toward the holiday lights. While the night-shift nurses arrive smelling like dinner. They nod at me politely on their way in, and I curl my fingers around the armrest on this bench to stop myself from stalking and killing one of them. I'm not angry at the people here, I remind myself. They're caring for James when I'm not allowed to.

And then I smell *him* and look up in time to see Howard hurtling toward me like I'm his final destination. (I could be if he wanted.) Even though I look like death—so pale that my veins are visible, dark circles beneath my eyes, hair a mess, cheeks hollow—after having stayed awake all day, starving in the closet of my own bedroom, he doesn't stop. Doesn't see the monster I'm seconds away from unleashing.

Instead, he collapses onto the bench, sobs racking his mortal body as he curls against me. I try not to flinch when he buries his face in my neck, a position I'm usually in—usually *dangerous* in. But Howard is not. *I need you,* he wrote, and I'm here. I'm here for him with the whole of my undead heart.

I hold him, because how could I not? Born generations after me, this talented, generous, empathetic young man is still facing indignities—still being told to prove he's worthy of respect and care. Forget strangers in alleyways; I could rip out the throat of everyone who's made him feel this way. I'm hungry and angry for myself, but even more so for Howard.

"I'm here for you," I say against the fall of his hair, against the shudder of his body. "Forever, if need be."

He doesn't stop right away—can't stop, and that's okay. It's okay to cry, feels good to cry. My father always told me, *Real men don't do that.* My father is dead. Howard can cry on me all night if he wants to. But eventually the tears stop coming, and he dries his face on his sleeves. When he looks up, his eyes are red and glossy.

"Sue was incredible. Passionate, smart, informed—as much as any adult there. *More* than most of them."

I can hear the *but* on the edge of his tongue, feel the frustration in his body. The tension.

"They couldn't even look at us," he spits, clenching his fist.

I wrap my hand gently around his and squeeze, asking him to open it for me, to allow me in. He does, twining our fingers together. We make a new fist as one.

"We were in the front row—Phoenix started crying. Imagine watching a student cry and thinking you know better." Howard shakes his head, strengthening his grip on me. "And some of them are parents—*our* parents, even. Like Sue's mom—have I mentioned she's the worst?" His words bite.

I have a few of my own but let him go on. I let him feel his anger like I feel mine: raw and gnawing. I half wish a board member would find me in a dark alley, so I could vote against *them*. With my fangs. Their suffering would taste so sweet.

Howard shakes his head, his eyes roaming for a moment. I assume he's reliving it. People often tell queers to *get over it*, like we can just forget the injustices. It feels like every time we cut off one head, another grows in its place.

"But I stood up." At this, Howard straightens. He looks at me steadily, no longer trembling or grasping.

I match his stance. "Good." Because I want him to know how proud I am. I want him to know he was brave.

He presses a pointed finger into his sternum. "I forced them to see me, even if only for a moment. Maybe if they won't remember

Sue's brilliant speech and all our contributions, they'll at least remember the hurt and anger. Maybe they'll have trouble falling asleep in their fancy houses tonight because they can't get our faces out of their heads."

A moment later Howard sighs, long and deep. He shakes his head and drops his eyes down to our clenched fingers. "Or maybe they'll sleep soundly—who knows. After the meeting, some of the guys from the lacrosse team were making faces and laughing at us. They were there to request funding for new uniforms, which of course they got. It's all a joke to them. And I couldn't sit and take it anymore. Not without making a statement, you know? Even if it was small, it still felt big."

He doesn't have to say more. I encouraged Howard to fight—to have hope—and they failed. No, they didn't *fail*; decades of prejudice set an unwinnable trap for them. Often, progress is slow. It isn't all throwing punches and bricks. It's lobbying and demonstrations. Being arrested a dozen times. Shouting into a bullhorn while people go on with their days, pretending not to hear you. Going out even though you know your happiness might get you killed.

If I could eliminate all the violence and discrimination, I would. Like, if I were truly superhuman, I would change minds en masse—convince parents to love their children and cops to follow their own laws, politicians to care about us, religious leaders to celebrate us. I meant it when I told Howard it was important to fight, that we have to. But it's also a long, hard road. One I've been walking since before even his parents were born.

"I'm . . ." Further words of encouragement die on my lips,

KELLAN McDANIEL

because I *didn't* make a statement. I might not ever be able to, dead as I am. I feel myself softening beneath his amber eyes. "James' house sold." I don't mean to interrupt—would have let Howard go on as long as he wanted—but the way he opened up has opened *me* up in a way I never really experienced with James. We didn't talk much about the hard times.

Panic flits across Howard's face as he tries to figure out what I'm implying. Unfortunately, it is *that*. "Wait, no," he says.

Denial: I know it well.

"Where—where are you going to go? Like, you have somewhere else to live nearby, right? I know your parents passed, but other family, maybe? You have to . . ." His nails dig desperately into my flesh, as if keeping me beside him now also keeps me off the streets.

I look down at our hands, afraid of the answer myself. But I have to tell him. Before James, I didn't stay anywhere too long. Silly of me to have grown used to it. To having a home. To trying to put down roots somewhere with someone—with more than some *one*.

"I don't know. I don't want to lie to you, Howard. You're important to me." The words slip out, but they're true. He is—has become—the most important person in my life besides James. And I might have to leave him. "I might not be around much longer—"

Before I can finish, a black SUV flies into the parking lot; Howard and I instinctively brace ourselves as if we might have to leap out of its way. But it screeches to a stop right in front of us, straddling two spaces. The driver's-side door flies open, and a middle-aged woman flies out of it, pulling her purse over her shoulder as she slams the door behind her. She's moving so fast, even with vampiric eyes it takes me a second to realize who it is.

"Speak of the fucking devil." Howard stands and levels his eyes on her, hands fists at his sides. "That's Mrs. Wolcott from the board. What the hell is she doing here?"

The last time I saw that face, it was between slats in a closet door and, before that, in family photos hanging on the walls. But then someone else gets out of the passenger side, hoodie pulled up over their hair, eyes red—probably from crying. Barely contained rage radiating through their stance.

"And that's Sue. Sue!" Howard calls to his friend as he stands.

His friend who is Jacqueline's son. His friend who is . . . James' grandson. The one I only ever glimpsed in old photographs, never updated from Sue's childhood because his mother never sent any new ones and no longer brought her son to visit.

I remember when Sue was born—not because I was there, but because James was so happy. And then, of course, because Jacqueline is rotten with hate, she almost never brought him around. I've never been in the same room as Sue because I had to hide whenever James' family came over.

For years, she's been ruining our lives . . . and now I know she's also ruining Sue's and Howard's. The worst of it is, I can't stand up to her. I can't make her look at the pain she's caused me the way Howard did at the board meeting. Yet again, I am forced to slip into the shadows.

CHAPTER 15

HOWARD

I stare at Mrs. Wolcott as she storms toward me, a confused look on her face, before bursting through the entrance. Why the hell is she here? I flip her off as soon as she turns her back, then catch Sue's attention. It's not hard.

"What are you doing here?" I ask, catching his shoulder.

"You're never going to believe it." His voice is hoarse, hands curling into fists as he explains, "My *bitch* mother put her dad in here, like, a month ago and didn't even tell me. I didn't even know he was *alive* still." He grabs onto me too, steadying himself. His fingers dig into my arm, and that's okay. His anger is mine. And his mom is the worst.

"Jesus," I mutter angrily—a reaction I can't seem to help lately. But the second I stop to think, to clear the fog of frustration in my head, I realize only one person has moved into Spring Meadows in the last month: James.

Sue pushes on while my mind races. "Yeah, we fell out of touch a while ago, but it wasn't by accident; it was her doing, her *plan*. I can't believe I didn't see it before—how Mom has been keeping me away from him."

"That's seriously messed up."

"You know what's even more messed up?" Sue's eyes are fire on mine. "She did it because he came out as bi to me. I was in middle school then, and I think he knew how much it would mean to me to know a queer adult . . ." Sue trails off, eyes reddening, head shaking.

"That *is* more messed up," I say because it's true, but also, James *can't* be Sue's grandpa . . . right? But when I look at his deep blue eyes, I see the same shade as James'. When I look at how his jaw has developed on testosterone and think of how they have the same slightly crooked smile, it all fits. Except for George. If James is the grandpa to both of them, that makes them cousins. But I know that Sue's mom is an only child. . . .

"You know she doesn't give a shit about queers. We're not people to her. Not even her own father or son. God! It was so important to me when he told me he was bisexual. Like, not just because we're missing almost an entire generation of older queer people—and we are. But because it meant someone in my family might finally understand me." Tears line his eyes. His grip on me tightens. "I hate her."

I agree—he knows I agree. So instead of saying anything, I pull Sue into a hug and hold him as tight as I can. "I'm really sorry," I say quietly. "Let's—well, you're here now, right? So let's go see your grandpa."

Sue nods and smooths his clothes, then his undercut.

The question is booming in my head. I have to ask it before we go inside. Otherwise, it'll inevitably be awkward when James recognizes me. "You know, I'm here all the time, and . . . if I'd known you were related, I'd have told you."

Sue looks at me with new hope in his eyes. "You've met him? Of course you have."

"Is his name James? James Bedford."

"Yeah, Bedford's my mom's maiden name." He shakes his head. "When I'm out of the house, I should change my last name to his. You know, the only one in my family who ever really tried."

"I think that's really special." I offer him a smile before leading the way. Because strangely, I'm the one who knows James' situation better right now, even though he's Sue's grandpa.

And George's *what*? The thought slaps me across the face.

I feel him nod. "Yeah." His voice cracks as he pulls back and wipes his eyes dry. "Fuck her. Let's go."

With a fake nod of confidence, I say, "Let's do it." My heart is pounding in my chest. It just doesn't make any sense.

The second we enter the lobby, his mom's voice slams into us like a bus. Behind the front desk, Ada stands with the receptionist, guarding her from an onslaught of anger.

"Mrs. Wolcott, please." Ada holds up a calming hand. "I'm doing my best for you, but most of our residents have retired for the evening, and we have a noise policy—"

"Has someone been visiting my father? Tell me who's been visiting my father!" she shouts in her *I want to speak with the manager* voice (and haircut to match).

Ada shoots me a look that begs me to stay back—and begs for

my sympathy. She has it, always. So much patience is required to manage this, well, *home*. And she does it so well because she loves cultivating that space for our elders. Unfortunately, she also has to deal with people like Sue's mom.

"What's she going on about?" I ask Sue under my breath, not trying to draw any attention or make the situation harder for Ada. I feel the answer like a pit in my stomach—that George bolted for a reason when Sue and his mom showed up. Suddenly I'm racking my brain, trying to remember if he ever called James his grandfather, or if that's just something I assumed.

"One of the neighbors called my mom to say they saw some young guy coming out of Grandpa's house, and now she's convinced that he has a secret family, eating away at her inheritance." Sue shifts his stance toward me, crosses his arms, and leans in. "I bet it's something way cooler, though. Like, he has a *kept boy* or something. God, I hope so," he adds conspiratorially. "Would absolutely serve my mom right."

Oh my god. Oh my *god*. "Listen, let's get out of here while she's, um, busy." Mrs. Wolcott is now attempting to commandeer the receptionist's computer. "I know which room James—I mean, your grandpa—lives in."

Sue's face lights up. "It'd be so good to see him for real after so long. Lead the way."

Suddenly I'm filled with dread. As if suite 217 is a black hole and every step toward it further crushes me. No turning back now, though. I put a hand on Sue's shoulder so I won't tip over, but also so I won't run off in search of answers.

Who the hell is George?

CHAPTER 16

GEORGE

There's an old oak tree to the west of the building with a view of Spring Meadows' gate—and James' window. I see Sue and Howard cross it before disappearing. My vantage point isn't perfect, but it's enough to see if Jacqueline visits him and, better yet, when she leaves.

Leave. She doesn't deserve to be in Spring Meadows, much less James' room. She's not the one who's loved or cared for him for decades. Who's woken up beside him for the past twenty years, and helped with the buttons on his shirts when his fingers could no longer manage such detailed movements, and who relived high school memories when he got confused.

My knuckles burn, and I look down at the five holes I've pressed into the oak branch. I release my grip on the tree and flex my fingers, take a long slow breath. She doesn't matter and will be gone soon. As if on cue, I watch her barrel out the front doors and into her SUV, Sue trailing with a wistful look over his shoulder. As soon as he's in the car, they fly down the driveway and through the gates, back to a life where Jacqueline can pretend her father doesn't exist.

It's all I can do to pretend *she* doesn't exist.

I find James' window again, because even though I don't belong at this old folks' home, I belong with him, whether his family thinks so or not. I don't want to risk going through the front door, so I climb. I'm still starving and exhausted, so my muscles burn as I haul myself up the side of the building, fingers seeking purchase in cracks and on ledges, until I'm at his window. I heave myself up onto the sill, pop out the screen, and push up the window.

But when I slip inside, I find—oh. I find Howard. Standing beside James' bed. His heart is pounding in his chest. I can hear it—feel it even—like the whole room is pulsing. I don't have to ask to know that he's confused, and I search for the right words to explain.

Before I can even try, James turns to him and says, "You must have questions."

"I do," he replies in nearly a whisper. Howard clears his throat and shifts his stance. Gravity lines his forehead when he looks at us. "But I want you both to know you can trust me." With that he locks the door, making a space only for us. This sterile, hotel-furniture room almost feels like a home with the three of us in it, lights dim. He faces James, not me, and asks, "Who is George to you?"

My head swivels between them, desperate to know the answer. After so long, I get to hear James acknowledge me to another person. Acknowledge our relationship. A thing that has literally never happened. I hold my breath. (Not that it matters.)

"Who do you think he is?" James asks, rather than answering.

"I don't know." Howard hesitates. Like he has a real idea but is afraid to speak it. "Like, a secret grandson? Or son? From a secret relationship?"

"No." James' voice is soft and kind, the way he has always been with me.

Then Howard turns to me, holding out a wondering hand. "Are you—are you a rent boy? And James is, like, your daddy or something?"

My held breath comes out as a hearty laugh. A real and good smile etches itself onto my face as I see the same on James'. Howard is . . . well, no other boys are like Howard. Who but him would have offered that without judgment? Would understand what that meant if it were true? And it technically *is* true.

I walk over to James' bed and sit on the end, taking his hand and meeting his eyes. "In a way, I kind of *am* a rent boy. You *have* funded my life for the last twenty years, and you're more than old enough to be my daddy."

"Grandaddy, even." He winks back.

I turn my smile on Howard, who could not look more confused. "Forgive our jokes. I am not James' rent boy, though some of the best people I've known in my existence have been, by the way. I know you're not disparaging rent boys."

"No!" Howard's sincerity warms my cold, dead heart. "Not at all. You know I wouldn't—"

"I know, Howard." I pat the other side of the bed, offering it to him. "No more of this standing awkwardly on opposite sides of the room like we might draw pistols at dawn." I'd be dead at dawn anyway. "Sit with us."

When I feel James' eyes on me, I meet them. I feel decades of relief when he nods. It's time. My first coming out, really. Well, in this sense. I've certainly never told anyone I was a vampire. Only James. It was the early 2000s; he'd just lost his wife. I considered waiting a few years to give him time—how much time do mortals need to grieve? But I forged ahead, knowing that was just what I'd asked myself to cover my real fear. That James had forgotten me, would reject me—would be *scared* of me. I remember standing on the stoop of his house, not yet *our* house, fixing my hair, wondering whether the truth would've gone down easier if I'd styled myself like he last remembered seeing me in 1960.

Everyone changes, though, even those of us whose bodies literally can't. I wore a pale-wash denim jacket and jeans with a clean white T-shirt from the drugstore. My hair . . . well, my hair hadn't changed. I realized after a couple of months of being a vampire that my hair no longer grew. Which meant that if I cut it off, it would likely forever stay short. So, though my fashion had shifted with the decades, my hairstyle was forever the same, which was fine with me; I liked my shaggy black curls.

None of my fretting mattered in the end. James opened the door and stared at me like we were starring in our own episode of *The Twilight Zone*. I'll never forget how he reached for my face, tears rimming his eyes. I closed mine because I too wanted to make sure I wasn't dreaming. I wasn't.

And though he should have been scared of me, he wasn't.

Will Howard be?

I open the drawer of James' nightstand and find the familiar black-and-white photograph. Frames are for photos that sit on credenzas or are hung on walls. But this one we could never keep where others might see it. I had it laminated not long after we got back together, afraid that it would fade and crease even more with time. No, this one's only for us. And now for Howard. That feels special.

I offer it to him across the bed, and when he takes it, I feel his heart jump. It quickens as he recognizes me—as he tries *not* to recognize me—because I look the same. I will always look the damn same while everyone around me ages and dies. Who will I grow old with?

"What is this, some kind of vintage photo booth...?" He looks to me, to James. He probably doesn't recognize the latter now that he's older. The two of us were eighteen years old in that photo. James had finally saved enough for the convertible he'd had his eye on in the used-car lot. It was one of the few places we could be together without question. Nothing particularly gay about two young men sitting together in the front seat. The driver's hand on the gearshift. The passenger's hand on the driver's thigh ... Okay, it was obviously very gay, but when we were flying down the highway, our hair tousled by the wind, no one could see us for what we were.

"There weren't many places we could go to be ourselves," I say, looking at the photograph with Howard. "After prom, we piled our few queer friends into the back seat and drove it out to the county, down roads that weaved through woods and past long driveways to expensive houses, coming out by the reservoir. We stayed there all night and watched the sun rise together. Our friend Donna was our historian—she was going to major in photography and carried her camera everywhere. She caught us lying on the baby blue hood, holding hands and staring into each other's eyes." I rub my thumb lovingly over James' supine image.

"Moments before she snapped the photograph, we'd kissed— an act we didn't dare capture on film. Those moments were for us and those we trusted. Even developing the photo personally in the school's darkroom was dangerous for her as much as for us." If anyone were to really study the photograph, they'd see it: the flush on our cheeks, the pout of our lips, our mouths hanging slightly open, our chests heaving. In our own world, we were.

"There are pictures of her and her boyfriend, Franklin, from that night too. Before *selfies* were a thing, she aimed the lens on herself, and why shouldn't she have? We offered to take it, but even her bad photographs were better than our good ones. Donna had this incredible wardrobe, and when we got to the reservoir, she changed into the outfit she wanted to wear to the dance but wasn't allowed to. Out by the water where only the stars could see us, she could wear what she wanted, kiss who she wanted, own her image, without fear of being stopped by a fucking cop.

"You know, back then, there was this three-article rule. The police could stop you on the street and check to make sure you were wearing three items of clothing that 'corresponded to your gender.'" I can't help but scoff as if it's still on the books. I feel its sting as if it is. I let myself be afraid back then, because I didn't want to get arrested or frisked or beaten. I never let myself try, experiment, feel. Donna did. After she died, I went to her grave and vandalized her headstone. I drank a man to death first, so I'd be strong enough to scratch her birth name from the stone and carve in her real one.

"I don't get it," Howard says quietly. Like if he speaks, he might break the spell of the past and time-travel us all forward. I think on a subliminal level he knows, but the reality is . . . challenging. "George, is this you? It can't be."

James slips the photograph gently from between Howard's fingers, glances lovingly at it for a moment, then stashes it safely back in the drawer.

Now, I take Howard's hand—a comfort, I hope—and look him in the eye. This passionate, creative boy who has been there for me like no one has in decades. Who has understood me the way I never thought anyone might again. He deserves the truth.

"Summer, 1960. I remember the Baltimore humidity made my graduation robe stick to my body. After the ceremony, and after we were able to shake off our families, James, Donna, Franklin, and I changed and went out on the town. And when we couldn't dance any longer, we piled into James' car with a terrible bottle of vodka Franklin had stolen from his parents and drove down to the bottom of the peninsula. I-95 was barely under construction in Maryland, so we used to go park under a bridge and drink and look over the water. The bridge isn't there anymore. It was demolished for the highway. But I remember it like it still stands. The cement curve above me and the colorful graffiti that decorated it. The smell of a split garbage bag. How I could actually see the stars that night.

"I should have let James drive me home, but Donna and Franklin had a curfew, and the walk wasn't terribly far. I lived just on the north side of Locust Point. So I kissed him good night—all of them, actually." I pause, remembering the chill of terror in the moments that followed. "And as I watched them drive away—I could still see James' taillights—I felt—" My voice catches. James reaches over and takes my hand. "I felt the pressure of fangs clamping down on my neck. Of bony hands holding me as whatever it was drained all the blood from my body." It's hard to look Howard fully in the eye while I describe the night I was turned into a vampire, but I try. "I know I said 'whatever it was' rather than name it. I never really saw the thing, but it felt like it had never been human. Like a monster. I thought that was it for me, that I would die under that bridge and never see my friends again. Never see James again. Never go to college.

"And I never did see my friends again—or go to college. But I did find James decades later, around the turn of the century. I knew what I was by then, knew the morning after the attack, and even though I still wouldn't call the monster that attacked me a vampire, that's what it had turned me into."

Howard's pulse races.

Mine does not exist.

"Here." I take his hand before he can say anything and hold it to my chest. "Do you feel that?"

His hand twitches before relaxing. Before sinking into the moment. "No, I—What am I supposed to be feeling?"

"Nothing." It's hard to feel *nothing*, though, so I move his fingers up to my throat, press two against what used to be a pulse point but now is also . . .

"Still nothing," Howard says, his fingers trembling slightly as I release them.

"Not for sixty years," I say. "Same length of time I've had these." I touch my tongue slowly to my left fang, baring it as nonthreateningly as possible.

"Oh, you . . ." Howard's curious eyes finish his sentence for him. "Can I touch them?"

"If you're careful. They're sharp. I'd rather you not bleed in my presence. Temptation comes more easily when I'm drawn to someone." I watch a rosy blush creep across Howard's cheeks as his eyes linger on my mouth. Now that he knows I could do more than kiss his full lips with it.

The two of us scoot closer on the bed's colorful quilt. He rests his palm against my cheek, and I close my eyes, lean into his touch. I almost forget why we're here, I want him to kiss me so badly. I remember what he asked when the pad of his thumb grazes the point of my fang. It takes all my willpower not to pierce his soft, fragile skin. I wait until Howard is finished exploring and withdraws. He clasps his hands together in his lap as we sit knee to knee.

Finally he says to James, "Mrs. Wolcott's your daughter."

James answers, "Sometimes to her dismay."

Howard's brow creases. "And Sue's your grandson."

"Yes. Sue is my . . ." James blinks his glossy eyes but leaves his feelings there. This is perhaps his first time naming who Sue really is to him. He smiles as he says, "Sue is my grandson. I regret that I haven't seen him for some time now."

I can feel the edge of them, that a reunion and conversation happened while I perched in a tree like an animal in the night. I should have been there for it. I wish I had been there for it. But I know what matters most is that it happened.

This time Howard closes *his* eyes, rubbing a hand across his brow as if he can rub the information right in. Make it all make sense.

"I'm sorry," he says, his head now fully in his hands, voice muffled as he looks down to the bed for answers. "It's a lot to process."

I reach for Howard, desperate for him to understand, but James catches me. Places my hand on my own knee. He's right. I shouldn't push. This is a lot of information for a mortal boy—one I care for deeply. Howard deserves space.

"It's getting late," James says, and Howard does look up at him, an old man with wrinkles and white hair, easier to face than one with fangs and no heartbeat. "Do you think you could drive George home so that he can get some things? She may not know the full truth, but now that my daughter's aware he's been visiting regularly and that I've become close to him, she's going to make his life very difficult."

Howard's nodding before he speaks. "Of course." And even though I can literally feel his fear, his words are warm. He meant what he said earlier: that we can trust him. Because I can feel that too. "Of course."

KELLAN MCDANIEL

CHAPTER 17

HOWARD

We walk to the car silently. Get in and buckle up silently. Pull out of Spring Meadows—silently. The drive home takes us onto the beltway and then onto I-83. There's something almost meditative about driving at night with the windows up, like we're in our own little universe.

Where I am driving a vampire home.

A *vampire*. A part of me can't believe it, even though George is clearly sitting beside me with his fanged teeth and his memories from long before I was born. A photograph to prove he was there. And though my brain is screaming that evidence can be faked, my heart knows it's not—it makes too much sense.

I've never felt his heartbeat, not when our bodies were pressed together for a kiss and not just when he guided my fingers to his pulse points. I look at my hands on the steering wheel, remembering the sharp point of George's fang grazing my finger. A shiver slides through me as I realize that even a gentle *push* would have broken my skin, bled me. How I put my hand in a vampire's mouth but also how he let me—how intimate it was.

On the underside of my wrist, I notice my pulse. Maybe for the first time, I become aware of the blood pumping through my body. I risk a glance in George's direction—at his neck, at his arms resting in his lap—and I see it: total stillness. Impossible and inhuman. My heart rate skyrockets as I clench the wheel—can he feel it? Should I be scared for my safety?

If George is what he claims to be, he probably could have killed me at any time. But he hasn't. He's been the opposite of scary— kind and generous and engaging and smart. And so, *so* hot. Like, I can't stop thinking about kissing him, even knowing how dangerous his mouth is. I risk another look his way, this time at his face. He's beautiful.

It hits me suddenly, as if it hasn't been on my mind the entire drive home. Oh my god. I've been dating . . . a vampire? Wait, are we dating? Does going on one date count as dating? How long do we have to date before I can ask if he'll be my boyfriend? And do I really want a vampire for a boyfriend?

Wait again.

Summer, 1960.

That's more than sixty years ago.

I remember the Baltimore humidity made my graduation robe stick to my body.

KELLAN MCDANIEL

George had just graduated, so he was, like, eighteen at the time.

Which means—"Holy shit, you're like eighty-something."

That's how I break the silence.

George chuckles softly. "I am."

"No wonder you're so mature—god." I run a hand through my hair and find that I'm sweating a little. I roll down the window down and let the breeze ruffle my hair just as much as he's ruffled me inside. I remember the tenderness with which James and George held hands as we sat together on the bed, while they reflected on their graduation day. It's the same tenderness my dziadzi and oma used to share. The reason that George and James seem so close . . . is because they've been in a relationship for decades. And I can't help it. The reality of it all is too much. I throw my head back and laugh. The wind takes my words. "I fell for a fucking senior citizen!"

And then George is really laughing. He puts his hand on my knee, and despite what I know about him now, I still want it there. I *want* him to touch me. I'd take his hand, but I'm trying so hard to focus on driving and not killing . . . myself? Could I even kill George in a car accident?

"Go on," he says. "Ask me—whatever you want."

"You're immortal?" I figure I might as well start with the basics.

"Yes."

"But, like, how immortal? Is this a Buffy wooden-stake-to-the-heart situation or—"

"I would prefer not to test that one."

"What about sunlight? In *Twilight*, they could technically go out during the day, but—"

"I do not sparkle."

I shrug. "It wouldn't be not hot if you did."

"Unfortunately, I can't go out during the day. Sun is the one thing I'm one hundred percent sure will kill me."

I risk another look at him when my eyes should be on the road. "Have you . . . tested that one?"

George's voice suddenly sounds nostalgic. "That first day, after I was attacked. Like I said, the thing that bit me wasn't like Dracula or Lestat or Edward Cullen. It was a monster." His fingers dig into my leg, and I don't get the impression he's trying to hurt me. More that the memory hurts *him*. "Neither of us stuck around for orientation. I woke up the next morning to the scent of my own burning flesh. Sent me scrambling into the shadows. I was terrified, but exhaustion won, and I passed out. I woke up again after the sun had set, only slightly refreshed and still terrified—but no longer burning. From then on I knew to stay out of the sunlight."

"But how did you know what you'd become? That you were, like, a vampire?"

"I sort of knew on an instinctual level. Something had changed inside of me. A deeper, predatorial urge gripped me: the desire to hunt, a craving for blood."

I pull off I-83 and onto St. Paul. It's not the fastest way home, but I like the straight slide downhill, and not having to deal with the car and foot traffic in the city center. As we drive beneath streetlamps, I glance at George, who is, indeed, not sparkling. But it's impossible not to see him in a new light, so to say. Reminds me of how, once I realized I was queer, I saw not only myself but the *world* differently.

I see George like that now. Knowing him more intimately, what he is and what he's been through, makes him all the more beautiful. I kissed a vampire. And I want to do it again.

And again and again.

I bite down on my lip to suppress the urge. Force myself to focus. To not think about running my tongue over his fangs. Feeling them in my neck. "Have you ever killed anyone?"

"Yes."

"On purpose?"

A moment of hesitation. "Yes."

I want to know what that felt like and why he did it, but probably not while I'm trying to change lanes. "Are you—not that you're not strong, but—"

"Howard," he says, laughing. "You're not going to insult me by stating the obvious."

"I don't know, most depictions I've seen—*The Vampire Diaries*, *Twilight*, *Interview with the Vampire*, even *What We Do in the Shadows*—they all have these powers. You could be hiding them, but in all the time we've spent together, you've mostly seemed . . . normal."

"I mostly am normal," George says. "At least to my knowledge. And I'm out of the loop on most modern pop culture, though I read *Interview* and watched the first *Twilight* movie. But I am well versed enough in vampire stories to say that they're mostly inaccurate—at least as to myself. My body heals wounds yours never could, but it's slow and painful. I can't fly or turn into a bat or run faster than a train or walk straight up walls, though I can climb them more easily when I've . . ." His voice trails quietly off.

After a moment I ask, "When you've what?"

He retracts his hand.

"George, I'm not scared," I say. "I probably should be, but I'm not. Even knowing you've killed. If you'd wanted to kill me, you would've by now. We've been alone together lots of times." And I find myself thinking, *I want to be alone with you lots more.*

He hums softly to himself. "When I've fed. When a mortal's blood is pumping through me—that's when I feel most unnatural, supernatural, preternatural. Least *normal*. When I feel faster and stronger. Like if I jumped hard enough, I could shoot straight up to the roof. If I pushed myself, I could give that Edward Cullen a run for his money in a footrace."

I almost start laughing again. My octogenarian vampire would-be boyfriend is comparing himself to Edward Cullen? I want to ask him under what circumstances he saw *Twilight*, but that doesn't seem particularly important compared to, well, everything else. Like, "You said 'as to myself' a minute ago. Are there other vampires? Do you know any?"

He shakes his head. "I want to say I wish there were, that I might have had company all these years. But I'm not sure I should wish this existence on others. Not that it's terrible, but I imagine few are truly compatible with the lifestyle. I've never met another vampire, which seems strange. I can't be the only one. In the decades since I was turned, there have been moments when I've searched for others without luck. No one found me, either." He pauses. "Remember when you told me you were lonely, and asked if I ever felt the same way?"

I nod, remembering the conversation vividly. I'd dared to be vulnerable in front of him. Never did I imagine his loneliness was tied to being the only one of his kind that he knew of.

"There's only so much I can share with mortals, no matter how close we become." George pauses for so long, I glance sideways to make sure he's okay. Contemplation rests supernaturally still on his face. "Well . . ." And then his hand is back on my leg. "Most mortals."

The shiver that slides through my body comes not only from his touch, but from the implication. That I'm mortal and George is not. That he's lonely and about to become even more so.

Just then, a drunk pedestrian charges across the street, and I slow down as we drive through the throngs of bar-goers in Federal Hill. We'll be at his house soon. The house that sold. At which he is no longer safe because of James' daughter. Who is also Sue's mother. Fuck.

"Can I ask—"

"I already said you can." George slides his hand up to my thigh, and suddenly I have to work even harder to focus.

"Well. I wanted to ask about you and James."

"Oh."

"And that seems more private, somehow, than details about your, uh, vampirism."

That earns me a smile—and thank god. Because I really don't want to butt into what seems like a really special relationship.

"Ask," George says, slowly. "Ask and I will answer honestly in such a way that doesn't breach James' trust. But James and I have built that trust over decades. He knows I'm having this conversation with you. He knows how important it is."

I gather my thoughts. "At Spring Meadows, you said you and he didn't find each other again for decades, but it sounded like you were high school sweethearts." We're both silent for a moment while I put the pieces together. While George lets me. "Does that mean, after you became a vampire, you didn't go back to him?"

"No." Then it's my turn to wait patiently while George puts his past together for me. "I was . . . I should have been braver; I know that now. It's easy to say that when I know it worked out for us in the end. But right after it happened, I was terrified of *myself*; I could only imagine how James would feel. I might not have been the monster that attacked me, but I was a monster regardless. An undead thing that hunted humans and drank their blood. A predator whose loved ones suddenly made him salivate. What if I'd lost control and attacked James? I could never have lived with myself. In those early days I was driven by my cravings, and remember, I had no vampire teacher. I was unsure and scared of so much back then. That I should subject James to me—that he or *anyone* could love me . . ."

I could love you. I don't say it, but the thought flutters through my mind nonetheless. "Well, he did—does," I correct myself. "Then and now. I can tell things didn't go the way you hoped, but . . ."

"It's complicated," George says. "It wouldn't be fair of me to write off decades of James' life—to wish it had gone differently. Those decades I spent alone made me who I am, just like those decades of college and family and a home made James who he is now. And I love that person."

164　　　　　　　　　　　　　　KELLAN McDANIEL

It makes sense; I can't hold George's fear and hesitancy against him. But it also sounds so lonely and sad. To feel utterly alone in the world, to feel like you have no one you can turn to.

"It's not that I didn't see James between our decades together. I watched him during that first summer from the shadows. Watched as he and Donna and Franklin canvassed the local neighborhoods, looking for me. As they put up posters with a picture of me that Donna had taken. But I ripped them down—I had to. Couldn't risk being found like I was. I watched her and Franklin move forward while James grieved. And eventually I watched when he left for college."

George grows quiet, and I wait, imagining what might have been if he'd just—

"I almost revealed myself to him once." A wistful look crosses his face—a memory, I assume. Maybe one he'll recount for me someday. "But every mortal I passed reminded me even more of how different I'd become, of how risky it was. I was cold. Unnatural."

I give him a moment before I ask my next question. "How did you find James again, so many years later?"

"Ah. I was back in Baltimore, working the night shift at Papermoon. Do you know it?"

I smile. "I know that place. Sue and I like to go there, but they're not open overnight anymore."

"Oh, damn," George says. "It used to be one of *the* late-night spots. Yours truly used to wash dishes there. I made enough to rent a shitty basement apartment nearby. I just happened to pick up a local paper one of the guys had left on the counter, and there in the obituaries was a photo of James and his recently deceased wife. I went to him the following night."

I nod, listening, digesting, trying to imagine what it must have been like for James—to be an old man, and suddenly there's your high school boyfriend at your door . . . *looking exactly the way he did back then*. I decide to save further questions about that night for another time.

"How did you make things work?"

He looks at me quizzically.

I pull up to a stop sign and then turn onto his street. "Like, he's a human—or a mortal or whatever—and you're a vampire." I hope it's not too obvious why I ask the question.

"Oh. There were definitely adjustments that needed to be made. He had to learn to live at night, and I had to overcome my fear of putting down roots. But we're partners—through everything. He's been my rock, my person I always come home to."

He looks at me and must notice my furrowed brow. "But that's not really what you're asking, are you?"

"I mean, it's not *not*, but also . . ." I shrug.

"We shared a home—yes, a bed. But others' beds too. And I fed on James, as well as others, mostly men."

My mind is spinning; his answers have only created more questions, and I'm desperate for more details. But they'll have to wait, because we've arrived. I double-park in front of his house. We both glance at the SOLD sign, and I can't help but think how, when James dies, George will lose this home *and* the one in James' heart.

"I know monogamy hasn't always been the standard," I say, "and that it's been ingrained in society by religion and conservatism. Polyamory and open relationships certainly weren't touched on in our terrible sex ed class. The idea of following some dating-to-marriage script just because I'm *supposed to* does nothing for me." Intellectually I know how I feel, but I've never been put in a position where I had to consider the real-life consequences. "But Oma and I watch old romances practically every night. Part of me still wants the fairy tale, you know? Even if that whole concept is kind of fake."

George shrugs. "It's not fake if it's real for you. And you have a lifetime ahead of you to consider what you want. You think James and I expected our lives to turn out this way?" The smile he offers is weak but feels true. Like he's proud of what they made, even though he was attacked by a monster and James is now dying.

"You're right," I say. "I have time. And I have you." I can't help but feel ridiculously romantic bringing our hands to my lips and pressing a kiss on George's knuckles. That earns me a glowing smile.

Tonight has been huge. I kissed a vampire. I'm considering what our future might be like. I should—I need to think as carefully about this as George and James have about each other. Honesty. Openness. If that's what I want, I have to lay the foundation now. So I take a deep breath. "I like you, George. And I believe in accepting people for who they are. So thank you. For sharing with me. Your trust means a lot. I'm still going to need time to think this through, think about what I want and what this means. Give me a few days?"

He nods. Pulls on the door handle but doesn't get out.

What if it doesn't work out after all this? I've found the perfect guy—hot, caring, passionate about my interests, and queer in such thoughtful ways—but he could still not be perfect *for me*. Relationships fall apart over expectations like monogamy and openness. Hell, they fall apart over not doing the dishes. The thought sinks into me like a set of fangs.

But then, to my relief, he says, "Take your time. I have all eternity," and steps out of the car. The door slams shut, and I'm prepared to watch him walk to the door when he doubles back and leans in through the passenger window. There's no hesitation when he says, "I like you too, Howard. And thanks. For being so open about this. For listening. For seeing me as I am. You have . . ." George sighs and rustles up a smile that could be sunlight on his face. "You have no idea how good that felt." He pats the open window ledge. "Or maybe you do."

PART II

CHAPTER 18

HOWARD

I can't stop thinking about George. The drive to school this morning was a blur, every class an hour of gibberish I don't remember. Even when a handful of lacrosse players bumped me in the hall, I barely noticed. How am I supposed to focus on calculus and the invasion of Normandy or whatever when I've just learned he's an immortal vampire with more than eighty years under his belt, and that soon he'll have nowhere to live? Never mind that the sun will be setting in a few hours, and George will be waking up.

I really need to clean up my locker, I think as I rummage through it for the right textbooks. (What even is my homework?) I wonder if George might come in one evening after school lets out to stand guard while I organize it. I'd feel a little more secure knowing a vampire was standing by.

Have you ever killed anyone?

Yes.

On purpose?

Yes.

"Did you hear?"

I jump as Sue runs up alongside me. "Jesus!"

"No, not him."

"You scared the hell out of me."

"Sorry." But he looks serious. Like this maybe isn't the hot gossip I thought I was about to get. "It's just . . ."

"What?"

"Teddy Holley. Christof's older brother."

I've heard stories about him; he's sort of famously always getting into trouble. "What'd that asshole do now?"

"He died."

"What?" I recoil in shock.

"Yeah. He was found in an alley last week and has been in a coma ever since. But he just, well . . ."

"Died," I finish.

"Yeah," Sue says distractedly. He holds up his phone to show me an article with a photo of Teddy. "His dad's stepping down from the school board to take some time with his family."

I take his phone and enlarge the image. It's the man who stalked me and George after we left The Charles. When George sent me ahead and returned—alone. Threat gone. Stalker gone. Teddy Holley gone. I remember how pale and out of it George had looked at the beginning of the night, and had chalked that up to him mourning James. That his, well, his grandfather—or so I'd thought at the time—was dying.

But then he came rushing up to me, full of life and energy. A smile on his face before his lips were on mine, before we were kissing right there in public, our stalker nowhere to be seen.

George's words prickle on the back of my neck: *When I've fed. When a mortal's blood is pumping through me—that's when I feel most unnatural, supernatural, preternatural. Least* normal. *When I feel faster and stronger.*

I glance between Sue's phone and a growing commotion down the hall, where a half dozen lacrosse players are clapping Christof on the back. Straight-dude attempts to comfort one another, by the looks of it. And Christof looks the most pathetic I've ever seen him—not a hint of the usual haughty fucking smile on his face. No energy in his walk. Not feeding off the crowd. Ignoring them, actually.

And then, down the hall, he turns my way. Catches me staring. And I know I should offer him a sympathetic look, but instead I feel years of anger and frustration boiling up inside me. Bubbling over. I feel the muscles in my face tense, and then it happens. The same look he gave me after the board voted down the QSA's proposal. A *boo-hoo.*

It feels good when Christof's eyes widen and he returns solemnly to the contents of his locker. "Well, then, I guess that's one less homophobic asshole in the world," I say, handing Sue back his phone.

"Cold, Howard," he says. "Cold."

I don't find it in me to apologize—because I'm not sorry. Teddy was following us with intent; I could *feel* it. Sue wasn't there. He doesn't know how terrifying it felt on the street, wondering if we were about to be beaten or killed. I really thought, *This is how it ends.* Two queer boys becoming a footnote in the *Baltimore Sun*, with dozens of conservatives yelling about how it's what we deserved.

"Let's just go." I glance at the time. "Meeting's about to start."

I feel Sue's eyes on me the whole way to the library reading room. And not an ounce of guilt stirs inside me.

When we arrive, everyone's sitting and facing Mrs. Sullivan like she's about to teach a class. We melt into our seats, and I look around at the others nervously. I know it's serious, because Tiana's book is closed on the desk and Gray's phone is fully off. Did we miss something? Mrs. Sullivan stands, walks around to the front of the desk, and sits on it.

"Now that you're all here—"

Sue's hand shoots up, but he doesn't wait to be called on; this isn't class. "Phoenix isn't here yet."

Mrs. Sullivan deflates, the rest of her sentence breathed out in a long sad sigh. She takes off her glasses and fits them on top of her head, the rainbow beaded cord dangling against the sides of her face. "Phoenix . . . Phoenix has withdrawn from Wyndhurst."

"What?!" Kenna's on her feet in an instant, like if she runs down to the dance studio, Phoenix might be there.

"Why?" Gray asks, already turning on his phone to text her.

Tiana puts her hand over his and pushes his phone gently back down onto the desktop.

"I'm really sorry. I can't discuss private student—"

"It was the board's decision, wasn't it?" I ask.

I can still feel her hand in mine that night when the board voted against us. Still feel her tears on my shoulder when I hugged her. It's been hard for all of us, but Phoenix was surrounded by it: the wrong pronouns constantly; binary changing rooms; the wrong dance roles, no matter which ones she tried out for. Sure, her dance friends were supportive, but the school wasn't. Isn't. And she could only spend so much time in the safety of her bubble before she felt the sting of being misgendered or mocked. Was forced to endure praise for performing so well at a thing she hated.

"Well, it wasn't—" Mrs. Sullivan cuts herself off. Seems to realize we're not going to let this go. "I mean, I can't confirm anything, but it wasn't unrelated to the board's decision. Her . . ." She looks between us and the door, then lowers her voice. "She cited mental health reasons. And I can't say anything else—shouldn't even have said that, but she did ask me to tell you all. . . ." She rubs her hands over her face and fits her glasses back on.

By then, everyone has their phones out and is texting Phoenix, me included.

When we're done, we just sit there in silence, still processing. It's not disbelief, because I absolutely believe this school could drive queer students out. I know the pain of it firsthand, even if in different ways. All of us do. We all get it, and we all hate it.

"You shouldn't give up," Mrs. Sullivan says, but it doesn't have the same vigor that George had, and I find myself remembering his *vigor* after he . . . after he killed Teddy Holley. He was so full of life in my arms, lips pressed against mine, body warm. Already I can think of people I wouldn't miss in the least. More Holleys, the lacrosse team, their shitbag parents on the board.

"Are you saying Phoenix gave up?" Tiana says.

"No! No. You kids should always do whatever you need to do to take care of yourselves, even if that means taking space. But if you can stay, if you have it in you to keep trying, keep fighting, then you should. And I'll continue to stand beside you. I know I could step up more—I already talked to the board members who voted in your favor and asked them what they thought might sway the others. I want to make an effort to be more involved with them. If I'm asking you all to do that work, I can do the same."

"You can't just change people like that." There's an edge to Gray's voice. And I can't help but notice that he glances at Sue like it's his fault. Several other eyes follow, landing on our president like he made his piece-of-shit mom vote against us—and after he gave that incredible speech.

But Gray's right. You can't just change people. Just like the world is better off without Teddy Holley, maybe it'd be better off without the six who voted against us.

That's what they think of *us*, though: that if we all just disappeared, the natural order would be restored. We should be better than that—have to be if we want to be taken seriously or get anything done. Go through the appropriate channels. *Murder* is what people always mean when they say "disappeared," anyway, and murder isn't justice.

I need to redouble my focus on the QSA.

As if that will work, though.

How many more students need to suffer while progress moves through the school board at a glacial pace? Maybe we'd all be better off if they *were* dead. Teddy was practically hunting George and me, so why should I feel bad for wishing the same on him? Why do I need to rise above them? I wouldn't shed a single tear for any of them, and I'm sure Phoenix wouldn't either. She would still be here if they weren't. We would have access to better facilities and protections—feel safer, achieve more, have more goddamn fun— if they weren't. This is our school. We're students. We deserve a better future, and the six board members who keep taking that from us?

They don't deserve one at all.

CHAPTER 19

GEORGE

The rev of an engine shocks me awake. Everything hurts—immortality didn't gift me comfort, especially not in this cramped electrical closet in the basement of a cold parking garage. Bright light pierces the crack between the doors, and I recoil instinctively, curling into the fetal position.

But the light doesn't burn. Headlights. I'm still shaking as I exhale. This was the most secure place I could find on such short notice, and I'm still terrified a maintenance worker will open the doors and force me onto the street, or call the cops, or—I could always kill rather than be killed, but . . .

Outside, the car engine revs again before tires squeal away over pavement. Alone again. At least until I overhear a family trying to get their children into the car. Their little feet echo across the floor, a shadow blocking the light that shines on me for a moment too long, like someone's lingering right in front of me. I get no more sleep while their parents herd them along. I can't relax even when they're gone because there will only be others.

The night Howard dropped me off, I spent hours roaming the house, taking in everything I could, reliving old memories. Just before sunrise I packed a go bag that I stashed down in the basement. Now that the house had sold, I knew my time there was coming to an end. And then I slept one final day in my and James' bed. Not that I actually *slept* that final day. Just lay there for twelve hours on the mattress, next to the dent James had left behind on his side. Wrapped the bed linens around me like a child protecting himself from monsters.

That's me now, though—the monster. And I miss my bed.

Close—I'm too close to people. No wonder the monster that attacked me lived under a bridge. Maybe I should do the same. Let go of any shred of humanity still lurking inside me. Let myself become the monster, rather than someone wishing he was spending Thanksgiving with loved ones at a table set with food he can't even eat. Might be inevitable anyway—I'm the only vampire I'm aware of.

Besides *it*.

I'm an *it* to James' daughter, who came by to install a new alarm and change the locks. I was sleeping in the basement, thankfully, so she didn't see me. But that night the sensors went off when I broke out—I had to smash a window because I couldn't unlock the new deadbolts.

I'm an *it* to the cops who chased me away from my own home when I returned for more of my things. I don't suffer from the cold the same way mortals do, but I still feel it. James' wool sweater adds another layer of warmth under my coat against the cold air and concrete.

My whole life was with him in that house, and now, because of that horrible woman, it's in a duffel bag I'm currently using as a lumpy pillow in a garage. It's not with James at all, because how the hell am I supposed to get out to the county like this? My bus pass expires in a couple weeks anyway, and I'm worried that if I use any of James' accounts to buy a new one, his daughter will sic detectives on my trail.

Sixty years of immortality and this is what I've become. All those vampires Howard talked about had money saved and invested. Had others they considered friends and family. Had beds to sleep in.

Howard.

I almost wish he was here, but I wouldn't want him to see me like this—not only because of how I look and smell, but because I've had decades to get my life together, and here I am, a struggling immortal. I slide my hand into my pocket and reassure myself of the small wad of cash I managed to save from the house. It's enough for a week at a motel, but I have to make this money last . . . who knows how long.

I feel a shift in my energy, signaling the sun has set. A whimper escapes me as I stand, stretching stiff muscles out of contorted positions. I breathe out purposefully, watching my breath fog in the late November air. I don't feel the cold as keenly, being cold myself, but it's certainly not as comfortable out here as it is in a home with a thermostat. I'm weak; I need to eat. As I steel myself to go in search of food, I feel my pocket vibrate. I pull out my phone—a text from Howard, the first time I've heard from him in a few days when he wrote a reassuring, Thanks again for being so open with me. Just wanna make sure you know I'm thinking about you even though I need a little more time lol

I open it.

Howard: Where are you? It's urgent.

Howard: I'll come pick you up.

I let his offer take me. Don't try to hide or ignore it. I need him and need to get out of this garage. Need to—whatever is urgent, we'll deal with it together. So I gather my duffel, run my hands through my hair (it doesn't help), and slip out into the streets.

Me: I'll meet you on a bench outside Latrobe Park.

Because I can't wait for him at my home or even on my stoop— not even on my street. Not when there are cops keeping an eye out for me. But Howard's coming. Howard's coming, and it's going to get better. It's going to be okay.

I tap my heel against the concrete so many times, I worry I might make a dent in it. The last time Howard texted urgently, he ended up crying on my shoulder. And now after days of us not having talked . . . I dig my nails into my palms, imagining a bully hurting Howard or the school board screwing over the QSA again.

Please be okay, please be okay.

I look up at the sound of tires and can't hide the relief that crosses my face just at seeing him and knowing that whatever it is, he thought of me and we're going to work through it. I hook my duffel casually over my shoulder like it's not full of keepsakes and dirty underwear, then slide into the passenger seat. When I catch Howard's eye, there's no judgment at my disheveled state, but there is sorrow. Oh no.

I drop my bag to the floor and pull on my seat belt, gaze unwavering. "Howard, what is it?"

Howard takes a deep breath. "I'm so sorry, George."

I know. Before he can continue, I know.

"It's James. He passed away this afternoon."

His words sound distant and rippling, as if we're underwater. "Oh," is all I can manage.

Howard slides his hand over mine, threads our fingers together, rests them on my lap. I don't mean to squeeze him as hard as I do, but I need to hold on to something. To someone. And Howard isn't James, but he's become one of my people. My *person*, singular.

"I, um . . ." I try to say something, anything, but can't. Can only think of our home and the last time we were there together. The last morning we lingered in bed, facing each other, with the covers pulled up over our heads like we were teens at a slumber party. It was night, obviously. Dark and still. And we were alone—together.

But then he died alone in that place. And the Spring Meadows staff likely called Jacqueline, not me. Not his true heart.

"I can take you." I feel Howard's eyes on me, and when I meet them, I realize I'm crying. I thought I'd lost the ability after crying my eyes out dozens of times while holding dying men in hospitals, men whom I had to fight to be near as AIDS withered and took them. I've mourned so much, lived with generations of grief for so long, that I'd almost forgotten what it feels like to let that go.

Howard pulls a handkerchief from his pocket—because of course he carries one—and wipes it gently across my cheek. Crisp white fabric, now stained pink. "Oh," I say again. Then, "Sorry. Blood even in my damn tears."

"No, don't be sorry," he says, reaching across to retrieve something from the glove compartment: a plastic dispenser that he pops open and retrieves a moist towelette from. Howard takes my chin gently between his fingers and turns my face, wiping away fresh tears before their pale pink tinge can stain my moon-white face. "George, I . . . Even though you explained to me . . ." He struggles to string together a complete sentence, which is fine because I know I would do the same right now.

"You don't have to—"

"No, I just mean . . ." He gestures as if he can literally grasp the answers. "I know I can never fully understand your loss." And then Howard is crying too. "You deserve to have grown old with him if that's what you'd wanted. You deserve more than being chased from your home. You deserved to be with James and to be seen. I just wanted to let you know that even though it was too little, too late, I saw you. I see you."

Faster than Howard can comprehend, I unbuckle my seat belt, lean across the console, and pull our bodies together, resting my forehead against his. As I draw a ragged breath, I smell the salt of his tears and the iron of mine.

"Thank you," I whisper, our breaths hot against each other's mouths.

Howard wipes our faces clean, presses a kiss to my cheek, and settles back into his seat. "Buckle up," he says. "I'm taking you to Spring Meadows to say goodbye like you deserve."

Howard pulls up to the security gate at Spring Meadows. I'm lying on the floor of the back seat, hidden beneath what are now considered vintage sweaters. I bear it because he sees me. After he parks, I sneak out of the car and in through a back door. Howard is a known quantity here. The staff and residents don't mind him waltzing through the front door, don't mind him disappearing down a back hallway—though they might if they knew it was for me.

I, on the other hand, hold my breath. I hold it for the entire ten minutes from gate to interior while the air burns in my lungs. Howard takes my hand, pulling me along and holding me close. I shouldn't feel so vulnerable—I'm a vampire, and it's night, and I could kill anyone here—but I do. Just like I can't step foot in daylight, I've never been able to stand beside James, not as we truly are.

Were.

"That way," Howard whispers, pointing. "To the west stairs. I'll go first."

He takes my hand and leads me through back halls I didn't know existed, until we emerge on the other side of reception. We glance over our shoulders—it's quiet. Ada stands beside the receptionist at the front desk, thumbing through a pile of forms. No one is screeching or running. Finally I release the pressure in my lungs. Howard has this, has me.

Until we reach the stairs.

"You!"

Every hair on my neck prickles to attention at her voice. His daughter's.

"Stop! Stop him!" she shouts as she begins to run toward me.

No one does. The receptionist must recognize me, and Ada's jaw just drops as she looks between Jacqueline and Howard and me. Sue is quick at his mother's heels, trying to get to Howard, to his friend. He doesn't know me. Especially not like Howard does. No one knows me now, except Howard.

I stumble up the first few steps until Jacqueline cuts me off, blocking my path with her body. I have decades on her, but by all rights she stands with the authority of adulthood, while I will never appear as more than an unruly teenager. She talks down to me like I'm less than that. "You're the one who's been taking advantage of my father—I've got footage of you sneaking around the house, and my neighbor has seen you with him. What is *wrong* with you?"

"I'm—" I can't defend myself. Well, I could, but only if I want to be arrested for murder. There are too many witnesses, and one of them is James' grandson. Howard's friend.

"You're what? A deviant?" she offers, practically spitting on me.

Howard's body presses against my back as he steadies me. Grasps my arm from behind. Tries to protect me. As if I need protecting from this mortal. I'm salivating for her blood.

I can hear Sue's heart racing in his chest. See his mouth hanging open. And somehow I sense he's lightheaded. That his pulse shouldn't be so slow. Blood shouldn't be doing that.

I clamp my jaw shut so that I won't scream at Jacqueline. So I won't clamp my jaw around her neck. I wouldn't drink neatly like I did from James—or even as cleanly as I did from that drunk bigot in the alley. I would rip her fucking throat open, exposing a column of muscle and arteries. Of spine and esophagus. Bleed her out onto these stairs that are younger than me.

She's James' daughter, I remind myself.

"Did it feel good, abusing an old man? Corrupting him and turning him against his family?"

Howard holds me tighter—he can feel me twitching, using every ounce of vampiric strength to restrain rather than unleash myself.

Not in front of James' grandson. Not in front of the boy I'd like to kiss again—without him imagining a monster's mouth on his, blood dripping between our lips. "Don't," I growl, and I can already taste her. How easily the wet meat of her insides would tear away from their bones. How sweet she would taste.

"Howard, I don't understand, what's—" Sue begins, breathless, knuckles white where he grips the railing. Gathers himself. "Is this—are you dating Grandpa's rent boy?"

Roommate, rent boy, friend. None of them bad, but none of them right. Each of them aimed at me, at one time or another. He doesn't even mean it. I can't be here. Cannot kill—

"Let's go." Howard is pulling me back down the stairs, toward the lobby. "George, *please.*"

He doesn't answer Sue. Doesn't bother with Jacqueline. Is only with me, is only mine. And I let myself be his—especially now that I am no one else's—and be rushed through the lobby and out the front door. Down the garden path and among the strings of twinkling lights.

They blur and soften as bloody tears blot out my vision. As they run down my cheeks and stain my shirt. As fury and frustration and grief wrack my body until I am clinging to Howard. Until I can't stand any longer, and he helps me slowly to my knees, then to the hard autumn ground. He holds me.

CHAPTER 20

HOWARD

Digging up a grave is kind of like digging a garden. Same metal weight in my hands, hoisting dirt. Same sweat and calluses. But no garden is six feet deep, and the work is rarely done at night or this late in the year. I do it now with George.

Insisted, actually.

Because James died alone without his partner beside him. Because George was hiding in a parking garage when it happened and had no easy way to reach Spring Meadows. Because he was not invited to the funeral—of course he wasn't—not that he could have gone, since it was during the day. He wasn't even given a say in the preparations or in the selling of his own house or possessions. Obviously won't be invited to review James' will.

So I'm sharing the work with him. The way he led me into the cemetery, how he picked up the shovel and threw his weight into that first heave, I could tell he'd done this before. I closed my hand over his immediately and took it. "Let me."

"I'm stronger."

"Not right now, you're not." I meant how pale he seemed from not having fed, but also . . . "You don't have to be strong about this. Not alone, at least." As soon as the shovel was in my hands, I said, "Tell me about it—the other graves you dug up. Because I'm part of it now."

As he begins, I sink the metal blade into the dirt, press it deeper with my heel, and haul away another shovelful.

"The first time I put shovel to earth was for Twyla Horne, whose parents cut her hair and buried her in a suit."

I pause, roll my sleeves up over my elbows, and then keep going. George's story fuels me, reminds me that I'm part of a community that's thrived in our own ways, even when others have tried to end us.

"I didn't tell anyone because I wasn't sure I'd be able to pull it off, so I spent the whole night fidgeting with the wig and dress on my own. Bodies are heavy when there's no life to lighten them."

I dig for Twyla.

"The next grave was Bryce MacLaren's. I collected letters and trinkets from our friends and laid them to rest with his body, where they belonged. His family didn't invite us or his partner, Bobby Reed, to the funeral. We didn't even know it had taken place."

I dig for Bobby.

"As if I trusted his family not to 'clean up' our offerings at Bryce's headstone. No, they went right into the casket so that he'd have them for eternity. That and a swipe of glitter across each of his eyelids. We used to call him Sparkles."

I dig for Sparkles.

"I've never brought anyone with me before now," George whispers.

I lodge the blade into the ground and give myself a moment to catch my breath as I gaze upon him. Even though my arms already ache, my heart aches more. For those he dug up before, for their friends and chosen family, for James now, and for George through all those decades alone.

It sucks being out at school, but at least I *can* be. Not that it's fun. My parents didn't want me, but thank god Oma did. The lacrosse team gives me bruises on a regular basis, and the rest of the student body stares and whispers on a good day—but I have my friends in the QSA.

Or I did.

Phoenix is gone. I still have her number, of course, but she's slow to respond to texts and rarely engages, like it's too hard to interact with someone who reminds her of the school that drove her away. I don't blame her.

At least she was able to leave when the weight of the school board and bullying became too much to bear. Not that it was a great solution, but Sue is stuck with his mother all the time. Imagine having a parent who doesn't love you for who you are. Who talks about deviants and corruption around you as if she doesn't place you in the same category.

Mrs. Wolcott probably expects Sue to ignore it, to understand, to forgive her. Probably thinks he'll change. That's why it took him so long to get on testosterone—she wouldn't take him to the right doctors. Made him pray about it with their family minister or whatever. Wasn't until his dad took him to the doctor—out of state—that Sue could even speak freely about his needs. He's the only one I know who's glad his parents are divorced. Well, almost divorced. Apparently, his mom's church *doesn't look fondly* upon that kind of thing, so they're technically only separated.

She doesn't deserve Sue.

I wipe the sweat from my forehead and pick up my water. I tilt it back and chug, the cool water sliding down my throat. I start thinking about how George doesn't have the same needs as me, has no need for water or food, even air. He thrives on what keeps humans alive. I glance at him as I finish drinking. He takes the bottle from me, twisting on the cap, and then holds out a hand like he might help with the digging. But I don't let him—not yet, anyway.

Because I don't feel like I'm only digging up this grave, but the latest in a long line of wrongs righted. Of the dead respected and honored like they weren't by their bio families. When George told me the fight was worth it, this was what he meant. When he told me it wasn't about any one of us, this was what he meant. That we're digging up graves to honor those who've come before us. That we're all pushing against our local school boards and parents until they collapse beneath our weight. Until we make our square of the world a little better for ourselves and others. Join our squares together. Make a quilt.

I want so much for George. He has spent the last twenty years hiding. He deserves a stake in his own life. To go on a date and not have to hide it. To meet the family, to be hugged by a bunch of overenthusiastic aunts and uncles and grandmas. I want to show him that—to be that for him. To be an *us*, not only in public, but around my friends and family.

My ability to help him is limited; I'm just a kid in high school who lives with his grandma. But there's something I can do for George tonight. I can shovel one heap of dirt after another until—

The shovel hits wood.

I steady myself on the wooden lid and hand the shovel up to George, who stands perched on the edge of the grave, the bone-white moon creating a halo behind his wild black hair. I've looked into his eyes so many times but only become aware now, while the light is behind him, how their silver seems to reflect and shine on their own. How the tips of his fangs glisten where they poke out from between his soft pink lips.

George could kill me—rip into my throat, leave me in this grave, and bury me with the dirt I dug out. Could, but won't. He's stronger for the blood he drinks, but he's also stronger for the people he's loved. And I plan to be stronger for him.

CHAPTER 21

GEORGE

Ever since I became immortal and started watching friends and lovers die, I've known it was my responsibility to make sure they moved on with dignity—a grace I will surely never be afforded. Who better to honor the dead than the undead?

Though tonight is familiar, it's nothing like the dozens of times before. Because tonight is about what *I* need to move on.

I used to wish more than anything that James and I could have grown old together, but a small, guilty part of me is glad we did not. Were I mortal, we surely would have made a home in lively bars and with lovely people, and so many of them died young from a disease doctors refused to understand—we could easily have met the same fate. Instead, well . . . Instead, here I am, more than sixty years later, standing in front of my love's grave with a shovel in hand.

JAMES DOUGLAS BEDFORD

BELOVED HUSBAND, FATHER, AND GRANDFATHER

FOREVER IN OUR HEARTS

I huff a rude little laugh. "Forever in our hearts"? Only until they stop pumping blood. Mine is the only heart that will keep James forever—or at least until I decide I've had enough and walk myself off into the sunrise. I used to think that was how I'd end it, that I would inevitably end it. Because who really wants to live forever when those you love keep dying? But here, now, I realize how many lives I hold inside mine. I'm not my only responsibility. I am the keeper of so many names forgotten, those whom others have tried to scratch from history. Who else knew James like I did? Who else will go on knowing?

I hear the shovel strike the top of the coffin. Howard looks up to me and passes me the shovel, which I toss to the side. I lift Howard from the grave, steadying him beside the pile of loose dirt, before climbing down into it. Howard has done the brunt of the work—for me, for James. I push a few handfuls of dirt to the side. I wonder how much they paid for this coffin. To tuck James away in a neat little box lined with silk, as if that can contain all of him. I'm glad that when I go, I'll go in a burst of flames. If I were mortal, I'd have wanted to be cremated. Let my body be fire and ash and wind, grass and soil and food.

I feel around for the latches. I've got to open it—am going to open it. Look at him one last time. If I'd been there with him when he passed, as I should have been, this might be easier because I would have experienced it, watched the life leave him, felt the last of his breath against my cheek, heard the last few beats of his heart.

I do it—I heave the lid open. Inside, James rests like a facsimile of himself. I've been close to death before. Touched it, caused it, held it lovingly in my arms. Experienced it. But nothing prepares me for how it feels now, as I climb into the silklined coffin. I fit in next to him as I have done thousands of times and stroke my hand slowly down his cheek. It's cold now, cold as it has never been. Cold like I am. Lying there with him, my head on his chest, I hear nothing and wonder whether he still has a heart.

I'd asked James so many times if he'd let me turn him. No, I didn't know exactly how. Still don't, really. But I've read enough over the years that I think I could figure it out. All that lore must come from somewhere.

I first asked on our one-year reunion anniversary. James was sixty-one or so at the time; he was growing older and would die, if of nothing else, of old age, and I couldn't stop thinking about when that might happen. I could stop it, though. Told him as much, and he replied, "I'm too old for that now, George."

I know he hadn't meant anything with his "now," but it pierced me like a set of fangs. *Now*, as if he would have been open to being a vampire if only I had offered earlier. Like when I'd first been turned, when I wasn't brave enough to face him.

How could I—

I didn't know—

I was so scared—

He was so alive, and I—

Regret, regret, regret.

Cursed to live with it forever. I don't know what would have happened, and I never will.

I curl against James, burying my face in his suit. I know this suit; it was his favorite. Dark forest green, and a white dress shirt with a little purple bow tie. *Splash of color,* he would say, as if green was a completely standard suit color to begin with. At least that child— his child—hadn't buried James in something black. Or a red tie, like he was a Republican businessman.

I should have just done it—turned him. Sixty's a good age; I don't know why James insisted he was too old. He was hot. A full head of graying hair. Lines, sure, but showing the depth of his age and experience. His body was weakening, but my blood would have made him stronger. Healed his aches and toughened his skin.

What a "Fuck you" that would've been to his daughter. We could have outlived her in that house. Queer before her birth and long after her inevitable death.

I lift my head to look into James' face. My beautiful James. The love of my life, both before and after I died. I will forever be grateful for the time we had together, but the deep ache coursing through me—I don't want to know this feeling ever again. And in fact I will never have to, not when the gift of forever runs through my veins.

Forever.

The soft light on James' face draws my gaze toward its source. Toward Howard, standing tall against the moon. Sweat glistening on his forehead. Bared arms covered in grave dirt. He grips the length of the shovel, his chest still heaving from the effort of digging. Strong on the outside and now within—always within. He just doesn't know it yet. But I know. Perhaps I will know him forever.

CHAPTER 22

'm home!" I call, pushing the front door open to find not Oma, but George. I smile as he brings his finger to his lips, a mimed *shh* while I set down my dance shoes, our silent joining as he glides over to me. If you're going to hide a boyfriend in your house, a vampire is highly recommended.

"Hi, Howard! How was folk dance club?" Oma calls up from the basement suite. She moved down there when I moved in. The suite has everything she needs, including a stair lift. Since she was already having trouble with the stairs up to the second floor, it just made more sense for me to take her bedroom.

As a result, it means I have almost total privacy on the second floor, and George has even more in the little attic we've reclaimed for him. The thought has me hot as I pull George's cool body against mine. He came home with me the night that James passed away, and he hasn't left since. It's only been a few days since we held our own vigil in the graveyard, not even two weeks since he moved in, but it feels like forever—in the best way. Like he belongs here.

"Hi, Oma!" I call over George's shoulder before resting my eyes on his. They are silver mirrors in the dim light of the living room. How can I always see myself in them—see myself in him?

"Must be hungry after all that stepping. Do you want dinner?"

"Yes, please! But just a little. I have a date, remember?" I respond, smiling at George.

"That's right! I finally get to meet your mystery man," she says. I can hear her getting settled in her seat to come up.

George tilts his head, eyes still on mine. "I should go," he warns.

I nod. "I'm excited for you to meet her," I say quietly, sliding one hand around his waist and brushing the waves of black hair from his face with my other. Kissing his exposed brow. I could kiss him more—press my lips to so many places—but not with Oma on her way up. "She's been asking about the boy who's made me so happy."

"Has she?" Swear to god, George blushes. Whatever blood's inside him rises to his cheeks.

Seeing it has me longing for the privacy of a closed door. A locked door and the pattern of George's body beneath and beside mine, fingers teasing at hems, knees rubbing between legs. This is all new to me, not only the making out but acknowledging that my boyfriend is mourning his partner of over twenty years, which is not something I thought I'd *ever* have to consider. I don't think they were really physical toward the end in the way I want to be physical now. But I want to respect his process. We're going to have to navigate a relationship differently than two mortal people would.

George catches me fantasizing about him and snorts. "I should go," he says, nodding upstairs.

"Okay. I'm going to catch up with Oma and have dinner. Around seven, we can do the whole going-around-to-the-front-door thing like we discussed? To be honest, I've never been truly picked up for a date."

"Well, I don't have a car, you know, but . . . pick you up at seven?" He winks.

"You know it. My drama classes are about to pay off." I don't love lying to Oma, but how do I tell her that I'm dating a vampire who's older than she is, and, oh yeah, he's living in our attic? That isn't the kind of thing you casually drop. I plant a soft kiss on George's lips, then watch as he makes for the banister in two steps, hurdles himself over it, and silently ascends—

Right as Oma reaches the top of the basement stairs. I walk over and find her standing on the landing. "I've got some stamppot on the stove. With rookworst, because I know how much you like it," she says, smiling and kissing me on the cheek.

"It smells good." Though I admit I hadn't even noticed until she said something. That would have been the first thing I'd have noticed after getting home, but now the first thing I notice is George. Even now, as I follow Oma into the kitchen, he's all I can think about. How fast I can eat. How fast I can help clean up. How long until I can sneak upstairs to get ready for tonight. Not exactly a big reveal when your date's already in your bedroom, but I wouldn't have it any other way.

"So where are you going tonight?" Oma asks, bringing me back to the scent of smoked sausage and buttery potatoes. Of kale and onions. I breathe them deep as she lifts the lid and gives the pot a stir.

"Movies." I take two bowls from the cabinet and begin setting the little table against the wall. "Might stop at a diner after for a milkshake or something."

"Milkshakes." She chuckles to herself. "You boys remind me of me and your dziadzi when we were younger, ducking over to the nearest soda fountain after school. Nothing like a chocolate malt."

At her words I glance toward the stairs. Because George is actually older than she is—and I might as well be a senior citizen, given my interests. She's going to like him. I know it.

After dinner, I go upstairs to get ready—and alert George.

"How long should I stand on the stoop? And are you really going to change clothes again?" He grabs my collar and straightens it.

"God, you are such a grandpa sometimes."

"I'm sort of a grandpa all the time." He smiles and pecks me on the lips.

How I wish we could just stay in and do more of that. And then do even more than that. But I like existing in public—and not only in queer spaces, which will open up to me after I graduate, but also just at the grocery or hardware store, at the public gardens and the zoo—in order to remind people like Sue's mom that queers not only exist but have full lives. That we too buy toilet paper.

"Who knows?" I tease him. "Maybe I'll change one little thing about my outfit to see if you've been paying attention." I kiss him back before nudging him toward the stairs. "She's in the basement, but be quiet on your way out the front door; you know that one floorboard—"

"Creaks, I know. Left side of the threshold. Just another part of an old house's charm." George sighs like it's a lot but worth it. He lets himself be prodded quietly down the steps and out the front door, which I literally sprayed WD-40 on earlier so it wouldn't creak.

Actually, I do change one thing. I pull a denim jacket from my closet to go with my neon shirt and faded jeans. I don't wear the jacket often—and I'll have to wear my winter coat over it outside—but I think he'll appreciate it. Sue bought a grab bag of queer patches one day that we ironed onto our jackets and backpacks together. I had to buy a whole new backpack because it drew too much attention. It was like I was signaling, *Beat me up!* Sue still carries his and no one bothers him, so it must just be that lack of confidence he's always on my case about. So it feels even more right wearing this tonight. Displaying patches I've previously hidden. And double denim feels appropriate for the movie we're going to see.

I'm adjusting it when there's a knock on the front door. I look toward the stairs, breath held in anticipation, even though I saw George only minutes ago. "I've got it!" I shout, my boots pounding down the stairs, so Oma knows she doesn't have to. Still, I can hear the stair lift already. She's a woman on a mission, but I beat her to the front door.

"Well, don't make him wait on my account," she says as she finds her footing.

I unlock the door and fling it open. I don't have to fake my joy at seeing him, no matter how little time it's been. In fact, all I can manage is, "Hey," and a stupid smile.

But he's smiling back, trying to smooth down his curls, which, why would he ever? I love them. I show him by batting his hand away from his hair, taking it, and leading him into the house. Through the front door. It feels so official. Feels real.

Oma rests a hand on my shoulder for support as she joins us— and then moves it to George's before going right in for a hug. "So wonderful to meet the young man who's made my Howard so happy." I hear the smile on her face even though I can't see it.

George mouths, "Young man," to me over her shoulder with a conspiratorial wink before she releases him. "Well, it's a pleasure to meet you too, ma'am," he replies.

I guide them to the living room and notice that George has offered Oma his arm, which she gladly takes. "Oh, thank you," she says as he leads her to the old floral couch. "My knees aren't what they used to be."

"I understand," he says, which strikes me as hilarious.

My grandmother invites him to sit beside her and tells him about the movie she's planning to watch tonight while we're out, and this is all I've ever wanted.

I watch them interact, and he behaves the way he did with the folks at Spring Meadows. George is . . . "Polite" is not the correct word. "Polite" is how you behave at a parent-teacher conference or with an aunt you rarely see. George is reconnecting. Code-switching, almost. Because he's one of them: an elder. A queer elder—and the full gravity of that hits me even harder than before. That I'm with this person who's survived. And not only that but helped others along their paths, often brushing with death in ways they could not.

"I love that movie," he says, settling into the cushion like he's planning to spend the evening watching a movie with Oma rather than me. I can almost picture him and James settling in for the evening to watch *The Price Is Right*. "I can't believe I just forgot who stars in it. . . ."

I sit on the arm of the sofa. It strikes me that imagining George with James—imagining my boyfriend with his former partner—is not something my classmates would find endearing. But I don't just love that George is *old*; I love the decades that have made him who he is, and James is a big part of that. The bravery it took to go back to him after forty years, making a new life together, and the care he showed him until death did they part.

"Why do they make the keyboard so small?" Oma asks, leading George to help her. I lean over the two of them and look at her search results. A familiar face pops up, but I don't recognize him right away.

"Martin Sheen!" George lights up as he looks between me and Oma. "He was so cute. There was an article about the movie—

That Certain Summer," he says for my benefit, "in the paper when it came out—not a favorable article."

"Well, it was a big deal back in the 1970s to show homosexuality on television," Oma replies. "A lot of people were not happy about it. But I tell you—Hal Holbrook and Martin Sheen had such amazing chemistry!" She claps her hands in delight. "Where'd you find that review? The library?"

"That's right," George says, though I can tell from the way his eyes light up that he actually read it when it was originally printed. "I'm a bit of a nerd when it comes to queer representation in the media. And I do have a soft spot for leading men from the sixties and seventies." He crosses his arms and slouches a little, getting comfortable.

I raise an eyebrow. "You going to stay home with Oma all night?"

"Maybe he wants to hang out with me," she says with a wink. "I've heard all the cool kids watch movies with their grandmothers on the weekends. Or is that just you?"

"Wow." George grins. "She got you."

I laugh, unable to hold back anymore. "No one ever said I was cool, especially not me!"

George hoists himself to his feet with a nod to Oma. "Guess I should go keep this one company." And then he's sliding a hand across my back and leading the way toward the front door. "I'll give you a moment to say goodbye to Oma?"

I nod, smiling, and watch as he disappears onto the stoop.

As soon as we're alone, Oma gives me a knowing look and says, "I can see why you like George. Polite, smartly dressed, *and* a Martin Sheen fan."

"Thanks, Oma." Suddenly I'm overwhelmed. I blink, trying to stop the prickling at the corners of my eyes.

"What is it, hon?" she asks.

"It's just . . . when I lived with Mom and Dad, I never thought I'd get to introduce a boy to them. Not that I had many prospects." I laugh. "I love you, is all."

Oma rests a hand on my shoulder, balancing herself as she gently runs her free hand through my hair. "I love you too, kiddo. And you can introduce me to a hundred boys if you—"

"Oma!"

"What!" She grins. "It took me dozens of boys before I settled on your dziadzi, and I didn't introduce a single one to my parents. They were very strict, but I'm not. I just want you to be happy. And George seems to make you happy." Oma pokes my shoulder before releasing me. "But the second he stops, you let him go, okay? A bad boyfriend is worse than no boyfriend, remember that. You're not married yet; enjoy dating."

"Oma." I press my lips together but can't conceal my smile. With a kiss on her cheek, I say, "Thank you."

"Now go. It's cold out there! Don't keep him waiting."

I don't.

As we spill out of The Charles and onto the busy Friday night street, I feel high. Because this time I take George's hand without fear. This time I pull him to me and kiss his perfect pink lips beneath a streetlight, where everyone can see us.

"That movie was so messed up!" I say as we walk down the street.

"In a good way, though, right?" George asks.

"Totally."

"I saw it with two friends, Justin and Aaron, at this cool theater in Brooklyn back in the late eighties. I think we said, 'What's your damage?' for the next three years." George smiles at the memory.

"Do you know what happened to them? To Justin and Aaron?"

"I don't." He pauses. "I told you before that I've been lucky in my life when it comes to friends."

I nod, remembering. Can't help but think of my own friends. I'm lucky to have Sue, even when he seems to be existing on a different level. But I feel a twinge of regret that I never got closer with the others, with Tiana or Phoenix or Kenna or Gray. Will we even keep in touch during college? After? What if I go on to have *no one*? I hold George closer at the thought.

"The thing, though, is that all my friendships had to be short-lived. Because of what I am. I couldn't stick around long enough for them to notice that I wasn't aging. Which is why I moved so much. Before I got back together with James, I lived in Manhattan and then way out in Williamsburg. I did a little time in Hudson before returning to the city. And then I did a stint in Philadelphia and then in New Hope before coming back to Baltimore."

I'd pieced together as much from our conversations, but hearing the details, I'm reminded of his stories in the graveyard as well. Of people who meant so much to him during such short bursts of time. Not a talent I seem to have. Maybe I'll earn it as I get older, get out of school, and can get to know the queer scene better. "It must have been hard to say goodbye to so many friends."

"It was," George says plainly. "Letting go hurt every time. And it's not like we had social media for keeping in touch. Not that I could have posted personal details or pictures, anyway."

I let a quiet moment pass between us. Feels like George's entire life is on the tip of his tongue.

"But then"—he smiles—"I always got to make new friends. Find the city's queer bar, whether it was legal or not. Seek out the fliers for events and rallies. Fall in love with a place and its people all over again."

"Can I ask—"

"Always—you know that."

I feel a blush warm my cheeks. "It's not even really a question. I'm just wondering how different things would have been—would be—if you knew other vampires. Like, I know we already talked about this, but they have to exist; you can't be the only one. That would make you, like, a cryptid or something."

George snorts, another smile crossing his face. "Well, now I'm going to start calling myself that."

"You wouldn't have to if there were more of you, more vampires. Like, why did that monster attack you, and what stopped it from attacking others?"

"I don't—I honestly don't think about it anymore. It used to keep me awake, wondering why me, and if there were others who might find and kill me. Right after being turned, the idea of seeking out friendships with other vampires wasn't top of mind, given my single vampiric encounter. And like I said, I'd occasionally get the desire to look. But . . ." He slides his hand out of mine and across my waist. Pins prickle my skin where his fingers press against me. "You're making me wish I'd looked harder. It would be a different kind of friendship, I reckon. Sort of like the vampiric equivalent of growing old together."

I immediately start thinking about what it would be like to *grow old* with George. To be immortal. "It's never too late to start looking," I offer—a test, I admit. Not one he can fail, but *would* he look for other vampires? Or candidates?

"No, I do have forever." George chuckles. "But I'm comfortable right now. Just met this new guy named Howard. He's kind of my boyfriend."

And now I'm really blushing but also kissing him, because I can, and he makes me feel bold and alive. "I hear Howard is a huge nerd."

George slides his hand up my back and beneath my jacket. "A sexy one. The eighties looks good on you, by the way," he says, tugging the denim.

I pull him across the street—extremely jaywalking, but I've seen *Twilight,* and wouldn't it be thrilling if George stopped a car from hitting me? Not that I'm trying to tempt fate. "Well, I couldn't not with tonight's movie. How have I never seen *Heathers*? Like, I knew it existed, obviously, but just never got around to it."

He laughs. "Well, I'm glad we did. It's a classic for a reason."

"Probably because Christian Slater's so hot in it."

"So hot," George confirms. "It's been wild watching so many movie stars go from baby-faced teens to silver foxes."

"I had no idea he was so good-looking when he was younger," I say, pushing my way into the diner on the other corner. "I mean, I only know who he is because of *Rick and Morty.*" This diner isn't my favorite, but their shakes taste like heaven after a movie and a bucket of popcorn. Besides, I can't stop thinking about how Oma compared me and George to her and Dziadzi.

"What's *Rick and Morty?*" George asks.

"I'll show you later." We slide onto the last two stools at the end of the counter. I order a chocolate malt in honor of Oma. George orders a strawberry shake, and I give him a quizzical look.

"Mostly for appearances," he says, "though I do like the way they smell, and I can have a couple sips before I start to feel sick. Plus, they bring back good memories. I'm sorry; it's a bit wasteful." A look of embarrassment crosses his face. It must be so weird to have had this luxe life for such a long time and suddenly have nothing.

"Don't worry about it. Oma gives me a generous allowance." Now it's my turn to feel embarrassed. But George smiles, and then I smile, and we're both laughing it off.

While we wait for our shakes, he explains what soda fountains used to be like: how you used to get the shake in a glass, plus the metal cup it was made in that had whatever wouldn't fit in the glass. An extra treat.

He makes do without when ours arrive—actually makes do with one slow sip through his paper straw. I can tell he's savoring it. Wonder what it tastes like to him, given that he otherwise craves blood. Does blood just taste like blood to him, or are there flavors we mortals can't pick up with our boring taste buds? Not sure it's safe to ask now that we're crammed into a busy diner, but I book-mark the topic for later.

"I mean, was Christian Slater right to kill those popular kids?" I tilt my head back and forth, considering. It's a kitschy movie, but it's also a fantasy. "Like, I don't agree with it . . . but I don't *not* agree with him. Those jocks who spent the whole movie joking about sucking dick and calling people fags made me want to reach through the screen and do it myself."

"Veronica and the Heathers weren't much better themselves."

When I look up from my shake, George is holding a spoonful of his out for me to try. Is this—him offering me ice cream—like the equivalent of a mortal offering their neck to their vampire boy-friend? Either way, I love it. A romantic gesture that also makes me want to take his clothes off. I close my mouth around the frosted metal spoon and draw slowly back, staring into his silver eyes while I taste strawberries.

I swallow. "No, they weren't. But they weren't the real problem, were they? It was something his character said. 'The extreme . . .'"

"'The extreme always seems to make an impression,'" George finishes for me.

"Right. Like, maybe Christian was trying to make the world a better place by getting rid of the Heathers and the jocks. But they were just kids parroting what they'd learned from their parents and society and history. I'm not making excuses for bullies—like, there's this guy at my school that I absolutely *hate*, and I'd love to see him gone. But I recognize that some people need time to grow out of their ignorance or whatever."

"So who would you go after?"

"Well, if it were me, I'd get rid of the people in power. The ones who've shown us that they're not going to change."

I watch as thought lines furrow George's forehead.

"Like . . . the night you told me you were"—I glance around to make sure no one is listening—"a vampire, you said you'd killed before." I look at him to make sure it's okay that I've brought up this topic. He nods, signaling that I can continue. "You sort of implied that you'd killed some people on purpose."

"Yes, that is true."

I'm not sure how to phrase my next question. Like, do I just ask him point-blank if the people he killed were bad people? I can totally see George going after corrupt politicians or, like, the Family Research Council. The six members on the Wyndhurst school board who voted against us seem small in comparison. *Not* that I'm about to ask him to murder them. Still . . . let's say those members happened to disappear. It wouldn't just be the current QSA we'd be affecting. It'd be all the closeted queer kids, plus the ones who come after us. And we'd also be honoring those who'd come and gone.

George interrupts my thoughts by asking, "Like who?" I know he's asking what people in power I'd go after, and I've thought about it. A lot more recently.

"That guy, for one," I say, pointing behind George. He turns to look. A familiar face hovers near the cash register. I watch as the man pays with cash and doesn't leave a tip. Even this late on a Friday, he's dressed like he's on the golf course. "Mr. Percy. Out-of-touch old fuck on the board. Doesn't even have kids—like, why is he on the board of a school if he doesn't even have kids? If he was gone . . ." I don't finish my sentence. Shouldn't—especially not here.

"I know why he's on the board," George says. "Most people in power—politicians and what have you—who claim it's *for the children* don't actually care about the children." He offers me another spoonful, his hand to my cheek as he guides the cold metal and melting milkshake into my mouth. We linger like that, eyes on each other, forgetting Mr. Percy for each other. Slowly, George slides the spoon out between my lips. Kisses them softly. "It's about control."

CHAPTER 23

GEORGE

Howard has long been asleep by the time I slip out of his bed—not uncommon. We've fallen asleep together every night since I moved in (snuck in?), but he can't—and shouldn't—stay awake all night with me, and I can't spend days in his room. I can't risk a ray of sunlight peeking through the curtains or his oma deciding to brave the stairs, only to find me in her grandson's bed. So when he draws in a long sleepy breath and stretches, I'm not worried. If he woke, he'd assume I was only climbing up to the attic. He has school in the morning, so I do my best to be extra quiet, though I don't hesitate to press a kiss to Howard's forehead before leaving.

After twenty years of living in a house, I've almost forgotten what it's like to wander the streets at night. When I'm not living on them, there's a sort of thrill. The city asleep while I'm awake—like your parents going away for the weekend and leaving you home alone.

Mr. Percy lives in Wyndhurst. I've been thinking about him since we ran into him during our date and decided to do a little research. His house is freestanding with a cultivated yard. At least three times as wide as Howard's and easily worth over a million dollars. I imagine he fancies himself a concerned citizen—*looking out for his neighborhood,* he probably tells himself.

A familiar fire burns within me, one I haven't felt in a long time but have no trouble remembering. I answered honestly when Howard asked if I'd ever killed anyone, but I did let him assume it was for survival. In truth, I've also killed to protect my own. There was that one politician who planned to propose a mandatory sterilization bill for all "sex perverts." I would have gone after Anita Bryant, but she was too far away and too high-profile for me to kill, so I killed that politician instead. Local menaces were easier to disappear than national ones. Cops who made a point to beat and arrest trans sex workers. Doctors who locked their patients in isolation from family and friends and refused to even try to help them. There were so many of those, I was often drunk on their blood.

I lick my lips at the memory—tongue my left fang in anticipation as I slip between well-trimmed trees and scour the back of Mr. Percy's obscene house with a practiced eye.

I never shared that part of my life with James. The murder part. For all that I loved him, I don't think that he would have understood. He was never very political. Certainly he believed in equal rights, but he never marched in the streets for a cause. Demonstrations that turned violent made him uncomfortable. During the 2016 election, I joked about how I wished someone would assassinate one of the candidates, and he turned deathly serious, saying it was never all right to kill someone. Didn't he realize they would kill us? *Had been* killing us for decades?

For forty years, I lived among political, passionate queer people who were forever fighting for equality. When I found James, he'd spent the last four decades being perceived as a straight white man. The causes I held close to my heart were ones he'd barely thought about. Any time I brought up gay rights, he'd say something along the lines of, "It'll all work itself out in the end," a common refrain for those who've never had to do any fighting for their own rights.

I knew the "working itself out" had killed tens of thousands in our community and was continuing to kill many more. But because I loved him and because we had lived different lives and because, if I'm being honest, I was just so tired, I was simply happy that we'd found each other again. I don't doubt that James struggled with his identity, and I figured he'd made the choices that were safest for him. I'd say mine were dangerous—because they were—but I was also immortal. I could bleed out, for example, a homophobic homeowners association president or district councilman with little fear of consequence.

Like this Mr. Percy. Howard continually surprises me. He presents himself as naïve, but he knows a lot about how the world works. At eighteen, he's already aware that you have to think beyond the immediate annoyance. Beyond the schoolyard bullies. It would be a lie to say they don't make Howard and his friends' lives miserable, but the bigger lie would be to label them the problem when they're only the symptoms.

To find the real problem, you have to look up the ladder. To their parents. The school board. Local politicians, national committees, and the White House. We aren't far from DC, but I don't want to get ahead of myself. And Howard, whether he knows it or not, has presented me a concrete way to improve not only his and his friends' lives, but also the lives of the generations of students who follow him. To flip an entire school ecosystem.

If it were me, I'd get rid of the people in power.

"What if it were us, Howard?" I say to myself as I spot a window that is slightly open and begin my climb.

I loved James and will continue to carry him with me as long as the sun or a beheading doesn't take me—and I also find myself invigorated by the notion of being with someone so inspired and energized. With ideas that remind me of how I once was and how I could be again. How we could be together. Imagine, with unlimited years and vampiric power, what we might achieve.

Then again, he is only eighteen. I wasn't given a choice to be turned into a vampire. I only killed because of the position I found myself in, because I was a monster who fed on mortals. But early on I made a conscious choice to feed on the ones who meant to do our community harm.

Could I do this to Howard? Turn him into the kind of young man who sees murder as the first, most effective, and most thrilling solution? Watching his confidence grow has endeared me wildly to him. But I've had years to grow and learn. To weigh options based on history and experience. The testimonies of and collaboration with others.

I climb as if it is the rough stone wall of Spring Meadows. But when I reach the window, I don't fall onto a weathered carpet or creaking floorboards. Rather, I land dexterously on polished hardwood in a large hallway that has enough room for a small sitting area and bookcase.

As I glide down the hall toward the soft sounds of snoring, I know that I'm crossing a threshold. That this will be the second person I have killed since I've been with Howard. Shortly after I moved in with him, Howard told me that the man who'd harassed us after *My Beautiful Laundrette*—who happened to be one of his classmates' brothers—had been found dead. He had asked no questions, though it was obvious that he'd understood what I had done. And the gleam in his eyes made it clear that he wasn't upset. I didn't intend for that man to die, though I had done nothing to ensure that he might live. In that way, tonight is different. I know what I'm here to do: I'm going to drain Mr. Percy.

Howard could hate it. Just because he fantasizes about pulling a Christian Slater on the school board doesn't mean he can handle ending a life. What I'm about to do is extremely real. I've read some of the same vampire books he has, and even the more horrific ones can't prepare you for the moment when a heart stops beating in your hands.

There's a strong possibility Howard doesn't mean it. That when he finds out what I've done, he'll finally see me as the monster I spent decades hiding from James. I don't want to hide anymore, nor do I want to live with the worry I'll terrify the man I love.

I consider stopping, going back out that window, and returning to Howard's bed. But no. This is what I want. This is who I am. As I crack Mr. Percy's door open, I know there's no turning back. I watch his chest rise and fall in his monogrammed pajamas. An electric fireplace flickering in the ambient moonlight. Perhaps a death on the board will make the other members reconsider their votes. Might make James' daughter reconsider her vote.

Percy's little power trip ends now.

I launch myself across the room like a heat-seeking missile and land on his chest, rip his collar, and latch on to his jugular. I don't bother trying to manipulate his mind; I want him to feel every ounce of this fear and panic. Just as his blood starts to fill my mouth, he bucks and thrashes, trying to fling me off like a pest. He's a mass of sixty-some years—the kind of guy who probably played football in high school and college before "retiring" due to injury—and strong, though I'm not concerned.

"The fuck are you?!" He manages to get his arms under me and push me away. His eyes open wide when he sees my fangs, sees his own blood like lipstick smeared around my mouth. "What in God's name—" He slaps at the wet sides of his own neck, desperate to find the wound, stop the bleeding. While his hands are busy, I take the opportunity to knee him in the balls just for the hell of it.

He groans and reaches for them, and I watch the blood spill from his neck again. I straddle him, his arms now pinned beneath me, and latch back on to his neck. I feel Mr. Percy's heart speed up as it tries to pump his remaining blood to his vital organs. Feel him go limp beneath me. Feel him dying as I become more alive.

He sates me. I haven't had this much fresh, hot blood in my body since . . . Actually, I can't remember when. The homophobe in the alley was barely a taste compared to this man.

I let myself out that third-story window in a single leap and land easily on my feet. *I'm excited for them to find his corpse,* I think, as I lick the remaining blood from my lips. *Let them be afraid.*

Howard doesn't wake up when I pull my shirt over my head and wipe it over my mouth one final time. He stirs when my weight dips the mattress. I lay my head against his bare chest and take in his scent as I listen to his steady heartbeat. I drape an arm across his torso just as he wraps one of his around my shoulders, sleepily pulling us together.

"Where'd you go?" he slurs, his eyes still closed. His forehead finds mine, his fingers dancing up my bare back. "Your skin is so warm." Howard sighs contentedly and falls back to sleep before I can tell him not to worry about it.

CHAPTER 24

S ue's waiting beside my locker when I rush into school late.
Not technically late, not yet. I love sharing a bed with George,
but having a boyfriend who gets in and out of it throughout the night has disrupted my sleep. I'm dragging in the morning
more than I used to, though I wouldn't have my nights any other
way. Still, I've picked up an aggressive coffee habit, draining Oma's
decades-old drip machine before she's had a chance to have a cup.

"Hey," I say, looking both ways before opening my locker as if
I'm crossing a street where the cars are lacrosse players. Sue looks
like his mind is elsewhere. "What's going on? Did I miss something?"

Sue watches as my lock clicks open, as I swing the metal door
open with a creak. Our classmates flow through the hallway behind

us, voices low, faces grim. I do a double take at Sue, my backpack hanging off my elbow, travel mug pressed to my lips. Something's wrong. It feels like it did when Teddy Holley died.

Maybe someone even worse died.

"Yeah, you missed something." Sue crosses his arms and leans against the lockers beside me. "Mr. Percy, that old guy on the board, was murdered. Or at least that's what everyone's saying. Allegedly, his housekeeper found his body when she showed up yesterday morning. My mom got a call about it today as we were driving to school."

An "oh" escapes me. I'm not sad that he's dead; I just wished for it a few days ago. I was with George when I did. And then George wasn't with me for part of the night on, what was it, Sunday? He came home, his body warm, a metallic scent on his breath. And now this morning . . .

"Are you smiling?"

"Huh? No." My answer is reflexive. My attempt to hide my smile is also reflexive. But I'm not great at lying, and Sue gives me a look. I shrug. "Okay, yeah, I am," I say into my locker as I trade my backpack for my math book. "So what?"

"A man died."

"Yeah, a terrible one." I slam the door shut with a hard bang and lock it before glancing at my phone. We're going to be late for first period if he drags this out. Seems pretty clear-cut to me. "That man has been haunting the school board for a decade. I only wish he'd had the courtesy to bite it before Phoenix withdrew. We could have replaced him with someone who actually cares about queer students. Suppose we can now." Confidence settles into me like my morning coffee. "We should discuss who'd be a good fit for the empty board positions at the next QSA. If we approach strong candidates and act quickly—"

"Howard," Sue says. The warning bell rings. "Are you listening to yourself?"

"Yeah, and I feel like I know what I'm saying for the first time in ages." Like the person at the podium rather than the one sitting in the audience nervously holding hands with my neighbor, waiting for others to make or break my future.

"Even so," Sue says begrudgingly, like I've forced him to play along with my actually good idea. He can't possibly wish Mr. Percy were still alive and on the board. "My mom would never let us fill those slots—she'd just fill them with her friends. You know how influential she is."

"Well, then your mom had better watch her step." My gaze holds steady.

But Sue blinks. "What the fuck? I hope you're kidding; there's an actual murderer out there."

Suddenly Kenna comes around the corner, phone in one hand, books in the other. She stops beside Sue and rests her head against his, an unspoken greeting. But he doesn't take his eyes off me, even when Kenna asks, "Want to walk to Spanish together, babe?"

That was . . . I maybe should not have said that. Even though it's true. I wouldn't miss his mom for one second. Not that I'd want—I mean, I know what it's like to hate your parents. Unlike Sue, I left mine. I was lucky to have someone like Oma to take me in. I don't know if Sue has anyone like that, but Oma would never let someone she cares about live on the street, and neither would I.

See: the beautiful vampire living in my attic.

I glance at Kenna and know I could never even begin to explain what I said or why—or the situation I'm in. She and Sue are model queer students. Vice president and president of the school's QSA, they understand the system and work within it. They're smart and visible and speak up. They push over and over for change . . . even when nothing does.

But that's just the problem, isn't it? Nothing changes.

"Did I interrupt something?" Kenna asks when Sue doesn't answer.

"No," I say. "Sue was just filling me in on Mr. Percy's murder."

She makes a show of shivering, leaning even closer to Sue as if for warmth. "That man was a piece of shit, but the way he was slaughtered in his own bed . . ." A sickly look crosses her face. "My dad literally dropped me off this morning and is attending my practice tonight because he doesn't want me driving home alone after. We live in the same neighborhood. I admit, I feel safer having him drive me." She nudges me with her phone before pocketing it. "You have your volunteering tonight, right, Howard? You should be careful going out alone."

"No, tomorrow. Doesn't matter, though; I'm taking time off for a bit." I avoid Sue's gaze as I add, "One of the residents passed away, and it sort of hit me—"

He interrupts. "My grandpa." And then, softly to Kenna, "The one I told you about."

I don't know why this makes me blush—embarrassed, almost. Like I've been taking James' death personally because of his and George's relationship and overlooking that he was Sue's grandpa. That the two of them were deprived of years' worth of knowing each other.

"I've got to get to calc before Mr. Redd marks me late," I say instead of digging myself any deeper. "I'll see you later." I leave before Sue can get another word out.

I race home after school. George isn't up yet, but that's okay, as it's Oma I'm eager to see. Oma, whom I love and who I am very much glad is alive. I throw my arms around her and receive my kiss on the cheek.

"To what do I owe this burst of affection?" she asks, pulling my scarf off and hanging it on a hook beside the door.

"It's just been a day." I want to explain the tension I had with Sue, but I don't think Oma is ready to learn that her grandson is open to murder if it serves the greater good. Have I always felt this way, and George just made me realize as much? Or is it George's influence that has changed my way of thinking? I glance up the stairs and then at the front window. Afternoon light still filters through the curtains. "I don't know if you saw on the news—that man who was murdered."

"I did. I recognized him from your school's board meeting." Concern shows on her face. "You want to talk about it?"

"Not really." I follow Oma as she waves me into the kitchen. Brownies wait on the table, and at her gesture, I sit. She joins me a moment later with two glasses of milk. "You remember how Mr. Percy voted against the QSA's propositions?"

"I do," Oma says. She focuses on me, ignoring her brownie.

I bite into mine, thinking how different my life might be if I still lived with my parents, if Oma hadn't taken me in. It's so nice having a safe space at home; it can be easy to forget people like Mr. Percy exist until they're voting against my safety at school. Well, he specifically doesn't exist anymore. For the best. "I'm really lucky to have you. And that you told me to come live with you."

Oma waves me off like it's no big deal, but it is, really. After a sip of her milk, she says, "Easiest decision of my life. I have no room for a son who treats *his* son like a stranger. You deserved to feel safe." She offers her hand, and I hold it gently in mine. "I often wonder why he turned out the way he did. His father and I—we always taught him to be kind and respectful." She shakes her head, and I can tell she's sorting through memories, trying to find one that will help her make sense of things.

"I wish everyone had an Oma." I pause, taking another bite and considering whether I should say what's on my mind, especially after my conversation with Sue at school. I decide to risk it. "And I wish no one had a Mr. Percy."

Oma claps her other hand over mine, giving me a squeeze before letting go. "It's normal to feel like that," she says.

"Sue doesn't think so."

Oma pauses. She knows Mrs. Wolcott, knows the challenges that Sue has with her, knows that Mrs. Wolcott didn't stand up for the QSA at the board meeting. "Well, you don't necessarily know how he's coping. We all deal with adversity in different ways. I'm sure Sue's doing his best with the hand he was dealt," she says. "Did you fight about it, or . . . ?"

I tilt my head back and forth, considering. "Kind of. I said something I shouldn't have." I feel the echo of my earlier embarrassment, and yet . . . I'm surer now with Oma. "Like, I understand what it's like to have parents who'd rather you didn't exist. But also, I'm just not sad about Mr. Percy—and I don't get why Sue is." I shove the rest of my brownie into my mouth so that I won't keep going. So I won't tell Oma that I wouldn't miss Mrs. Wolcott, either.

"I know you've had a tough time at school," she says after a moment. "And it sounds like Sue's having a tough time at home. But you two have been friends for years. I'm sure you'll work it out."

"Yeah . . ." She's right. We *are* in different places, but we're still friends. I wash down the rest of my brownie and give Oma a kiss on her forehead. "Love you."

"Love you too, kiddo. I, for one, am very glad you exist. Now, go do your homework, and I'll call you down when dinner's ready." She smiles up at me as I hurry off upstairs.

What I *want* is to go to George, but it's not even close to sunset. Oma's right: I should get my homework done. Because then when my boyfriend wakes up, I can give him all my attention guilt free. I toss my backpack onto my bed, grab my books, and spread out on my desk. Before digging in, I glance up at a photo of me and Sue at junior prom and find myself wondering whether a vampire like George would show up in photos.

• • •

After sunset—after I've finished my essay on queer themes in *Twelfth Night*—I walk out into the hall. Usually by now George has come down. I'm feeling a little impatient to see him, so I find the pull for the attic door. It's one of those you have to climb up into: not much more than a crawl space, but big enough to fit a few boxes of decorations . . . and a sleeping vampire. I can hear Oma working in the kitchen, the radio turned up. I'm careful when I pull down the stairs, but I'm not terribly worried she'll hear me. Quietly I climb up, pulling the stairs and hatch closed behind me.

George is still asleep on the futon mattress we laid out for him, even though the sun's down. I mean, I don't wake up when the sun rises, so I don't expect him to immediately get up when the sun sets. It's cozy up here. We moved all the storage bins to the far side of the attic and wove a few strands of extra string lights through the rafters. Then we emptied an old, short dresser and fit the things from George's duffel bag into it, so he'd feel like he had his own space. I even brought up some good pillows.

He's splayed across the entire mattress. Talk about a monster; I couldn't fit on that thing with him if I tried. But I do try, and I force myself to fit. George draws in a sleepy breath and buries his face in my neck. For a moment I imagine him biting me. Mouth clamped down, holding me close, entwining our lives together.

A cold shiver slices through me when I feel his lips press against my throat.

"I'm awake," he says. "What time is it?"

"Dark."

"That's not a time."

"Almost six. Dinner soon—for me."

"And breakfast for me."

Most nights, when I head downstairs to have dinner with Oma, George climbs out my window to go find someone to feed on. He usually comes back within an hour or two, his skin warm, his cheeks a little flushed. I'm always curious about where he's gone and from whom he's drunk. But I also feel like maybe it's none of my business? Tonight, though, I'm feeling bold, so I ask, "Are you . . . is it rude to ask where you're going to eat?"

"No." He rubs his eyes and looks at me. "But you ask *where* like I'm going to a restaurant. I know who I'm going to feed on—sort of. When James was younger and healthier, that used to be him. But as he aged, it became more of a ritual between us, an act of intimacy rather than my main source of . . . nutrients."

A nervous laugh escapes me. "Now who's talking like he's going to a restaurant?"

George smiles at my reply. "I'm skilled at finding the people who enjoy a moment of my company and the thrill of a bite."

An act of intimacy. "So for these people who like to be bitten, is it, like, intimate?" I'm glad we're still in the dark, because I'm blushing, partially from embarrassment, partially from jealousy. Intellectually, I know that George is just feeding—he needs the blood to be strong and healthy. But still . . . it kind of sounds like the people who want George to bite them find it thrilling or arousing.

"It's personal, of course, in that I put my mouth on them. But you put your mouth around a spoon when you eat and don't love it, so . . ." He brushes my hair out of my face. "You can always tell me how you're feeling, and I can do the same. So now I'm telling you: when I do feed tonight, it will be personal, but it won't be intimate."

"Would you . . ." We stare into each other's eyes for a moment—as if there's anywhere else to look this close up. As if I'd want to look anywhere else regardless. "Would you ever want to drink *my* blood?"

"Do you want me to?"

My heart races at his question—was already racing at the idea, but now that he's said it, it feels so real. Possible. And his mouth is right there, my neck right here. I'm nervous, though, if I'm being honest. It seems like a big deal. Sure, I've seen plenty of movies in which the vampire tears open their victim's neck and blood goes spurting everywhere. But I've also seen and read plenty of scenes in which a human willingly gives themself to a vampire, and the act is erotic, almost like a vampire's version of having sex—an idea that gets my blood moving similarly.

"Yes?" I test the word, and it feels good, but also my face burns at the admission. "But not right now. Or, I mean, I don't even know if you want to."

George closes his eyes, a light smile playing across his lips as he presses them to my neck. I hold my breath as if he might sink his teeth in now—but he would never. Not unless we were both ready, I know.

"Not right now," he says.

I release a long, controlled breath and relax on the pillow beside him. We hold each other for a moment before I'm relaxed enough to ask, "Did you hear about Mr. Percy? That guy on the board I pointed out in the diner?" Just because I'm feeling bold doesn't mean I'm bold enough to flat-out ask if my boyfriend murdered a man. I don't want him to feel accused if he didn't.

"I've been asleep literally all day." George yawns as he says it, baring the full length of his fangs. He never used to smile—used to seem afraid to—but he does now. I like it. He shouldn't be afraid to show his teeth.

"Right." Not an answer to my question but telling enough—he's hesitant to talk about it with me. Which is fine, but I want him to know he can trust me even with this. So I act casual about it, don't push him. I also don't resist the urge to run my fingers through the mess of black waves on his head. Bedhead looks good on him. "Well, he's dead."

"Hm."

Hm?

"We should go downstairs," George says before I can push further. "Just in case your oma calls for dinner and we don't hear. This room is good for storing my things and not burning alive during the day, but don't hold it against me that I prefer your room and your bed."

"Not at all." I watch while he pulls on a pair of flannel pajama bottoms and a clean T-shirt before pressing his ear to the floor.

"All clear," he says with a wink. Oma's never shown any suspicion of us, but it's fun to pretend that we might get caught—it makes things feel even more illicit.

Quietly we relocate, pushing the attic door closed behind us. George settles onto my bed and leans against the wall, his expression solemn. I stand still, watching him—watching him watch me. We both know we left the conversation hanging.

Finally he sighs and holds his hand out for me, and I take it, climbing onto the bed beside him. When he tries to press my hair back into place, I can't help but think of Oma or Dziadzi wanting to send me off looking my best. I half expect George to lick his thumb and wipe a spot off my cheek next.

And he does reach for my cheek but rubs a dry thumb across it. "Life means something, Howard. Ask me how I know."

I place my hand over his and curl our fingers together in fists, bringing them down to the covers. "I know you're technically dead, George." He's still warm to the touch. "But—"

"I'm not *technically* dead, I'm fully dead. That thing's blood just brought me back to . . . 'life' isn't the right word, but it isn't *not*. I only mean . . . death is real. Ending a human life means something—I've never done so lightly. If we're going to be together, I want you to keep that in mind."

"They don't keep it in mind."

His forehead wrinkles. "What do you mean?"

"I'm not naïve, George. These people—Teddy Holley, Mr. Percy, Sue's mom—they don't care about my life. They don't take fucking care when it comes to people like us. Queers. You know as well as I do that our community has had to take matters into our own hands time and time—"

"Howard!" Oma's voice cuts me off. Freezes us both in place.

"Yeah?" I call out. I take a beat and whisper to George, "Probably just dinner."

"Sue's here!"

"Or not," George says.

"Shit." There's no time to get him up into the attic; where can we—maybe the window?

I'm halfway to my feet when Sue bursts into my room, not bothering to knock, and why would he? We're best friends. He barely knocks at the front door, much less my bedroom's. As the door flies open, I stand between him and George like a barricade.

Sue stops still, holding his bag out as if to drop it but unable to. He looks between us in shock before his bag hits the rug with a muffled thud. "I came to finish our conversation from earlier, but I can see you're busy."

I press an insistent finger to my lips, signaling a desperate *Please be quiet,* as I close the door gently behind him. Across the room George straightens up and moves to sit on the edge of my bed. Ready. Sue steps into the room like he's stepping up to the podium—with total confidence. His eyes roam George's body and then my room. I see Sue notice the clothes strewn about the room—some of them mine, some of them George's—and the extra pillow on my bed.

"It's not what it looks like," I begin, like everyone who's ever tried to deny that it is indeed exactly what it looks like. "He just needed a place to stay after . . ." I'm not sure how to finish the sentence.

"After what?" Sue asks pointedly.

The fact that Sue's decided to be aggressive is all the incentive I need to be the same. "After your mom put him on the street and threw half his possessions into a dumpster and sold the rest."

A look of guilt flashes across Sue's face, but he recovers quickly. "He's living with you? And I'm guessing we have to be quiet because you haven't told Oma?" Sue brushes past me, and George is on his feet in a heartbeat.

They stand face-to-face, almost the same height. Sue's hands flex and curl with an energy aching to go somewhere, to find a home. George stands unnaturally still, his eyes the only movement as he examines his . . . well, the boy who would have been his grandson in another life, maybe one where he could have been open, accepted. Where he might have known and been embraced by James' child and grandchild.

Instead, that grandchild asks, "Who *are* you, George?"

My instincts are screaming to protect him. To intervene, to answer. Instead, I trust. No doubt George has been in situations like this before over the sixty years he's been a vampire. He can handle himself.

I take a deep breath as . . . he takes Sue's hand? George examines Sue's watch, and then he looks him squarely in the eyes. "All you need to know is that I loved your grandfather very much." He lets go and returns to my bed, settling in for whatever questions come next.

Sue pulls out my desk chair and sits.

I stand awkwardly in between them, wondering whether I should relax against the wall and let them talk, or sit beside George. Show him he has my support. There are sides within the room now. Which one am I on?

"Sure," Sue says, leaning forward but not getting up. "But who are you? What's your last name? Do you have a family? Where'd you grow up and go to school? We know literally nothing about you!" Then, as if to himself, "My mom would lose her mind if she knew you were here."

That's what keeps me on my feet. "Sue, you can't tell her."

"I want to know," he says, his eyes turning from me to George. It feels like a threat.

George shifts to the edge of the bed. "My name is George Culhane, my parents have passed, and I have no siblings. I grew up right here in South Baltimore. We've probably walked by each other on the street."

Sue sits back, absorbing his blunt honesty. Suspicion still threads his voice. "Okay, so where do you go to school?"

"I don't—I graduated." George's eyes dart my way and then back to Sue.

It's clear that Sue doesn't know what to do with George's brevity. "Well, what about college?"

"Not everyone goes to college, Sue," I interject.

George decides to ignore the question. "You know what this world is like to queer people, Sue. You saw it firsthand at your school board meeting a few weeks ago. And you know what it's like to have a parent who doesn't support you, as does Howard, and as do I."

Sue drops his head into his hands and takes a deep breath, like he's wrestling with something. There's no consequence here, though. George isn't accusing him of anything; he's attempting to empathize.

"I think you've gathered that your mom was not kind to your grandfather after he came out," George continues. "Stopped helping him around the house, stopped visiting for dinner. Started coordinating family holidays without him. Just didn't call. And after he came out to you, she kept you from him."

When Sue finally looks up, he sniffles, eyes wet with tears he's determined not to shed, wiping at their corners. *It's okay,* I want to tell him. *You can let it out; you're in like company.* But I want George to have his say—and he says it so well, both of us listen intently to his words.

"At first she made excuses, said you were busy with school and extracurriculars. James wanted so much for you to succeed, so he didn't press. Maybe he should have." George pauses, as if considering that notion. "And then she stopped bothering to keep him updated. Did you know that she took him off your family phone plan, so he had to get a new number and you couldn't call him? That she forbade him from calling you? I think that was around the time you were about to start high school."

"That was when I came out to her and Dad." Sue shakes his head. "I thought he'd died," he says softly. "It wasn't until that night at Spring Meadows that I even knew he was still alive." At this Sue sheds a tear, letting it slide down his face uninterrupted. He feels it fully.

George gets up and crosses to Sue, taking a knee in front of him. He takes Sue's wrist again. "This was his watch. I'm . . . when your mother forced him into Spring Meadows, he left it for me. So I could count the hours until I saw him again." He *hmm*s to himself, as if remembering. "I have no use for it anymore, though. And I'm glad you have it. You should have something of his after being denied a relationship with him."

George releases him. "He missed you, Sue. He had photos of you all over the walls—all old ones, forgive him. Your mom never sent updated ones."

"She never took updated ones." Sue's anger rolls into a sob. He tilts his head back as if that will keep the tears in, but it's no use, and he wipes at them with his sleeve. "Did you know that she told me we're not having new family photos done for our Christmas cards this year? Said she doesn't have the time or money. Please—she sold Grandpa's house! But I know it's because she couldn't ignore the changes from the testosterone anymore. Like, she always hated how I dressed, but it was easier to lie to herself and others before my facial hair started growing in." He closes a hand over the watch and clutches it to his chest. "And all this time there was someone else like me in the family—her own dad." Sue shakes his head, fingers tightening around James' watch. "He could have been my Oma, but she never even let me know him. Kept us apart. What I wouldn't have given for . . ." He doesn't finish his sentence. Can't.

"I'm so sorry," George says. "I wish . . ." He places a comforting hand on Sue's knee. "I wish you'd gotten to see your grandfather like I did. It's not fair—what your mother did was cruel. You and I shouldn't have met like this. We should have been friends. We still can be."

I offer Sue my handkerchief. As he dries his eyes, I meet

George's and take his hand, pulling him to his feet. I press a soft kiss to his forehead. It's not enough, but it's enough for now.

And then Sue is standing beside us, tucking my damp hand-kerchief back into my pocket. "I don't know what to say besides thanks." He places his other hand on George's shoulder. "It's a lot right now, but I appreciate you sharing—seeing as I didn't get to know him, and you did."

"It's my honor," he replies, the three of us finally joined.

"I feel like I should hate her—my mom. After everything you just said. I *want* to. I probably would if she were just some woman on the school board . . . but I love her. I don't know how not to." Sue's words hit me like a fist to the chest. A feeling I'm familiar with. An ache within myself but also for him.

CHAPTER 25

HOWARD

"**A**re you awake?"

It's a dumb question—I know George doesn't sleep after sunset, but I can't just spit out what I'm thinking. Not tonight. And he always looks so peaceful in bed, still and quiet in a way us humans can never be. Disturbing him feels illegal, but you know the saying: *Be gay, do crime.*

I chuckle to myself as he answers with a breathy, "Yes, Howard. I'm awake."

Even though we've fallen asleep in each other's arms before, I still blush when George kisses my chest, cool lips to warm skin. He nuzzles against my shoulder and neck, breathing me in, and I do the same, burying my face in his dark curls. I can't believe he's mine—that all this is mine, could be my life forever. That I could be his forever too.

Forever.

That's always meant a century to me, if I'm lucky. But as we hold each other here on tousled sheets in the pale moonlight, I know George's *forever* is exactly what it means. That we found each other at what might have been the end of his life, had he been mortal, and now we're beginning a second one, a new one, together.

I seal the moment with a brief kiss before attempting to climb over him. We giggle quietly as I snag my fingers in his hair before getting my foot twisted in the sheets and tumbling onto the rug. "Oof," I let out dramatically. "Off to a good start."

George might not survive the sun, but his smile is just as bright and warm. "Good start for what?" As he slides his tongue against the tip of his left fang, a shiver slides through me. Not fear—there's no one I feel safer around than him. No, it's flattering, arousing—overwhelming, almost—that he shows me his desire this way. That he'd like to take a bite out of me, that he trusts me and knows I trust him.

I have to turn away as I imagine his teeth sinking into my neck, lips pressing against my skin. There's something I want for us first. *Then* we can discuss . . . well . . .

On tiptoes I reach up onto the top shelf of my closet and feel for the shoebox I shoved back there, far out of view. I find the box and pull it down, set it on the rug beside the bed so we can both see inside. The big reveal.

"I was going to do this earlier, before Sue showed up. . . ." Suddenly I'm nervous. Just because I want to share *forever* with George doesn't mean it's easy to expose myself like I'm about to.

240

I lift the lid an inch, peeking within . . . and then turning it so he can see too. Lacy stockings and underwear, a maroon bralette, and some kind of fur-hemmed gauzy robe that spills out onto the rug now that the lid's no longer containing it. As George sits up and scoots closer, I swear he blushes.

"I remember what you said about the three-article rule, and I couldn't help but think . . . maybe it'd be fun to try something new—for me, at least. Even though we live in a state where there are protections, clothes are still scrutinized. My school literally still has a gendered dress code; I can only imagine what it was like growing up in the fifties and living through a time where, well . . ."

How do I even begin to compare my life to George's? The climate is so different now. I'd be lying if I said things weren't better, but it's not all rainbows. Just because it isn't illegal to wear the clothes you want in many states doesn't mean that people aren't still killed for it. Doesn't mean assholes like the school board aren't out there protesting and lobbying that we hang those clothes up in the closet before locking ourselves back inside as well.

But then George kneels down on the floor opposite me and reaches for something sky blue and silky. "Oh, Howard," he says, rubbing it lovingly between his fingers. I can't help but wonder if his sense of touch is heightened the way his sight and hearing sometimes are. Like his taste is for blood. "These are beautiful. I . . ."

He traces his hand over lace and fur and gauze. Over elastic and bows and a rainbow of soft colors and fabrics. I spent so long curating them from vintage stores and indie boutiques where I was asked to show my driver's license. Even though I don't think the clerks were judging me—they seemed delighted to help a young queer guy find what he liked—I was still embarrassed, and annoyed that I was embarrassed. I shouldn't have to be.

I watch as George pulls out the bralette, the dark maroon like blood against his skin. I find myself browsing for something that matches—so that *we* match, but also something that I might feel comfortable in. A pair of black thigh-high stockings, the kind with the seams up the backs, and blush-colored panties. As our eyes meet, the same color creeps across his pale cheeks.

"I'm going to change in the bathroom," I find myself blurting out. Like we haven't changed clothes in front of each other—it's nothing new, and yet it feels huge. More vulnerable than being naked, even.

Relief floods me when he says, "Of course. Whatever you need," before taking my hand and kissing it like the romantic lead in a black-and-white movie. I squeeze his momentarily before turning toward the hall.

The door closes behind me with a quiet click, and then I make my way down the hall toward the bathroom. Another click and I'm alone, barefoot on the cold tile, clutching my chosen lingerie like it might escape.

I avoid the mirror, setting down the stockings and briefs on the edge of the sink while I pull off my clothes. No need to seem cool or whatever; no one's looking. My hair poofs out from the static of my shirt as I hop on one foot, trying to kick off my sweats and underwear with only my feet. George is probably slipping his lingerie on gracefully, beautifully. Me?

I face the mirror, naked in my little bathroom with fixtures that are older than Oma. At no point in my high school career have I ever wished to be a lacrosse or football player, but staring at my chest and shoulders, I'm wondering whether ten pushups would do the job.

Ew, no. Not on the bathroom floor. Besides, I look fine. Or at least George likes my body. Hopefully he likes it in nylon and satin.

With a deep breath, I pull the pale pink briefs up my legs, tickling every hair along the way. I chuckle to myself as I smooth them down before putting on the stockings, which are trickier than anticipated. When I was a little kid, my mom used to keep a pair in a plastic egg in her car. The number of times she swatted them out of my hands like I'd broken the law, and now I'm fitting my own over my toes, heels, calves. Stretching them up to the thick of my thighs, where elastic snaps them in place.

They feel tight but good. Make me feel powerful when I look myself over in the mirror. Like I could command an entire audience. I only need the attention of one boy, though, and he's already half naked in my bedroom.

I don't really have to be quiet walking back, but I am. It's the nerves; they kick back in as soon as I realize I'm walking down an open hallway in nothing but lingerie. Not that anyone can see me, but there's a sense of exposure here in this shared space.

Before I can get too in my head about it, I turn the doorknob and slip back into my room. George is standing and holding a pair of fishnets, but that's not what most draws my attention. No, it's the navy blue briefs that barely conceal his bulge and the delicate maroon lace that stretches across his chest.

That's when I realize I'm holding an arm across my own chest like I need to hide it. Like George and I haven't pulled each other's shirts off before. "What do you think?" I ask, sliding my arm only slightly down the front of my body.

George's body answers first, hardening against lace flowers, stretching blue elastic. His hand drifts south like he wants to touch himself, but instead he swirls a finger distractedly through the downy hair on his inner thigh. My mouth hangs open as I watch, as I mimic his motions. Because then I'm hard, too.

"Oh." I swallow, moving instinctively to cover my crotch, but George steps so close, he catches me before I can.

"It's okay," he says, silver eyes locked on mine. "You look hot— even hotter when you don't hide." Those few words tear down all my walls. It's only us two here, in our own private world. Safe.

Confidence finds me as I find my grip on George's hands, then his lace-covered hip. "Well, it's your fault for looking so good in a bralette." I glide my fingers up his sides and find its hem. We're so close, so bared, so together. Tentatively I move my hand to his chest, finding his left nipple with my thumb. I swipe it slowly across the sheer fabric, across the hard nub, and George gasps.

He looks up at me through dark, fluttering lashes, and as he presses a soft kiss to my neck, I can't help but think how his fangs would feel inside me. "How do you feel?" His words graze my skin before his lips plant another kiss on my collarbone.

"Like I want to . . ." Why is it so hard to say, after everything?

"Like you want to what?" He knows. He knows, and he wants me to say it, and that shifts my nervousness into further arousal.

"Well, I've never had sex before. I mean . . . you know everything I've done, because it's all been with you." I find myself thinking of everything George must have done, of his decades of experience compared to my weeks, and I still can't believe we found each other. How we fit so perfectly together, and how special it is that he shared himself with me. My boyfriend, the vampire.

"Do you want to have sex?" he asks.

"With you?" He's been living with me for several weeks now, and we almost always make out before bed, but I was only recently brave enough to reach down his flannels. But standing here with him, beautiful and hard, I know exactly what I want. "Absolutely."

Then he's kissing me with tongue and teeth—wet and biting. I might not have much experience, but I've had my mouth all over George for weeks now, and I know how to make him feel good. His right ear, *so* sensitive. I drag my tongue across the length of his jaw, then flick it up against his soft earlobe. He moans, wriggling in my arms, as I bite gently down, sliding his, "That tickles," into a moan.

"Do you want me to stop?"

"No."

I answer his consent with enthusiasm, sucking his earlobe between my teeth. George whimpers as I steer him back toward my bed. And he's putty in my hands, barely aware as his knees hit the mattress. I stop only long enough for him to fall onto his back— and for me to fall on top of him.

This I've done before, I'm good at, I want all the time. My mouth finds its way down his throat and the curve of his shoulder to the strap of his bralette. I slide it out of the way as George says, "You can take it off. If you want."

"Do you like having your nipples played with?" I'm asking because I want to know his tastes, but I realize suddenly how hot it is to speak those words. To speak about what turns us on.

Beneath me, George shrugs. "I liked what you did earlier. Depends. I promise to tell you to stop if it's too much." And then he's helping me expose his skin, remove the bra. Blood-red fabric revealing bone-white skin. "And hey." He stops me for a moment, looks me in the eye. "If anything gets too much for you, or you just don't like something, tell me, okay? I'm experienced, but I'm not psychic. I'm trying to check in, and I want you to enjoy yourself."

"How about we *both* enjoy ourselves?"

George smiles up at me. "That too."

"That *first*," I insist. "Isn't that the point of sex? For everyone to enjoy themselves?"

He opens his mouth—closes it. Opens it again. Finally his thoughts turn to speech. "You got me there, Howard." Then he gets me with a little pinch in my side.

"Oh, I'll get you all right," I say, grinning as I pinch his thigh, and soon we're rolling around the covers, bodies rubbing against each other's, hands slipping between thighs and exploring curves.

It feels so natural when I slide my hand beneath the hem of George's lacy briefs. The fabric is flexible and soft against the back of my hand, and he's so hard and smooth against my palm. This is it; this is heaven. Not only touching someone I care for but also being this open and intimate. This trusting.

I rest my full weight against George, grinding my own bulge against his thigh, furiously kissing his neck and chest and mouth. I want more—want to kiss him *there*. He clearly wants it, too, helping me pry free his panties. For a moment I let my fingers linger in the thick curls of his pubic hair, mesmerized by every part of him, of what he's baring to me.

I slide down the length of his body, wet my lips, and drop little kisses on each of his thighs. This is it; I'm going down on someone, just like I've always imagined. He knows I'm new to this; I'll be fine. Besides, how bad can a mouth feel?

I steady him with my hand.

Kiss the tip of him.

Drag my tongue along his shaft.

Wrap my lips around the head and *suck*.

George gasps, whimpers, *bucks*.

I gag.

Saliva floods my mouth as he apologizes.

"It's not your fault," I reassure him, swallowing.

"No, I should have controlled—"

"Well," I admit, "it's hot that you couldn't."

"I mean, you can keep going if you—"

I'm on him again before he can finish his sentence, not only doing my damnedest but also enjoying the hell out of it—of him and his delight of a body. And when I go too deep and gag again, George encourages me with a hand in my hair and with moans that inspire me to keep licking and sucking until he's bucking again and I'm tasting him.

I glance up to find George still panting, his attention divided between me and what I'm making him feel. A smile winds its way across my face as he reaches down to caress my cheek. Finally I breathe deep.

George bursts into laughter before pulling me back up toward him for a kiss. "You've still got to breathe down there."

"One of us has an unfair advantage there." I wink, wiping at the corners of my mouth.

"And would you like me to use that advantage?" he asks, rolling me onto my back. The cool weight of him feels so good against my bare skin; I can't help but reach back and grab his ass with both hands, pressing our bodies impossibly close together.

Then our mouths are on each other's again, hands in hair, nails digging into shoulders and thighs, delicate fabric stretching as we rub and slide and grip. George disappears from view, slowly gliding down my body. I close my eyes and arch up against his lips as they touch down on my neck, chest, nipples, stomach. It tickles the lower he goes—or I'm excited and squirming with anticipation.

I know what he's about to do.

"Is this okay?" George hooks his fingers in the hem of my pale pink briefs, freeing my erection devastatingly slowly. I prop myself up on my elbows to watch as he flicks his tongue across his fangs. "I promise not to bite."

Words feel impossible—anything besides the moans that escape as he gently rubs my shaft. I'm a bit worried I'll finish before

KELLAN MCDANIEL

he even starts. "Yes," I nod quickly. "Please, god, I really want your mouth on my—*oh, Geor . . .*"

His name melts on my lips as he takes half my length in his throat at once. I can't speak, can't breathe, can barely think. His lips and tongue are my world, his fingers reminding me of reality where he grips me. I have to bite down on my own arm to keep from being too loud, my other hand finding its way into George's hair.

"George, I . . ." I grab a fistful of curls, holding tight as I thrust deeper and the tips of his fangs graze my shaft. "I'm going to . . ." And then my body convulses, writhes within his hold, until I'm spent and he's kissing my legs and hips.

Crawling back up beside me, George flops onto his side, facing me, watching as I catch my breath. I feel an idle hand rub slowly down my thigh as he asks, "Good?"

It takes another moment before I can answer, and only then a whisper. "Amazing." I reach out, pulling him flat against me and breathe deep. Feels like waking up. In a way, I am. I lie with that feeling for a minute, just holding George, hot on cold, breathing and still.

But he stirs me again, and soon I roll over on top of him once more, already growing hard. George smiles impishly at me as I ask, "What do you want to do now?"

He laughs, resting his hands on the curve of my ass. "What would you like to do?"

"God." I smile. "So much. But not all of it tonight."

"Okay—then what about tonight?"

My eyes drift down between his legs. "I know there's a lot more to queer sex than penetration..." George will know all about it, and what if he thinks I'm, like, too vanilla, too heteronormative?

"Howard."

Queers aren't like straights. There are no "rules"; we've had to get creative. "Like frottage and rimming. Thigh—"

"Howard." His voice cuts through my thoughts.

"Yeah?"

"You don't have to give me the Queer Student Alliance podium speech."

I laugh. "I'm not!" (Ugh, I am.)

"I just mean," he says, resting a hand on my thigh, "we don't have to do other things in bed just to thwart heteronormativity and the patriarchy and so on, if you'd rather shove your cock in me."

"George!" I feel my face turn red but can't help smiling.

"Do you have lube?"

"Yes." I practically lunge for the drawer in my nightstand. "Free samples from a health seminar, so it's advertised to straight people, but I'm sure it's good enough for us *nasty* queers." I pause. "I've heard we don't have to thwart heteronormativity tonight."

"We don't," he says, smiling back as he brushes a cool hand against my warm cheeks. Even after all we've done tonight—what we're about to do—that simple touch means the world to me. "And do you have a condom?"

"Also yes." This time I reach for my wallet—and realize halfway through how *that* looks. "I've been carrying it around for a while, but... it's not expired!"

George doesn't say anything about it, doesn't judge me. With a kiss to my forehead, he slides my lingerie all the way off while I open the condom and roll it on like I've seen demonstrated. (Okay, so I've practiced alone, but I wanted to be ready—otherwise what's the point in carrying one?)

"Wait, I should . . ." I gesture between his legs. Sure, in porn they just dive right in, but I've read it helps to ready your partner.

"I'd like that," he says, relaxing onto his back. The way George looks at me as I press my fingers inside him, it's like we're in our own universe. Like nothing and no one could come between us.

And when we're both ready, he helps ease me into him with encouraging words, soft touches, and a lot of patience. Which is good, because I'm half overwhelmed with pleasure, half worried I'm going to do something wrong and hurt him. I try to focus, and George makes it easier, keeps his attention on me.

But there's something else I want, and I know it so suddenly in that moment that I pause my repeated refrains of *"Oh my god, oh my god,"* and blurt out, "George?"

"Yeah?"

I look him dead in the eyes so that he knows I'm serious. "I want you to bite me."

"What?" We both stop moving. "Are you sure?" he says.

"I won't die, right?"

"No," George says, baring his fangs in the bedroom for the first time. "You won't die."

I lean down for a kiss to seal our decision before thrusting into him again. Slowly at first as I find my pace, then faster as we come closer together. The thought of George sinking his teeth into my neck and drinking is almost more than I can take. I'm already so close when I feel his hand on my jaw and his mouth on my neck. Then he bites down, and I lose my breath, lose control, become enraptured.

The world ceases to exist around us—it becomes my house, my bedroom, George's body around mine, his pressure and his hold. The way his strong mouth clamps onto my neck as I moan and swallow. My whole body lights up with an ecstasy no one else can experience.

Only us. Only here. Now and, perhaps, forever.

CHAPTER 26

How am I supposed to eat lunch when I could be at home fucking my vampire boyfriend? I take a halfhearted bite of my turkey sandwich before setting it back down and giving up. At least my Tab goes down easy. God, it felt so incredible with George's fangs in my neck, blood pumping while I—

"Hey." Kenna slides into the seat beside me.

I glance over my shoulder to see if the others are far behind. Admittedly, I didn't wait or look for anyone. I've sort of been in my own world since last night. Haven't come down from my high. As I turn to face her, I glimpse the lacrosse team with their girlfriends taking up their usual three tables at the head of the room. Like, I know they're having sex—far more than I have— but it cannot be as good as what George and I did last night. It was more than getting off; it was . . .

The feel of nylon and lace against my bare skin.

George moaning as I bit down on his earlobe.

Mouths doing things that are still illegal in some states.

"Howard," Kenna says, at a volume like I should've heard her the first time.

"What? Sorry."

"Get your head in the game."

"I know, I'm distracted today. What's up?" That's when I notice how serious her expression is. "Is something wrong?" Not that the other QSA members and I aren't friends—we are—but it's usually Sue who feeds me the news I've missed. Wait. "Was another board member killed?"

It's a good thing Kenna isn't a vampire; otherwise she'd be able to sense how fast my heart is beating. But George was with me all night last night. I know that for a fact because . . . well, I was technically unconscious by virtue of being asleep, but we collapsed into each other's arms afterward and only woke up later to his sunrise alarm.

"No?" Kenna lifts a brow like I've said the wrong thing, and maybe I have. Apparently, it's wrong to acknowledge the world's a better place without people like Teddy Holley and Mr. Percy.

"Then what?"

She sighs, her face shifting to solemnity as Sue approaches. He slides his tray down on the other side of me, and suddenly it feels like an intervention. But for what? He sits, ignoring his tray. The two of them make eyes at each other.

"Then what?" I repeat, looking back and forth between them. I hate this. I wish George could be here with me, rather than me always being the one alone with a couple. Practically reading each other's thoughts, judging me for not crying over dead board members. I'm not a child; not only did I have sex last night, but my boyfriend's spent decades actually helping people, unlike the QSA, which never gets anything done.

I lose it. "Tell me!"

Kenna's gaze drops to her lap. "We weren't fast enough."

Sue fills in the blanks finally. "My mom filled Mr. Percy's open board position."

"She what?" I'm on my feet before I know what I'm doing.

Kenna reaches out, grabbing my sweater and tugging me back to my seat. "Howard, sit down," she whispers.

I slowly sink back into my chair.

"Look, we knew it was a long shot," Sue says. "But—"

I cut him off. "There are no buts, Sue. When are you going to stop pretending things are changing, and realize that the system sucks and working within it does nothing?"

"Jesus, I've never seen you so angry before," Kenna says, discomfort crossing her face. She gives Sue another look, like it's *me* who is reacting the wrong way.

Sue purses his lips like he disapproves, so I don't bother holding back. "We should be angry," I say loudly. "Fucking furious, actually."

Kenna glances around nervously. "Howard, people are looking. You're making a scene."

I am. Just like our community has done for decades, because no one ever fucking listens to us until we're making a scene. I feel bad about making Kenna uncomfortable, but I'm so sick of being quiet. Quiet has gotten me nowhere. Even Sue's brand of studied, nonviolent protest has gotten us nowhere. I look around the cafeteria at all the kids who just take shit for granted, who sit quietly as their peers—their supposed friends—get bullied and harassed and marginalized. And then I see him.

Christof, who has made my life hell for almost four years. Before I know it, I'm on my feet, my hands balled into fists.

"Howard, no!" The blood pounding in my ears blots out the sound of Sue's voice and the scraping of his chair legs across the floor.

I lunge, hitting Christof across the face so hard, it hurts. He stumbles back, stunned and blinking. For once I've caught *him* off guard. Good. I flex my hand, readying my throbbing knuckles and aching wrist for another punch. Because apparently, *action* is the only way anything ever gets done around here—real action. The kind you have to get up to follow through on. The kind George dealt Mr. Percy, and the kind I'm dealing Christof now. His dad and Sue's mom and all their shitty friends on the board will never stop stealing progress from us. They have to know we're serious, and they have to be stopped.

But before I can swing again, I'm shoved backward. "What the fuck?" Christof says. He looks shocked that I've hit him, which is frankly offensive. If I have to live with the threat of him in the halls, he should have to live with the threat of *me*. And it feels good to see him looking a little scared, off-center. It feels good to *finally* take up space and fight back.

I spring forward again, but let's be real, I'm no fighter. This time Christof easily dodges my advance. He grabs me by the shoulders and throws me into a cluster of chairs, the metal and plastic edges jabbing hard against my spine and skull. The wind's knocked out of me, and before I've had a chance to recover at all, Christof is on me. He grabs me by the hair and shoves my face into the floor. I feel a knee on my back, and now I can't move, can barely breathe. Christof brings his face to my ear. "Think you're tough shit, you little faggot, getting in a sucker punch?" he spits.

I squirm beneath him, trying to bend my knees and get my palms on the floor for leverage, but he's too strong.

"Enough!"

Suddenly Christof is off me. "I was just protecting myself, Mrs. Sullivan. He sucker punched me."

I look up to see Mrs. Sullivan and Mr. Grisanzio, the vice principal, pushing their way through the crowd of students who have gathered to watch the fight. Mr. G guides Christof away while Mrs. Sullivan crouches by my side. "Howard, what were you thinking?" she pleads. "The nurse is on her way; don't move."

Don't move.

I only just realized I've been *not moving* my whole life. Now, even if it hurts, it's time to take action.

My whole body pulses. I don't know what I expected, starting a fight. I'm not George; if I were, Christof would be dead right now, his blood on the cafeteria floor. Instead, it's only in my hair, on my lips, beneath my fingernails. The nurse said I was fine, but that doesn't make things better with Oma. She had to cancel her weekly knitting circle to come pick me up, which isn't a huge deal, though it is the one social thing she does regularly. And now she's disappointed—even though she hasn't said so directly, I can feel it.

"Howard, please come downstairs and talk to me," she calls up again, and I don't reply because I can't. "I promise I'm not upset."

I've always been her well-behaved grandson. The high school senior who spends Fridays watching movies and eating popcorn on the couch with her, rather than off drinking or party hopping. She's *never* had to worry about me before. Knowing she might have to now, I feel an inkling of shame.

A loud sigh, and creaking floorboards sound below. "I'm here when you're ready, kiddo."

But I can't afford to hold on to that shame if I'm going to make progress. Oma loves me unconditionally; she just said she's not upset. (She's not, right?)

I can't see the horizon from my window, only the houses across the alley and more roofs beyond them. Poorly hung wires criss-cross the rose-gold sunset. I'm desperate to know whether the actual sun has gone down. Desperate to see George.

The sky is purple and blue by the time I hear the trapdoor to the attic open, followed by my bedroom door. I turn, cutting the suspense, and know my face matches the early evening sky. That I'm bruised and swollen. And that's not the worst of it.

George gasps, quietly closes the door, and hurries to my side. "Howard, what happened?"

I don't start with Kenna's news. Don't start with throwing the first punch. Definitely don't start with getting the shit kicked out of me, because isn't that much obvious? Instead, I start with, "I got suspended."

He blinks as he takes my hands and holds them out. Like examining me will make it better.

He takes my busted-up hands gently between his and sits me down on the bed beside him. "Tell me what happened."

With a deep breath, I do, like someone who watched it happen rather than experiencing it. Talking through the reality of my situation triggers that shame again—a regret I didn't know was in me.

"What have I done?" I ask myself. "I've already asked my teachers for college recommendations—what if they write something bad about me now? And I've drafted my personal statement a dozen times, but what's the point of finishing my college applications anymore? It's not like they're going to accept someone who got suspended for fighting." It hits me. I knew it would. I've spent the last four years trying to set myself up to get far away from this place, and now, with one impulsive punch, I've probably thrown that away. All my extracurriculars, my studying. Keeping my head down, no matter how bad the bullying got. No adult cares that Christof deserved it, only that I started it.

"What does a 3.9 GPA mean when my transcript says I got fucking suspended for fighting? I'm going to get expelled, George. I assaulted Christof in front of, like, a hundred people." Crying with a swollen eye sucks, but the release is everything I wished that fight could have been. "What should I do?" I ask him.

His mouth hangs open and silent.

"Oh, so *now* you don't have any insight? Nothing from all those decades of yours in New York?" I don't mean to scoff, but hurt and anger squeeze my heart. "Of course you don't. I mean, how could you? You've been out of high school for, like, sixty years."

"I'm sorry. I don't know what to do here, Howard." George releases my hands and rests his on my knee.

"Don't say you're sorry—sorry for what?" I say. For the first time ever, the softness of his touch grates on my nerves. How can he stay so calm, so quiet?

"For . . ." I watch him struggle to answer. Of course, because *sorry* is just a platitude here. "For getting you tangled up in my problems," George says. "I—I was careless. Selfish. It's easy for me to forget how much life you have ahead of you when I see such a kindred spirit in you, Howard. It's almost like you've been here all along. But you haven't, and now your very real future is at stake, and that's on me." George's face falls, and he hides it in his hands, and that's when the tension flees my body. I sigh and take his hand in mine.

"It's . . . it's fine," I say as much to reassure him as myself. After losing everything else, I can't also lose George.

I cannot believe I gave up my future for a moment of satisfaction. Now I'm bloody and bruised and doomed to watch my bullies attend Ivy League schools on their parents' money, only to play sports and crush beer cans or whatever. They don't need college like I do. Don't need a fresh start, or a safer place to find and be themselves.

My mind is racing. Guess I'll have to find myself a job. Maybe Spring Meadows will hire me as . . . what am I even qualified for? "It'll be fine," I say again, and it almost works this time. "I don't need to go to college. I'm sure Oma would let us both stay here until I figure out a job or something. And once we save up enough money, we could get our own place—or travel like Louis and Lestat from the Vampire Chronicles, living large and seeing the world." I don't speculate on how much saving up would be required for that. Lestat had a lawyer and multiple bank accounts, whereas I have a monthly allowance from a grandmother who might not have many years left.

(Will she die disappointed in me?)

"Though Louis resented Lestat, didn't he?" I say, mostly to myself. Plus, they were both vampires. "Well then, maybe we could be like Veronica and J. D. in *Heathers,* ridding the world of assholes. Minus the bomb at the end."

"Howard. I'm so, so sorry," George says.

I nod. My brain struggles to imagine a future in which George and I are thriving. All I can see is the two of us living in a shitty apartment, working the graveyard shift at a gas station or . . . what else is open overnight?

No, I can't—I can't think like that. We'll figure something out. I say it in the hopes it will feel truer, pulling George against me, holding him tight. "We'll figure something out."

CHAPTER 27

GEORGE

I almost felt bad about leaving Howard's side tonight. Despite his panic and my regret and the tension I could feel driving between us like a spike—despite all that—he looked peaceful when I left him. I wish he could always be like that. I wish he never had to worry for his life or his future again.

This asshole sure won't have to when I'm done with him.

I watch him snore quietly from the third-story windowsill that looks into his bedroom. I hate that he also looks peaceful; he deserves a lifetime of nightmares, as far as I'm concerned.

Do I deserve the same for what I've done to Howard? For what I *want* to do to him? Even though he was having a hard time, his life was still on track. His teachers had probably drafted lovely recommendation letters. His transcript was nearly flawless. His résumé boasted of volunteering and the Queer Student Alliance among years of clubs and activities. It really wouldn't have been *boasting*, though, because I know he actually loves all that. And now he's "taking time off" from Spring Meadows for me and suspended from school for hitting another student.

I test the window, and it slides up.

I haven't felt a fire like Howard's in so long; it was easy, almost natural, to encourage the spark that was already there. But he isn't a monster yet and doesn't have to become one.

I'm eighty years old. I should've known better than to start a killing spree inspired by a young man with his whole life ahead of him. I showed Howard a solution to his problems he never would have reached for on his own. I did that. But after all those years of peace and complacency with James, my body was crying out for it: a return to the radical behavior of my youth. *This* is my true nature.

I drop silently into the room.

I also didn't hate what he said earlier—that we might stay together, rather than him running off to college while I watched from afar. What if we *did* travel or find a place of our own? We could. All those other vampires in books and movies save their money and invest and figure it out. We could figure it out.

Couldn't we?

I stiffen as the mattress squeaks beneath the sleeping man's weight, but he doesn't wake. He rolls over and smacks his lips together, his snoring paused as he settles back into a deep REM phase I haven't experienced since before Jacqueline moved James into Spring Meadows.

It's not too late—Howard has only been suspended. That might seem earth-shattering to him, but with the right recommendations and a good appeal, he could certainly still go to college, grow up, meet a nice mortal man like himself.

But what about you? a voice within asks. *What do* you *want?* I know I don't want to be alone forever. That I want the intimacy and companionship I had with James, though I never want to experience that kind of loss again. I want a partner in crime, which James never was, and which Howard maybe could be.

I walk slowly toward the bed. When I reach it, I bend down to his level. It would be so easy for me to kill him. Asleep, vulnerable. He's not big like that Percy man, even though he's a lacrosse player. I reach out and curve my finger through the air, tracing the purple bruise around his right eye.

Howard did that. And tonight I do this: Leave. Let Christof sleep. His reckoning will come another time. Quietly I slip back out the open window and down the side of the house.

CHAPTER 28

HOWARD

I can't help but feel like this is the last night of my life as I know it. Dramatic, I'm aware. If it's going to be, I'm going to try and enjoy it—forget, relax. Sue's still my friend, despite our diverging paths. When he texted to say he was picking me up for an early dinner on him, I didn't hesitate, and only in part because George was still asleep.

We browse our menus, even though both of us know exactly what's on order and what our favorites are—we've been coming to Papermoon Diner for years. But reading the menu at least makes the silence between us less awkward. Like, *Oh, we're just busy doing normal restaurant things.* Not at all ignoring the last few difficult conversations we've had.

"Want to split an omelet?" Sue asks, still pretending to read the menu.

"Sure," I say, even though it ends our charade. The omelets here are bigger than my face, plenty enough for two. We both flatten our menus on the table and look around like a server might save us from actually having to talk to each other.

Sue catches someone's eye, smiles, and places our order: the omelet, plus fries, and a milkshake for each of us to start.

When the food arrives, I dip one of the fries in my chocolate malt. Sue does the same, and I can't help but smile.

I wasn't lying when I told George that Sue and I like coming to Papermoon, though we don't make it here often. It's not convenient—the drive takes us north through Inner Harbor traffic. (Tourists, office workers, ugh.) The food is great, but we mostly come here because it's safe. The staff is awesome and welcoming. And I love the aesthetic—mannequins and old toys and dolls without eyes and a thousand candy dispensers. Everything is a different color, and the menu's in a font that would get your résumé rejected. Jocks and rich kids don't follow us here, because it's in the city, for one, but also because it's weird. Just like us.

We dutifully work our way through the plate of fries, avoiding conversation until Sue says, "So Tiana finally started writing her own book."

"Oh?" I perk up, glad for a topic of conversation that isn't me or George or my uncertain future. "Finally? I didn't realize she had plans to."

"Well, she mentioned it to Kenna once or twice, but I guess she finally took the plunge. And you're not going to believe what it's about."

I raise a curious brow. "I assume a queer young adult book, like the majority of her reads."

Sue grins and leans closer. "An enemies-to-lovers lesbian adult romance."

"What?!" The laugh shatters any lingering tension. "Tell me all about it immediately."

And he does, having been handed the first few chapters at the QSA meeting I obviously missed yesterday. Something about two rival space assassins who're supposed to kill each other but are obviously barely restraining their desire to make out in the cockpit.

"Wish I'd been there," I say, poking at one of the last few fries.

Sue pushes the plate toward me, a *Take them, they're yours.* "You will be soon."

"But what if I'm not?" I pause while our server sets down our giant omelet and takes away the fries plate. Sue cuts it in half and separates our portions while I continue. "Wyndhurst has a zero-tolerance policy for violence."

"Yeah, but kids get into fights all the time and are never expelled," says Sue. "See: Christof and the entire lacrosse team."

"See: their parents are all rich and on the school board," I counter with a sigh. Food will make me feel better, right? I cut myself a way-too-big slice of our crab, spinach, and gouda omelet and shove it in my mouth so I don't have to talk about my future. Sue does the same, and soon we're staring silently at each other again. "I just want to get out of here, Sue," I say once I swallow. "College was supposed to be my ticket, you know?"

He nods. "Yeah. I know, but . . . try to have hope."

I feel him nudge my foot with his beneath the table and smile—it's a weak smile, but still.

"Listen, even if the worst happens," Sue says, "you still have Oma; you still have me. You still have Tiana and Gray and Kenna and Phoenix."

"I guess," I say, even though I don't really believe him. They'll all go off to school and make new friends, and I'll be left behind. It's hard to stay in touch when you're no longer in the same school, let alone the same city or state. And are they really going to make an effort for the kid who ruined his future by getting into a fight and now works some meaningless job? God, I need to calm down. I'm getting way ahead of myself.

"Friends aside, you would still have options for further education. Expulsion wouldn't be the end." He sends me a text with a link that I barely glance at before an uncomfortable heat settles into my face. "There's homeschooling or the GED—you're really smart; you'd excel at either. And besides, you can spin almost any obstacle into a positive in an application essay. Colleges are looking for students who've worked hard and grown."

"Are they looking for queers who punch rich donors' kids in the face?"

Sue takes a bite and chews, glancing between his cooling omelet and me. Our server stops by and refills our waters. I sip the last of my milkshake.

"I don't think that's who you are, Howard. Or it doesn't have to be."

"What do you mean?"

"Just that . . . George has changed you. Ever since you two met, it's like you've been on another plane of existence."

"I'm right here."

"But you've *changed*."

"Everyone changes, Sue. It's called growing up."

"Or is it called, you met a guy, and ever since you've been weirdly cool with violence? Do you even really know him?"

"He literally explained who he was when you came over. What else do you want?" Frustration winds inside me. Sue will never understand. Never!

"I wasn't going to say anything because I didn't want to hurt your feelings, but—"

I snort. "Now you're worried about my feelings?"

"You don't look great, Howard. Like, you look real pale, and have you even noticed your hands are trembling?"

I set down the fork I've been holding and press my hands between my knees to still them. Sue isn't wrong, but he also isn't right. I can barely talk to him about George, much less explain that, yeah, just before the sun rose this morning, he went down on me and then fed from my thigh while finishing me off. The memory alone sends a ripple of longing through my body.

"If I seem stressed or whatever, it's because I'm probably going to be expelled and have to get my GED and lose touch with my friends and figure out how to hype up my expulsion like a positive thing on college applications." I glance out the window to check whether the sun's set yet.

It's devastatingly close.

"Look," I say, "I have to go." But as I begin to fish money out of my wallet—yes, even though he said he'd pay; I just want out—I feel his foot tap mine again. "What?" I glance at my omelet, unfinished. "I'm done. You can take the rest if you want it."

"It's not about the food, Howard. Just stay with me."

"I told you I have to go." Another glance at the setting sun.

"But we haven't just hung out like this in a while," Sue says. He follows my gaze before trying to draw me back. "At least finish your food."

"What are you, my oma?"

"No, I'm your friend."

Suspiciousness prickles along the back of my neck. Something's wrong. "What did you do? Why don't you want me to leave?"

"Nothing! I mean . . ." Sue shakes his head, clearly frustrated. "He's not good for you, Howard. You can't even see it; you're in so deep!" And then his eyes are glossy with tears, and I swear to *god*, if he cries over my life . . . "You're my best friend," he says. "I can't just sit by and watch some guy ruin your—"

I'm out the door before he can finish his sentence.

I've never run a red light in my life, but I do tonight. Still, I'm too late. When I pull onto my street, there's a cop car double-parked in front of my house. I park, unsure of what to do. I can see that the front door's open with only the storm door shut, which means they're inside. A buzz in my pocket tears my mind from the fear sinking into my skin. I fumble for my phone, because now I *am* trembling. It's from Sue.

Sue: I'm so sorry

Holy shit. I swallow hard as my eyes jump from window to window for any sign of what might be happening inside. Sue called the cops. He called the cops on George.

Sue: I thought it would be better if you weren't–

I don't finish reading his message. I open my texts to George and send:

Me: Don't come out of the attic. This isn't a joke

I shove my phone deep into my pocket, take a deep breath, and then head inside. I leave the door open behind me, hoping it'll encourage the cops to leave sooner. (Like, don't let it hit you on the way out. . . .)

Oma catches my eye and waves me into the kitchen, where she's sitting with a hot cup of tea. Two cops lean against the counters like they live here too. "Howard, hon."

"Yeah?" I drop my bag in the living room on my way in.

"These officers are asking about George. Mrs. Wolcott reported he's been seen in and around her home?"

"The home she's in the process of selling," a cop corrects her.

"Right." Oma shakes her head. "Howard, do you know . . . anything? I told them he's a sweet boy and that I can't imagine—"

"We can handle the questions, ma'am, don't worry yourself," says a muscular woman whose badge reads OFFICER HENDRICKS. She glances at her less impressive-looking partner, Officer Costa, who pulls out a small notepad from his pocket.

"Okay . . ." I look between them like I couldn't possibly anticipate what they're going to ask me about. Wonder if George can sense my heart racing from all the way upstairs.

"Is there a George Culhane staying here?"

I don't like the way Officer Hendricks says his name. I want to tell them both that he's my boyfriend and that he could rip their throats out, but that's exactly what I need to keep quiet. "No."

"When's the last time you saw him?"

Lie. I have to lie. When's the last time *Oma* remembers me seeing George? "A week ago? We went to the movies."

"Are you sure about that? It wasn't here in the house?" Office Hendricks asks.

Fuck. Sue would have told his mom that he saw George here. "I'm sure."

Officer Costa steps in front of the back door. There's barely any light left outside.

"What did you see?" he asks.

"Is that . . . relevant?" Why do I feel like saying *Heathers* is akin to confessing to murder?

Costa shrugs. "No, just curious."

"We like old movies," I say, avoiding the actual question. "So does Oma."

Officer Hendricks chuckles to herself and pushes up off the counter. "And you haven't noticed any suspicious behavior from him? Expensive or frequent gifts, evading questions when you ask where he's going?"

"I'm not his mom," I say. "I'm his boyfriend. And he's never given me a gift—he doesn't have to."

"Okay," she says, holding up her hands like I've offended her.

I'm trying to stay cool, but I'm still so angry after dinner with

Sue. He knew his mom had called the cops, and he drew me away from home on purpose.

It takes all my willpower not to curl my hands into fists. I bite the inside of my cheek as I stare out the kitchen window, watching the sun sink deeper and the light outside grow ever dimmer. My phone starts vibrating in my pocket, startling me, but I leave it be. I don't want to talk to Sue, and if it's George replying to my earlier text, I definitely don't want the cops to see that.

"You going to get that?" Costa asks when it doesn't stop vibrating.

They all watch expectantly as I reach into my pocket and draw out my—oh, thank god. "Just an alarm," I say, showing it to them. I'm so damn distracted, I almost forgot I added sunrise and sunset alarms to my calendar.

"Okay, well, you have our information, ma'am," Hendricks says to Oma as she and her partner walk past me and into the living room. "If you or your grandson remember or notice anything suspicious, please give us a call."

"Thank you, officers." Oma stands and walks slowly toward the front door with them.

That's when a floorboard creaks overhead. Every head turns except mine. I stand dead still, heart racing in my chest, blood pounding in my ears, body cold.

"You said no one else lives here?" Hendricks asks Oma, but her eyes settle on me.

Concern crosses Oma's face. "That's right, just me and Howard. But it's an old house. You know, sometimes it creaks and moans like an old lady's bones."

"Would you mind if we went upstairs to check, just in case?"

No! But I can't say it—not even if I wanted to.

"Go ahead," Oma says, taking a seat on her corner chair. "But I'm telling you, it's nothing." And that makes my heart sink almost as much as the fear of them finding George. Because Oma will know I've been lying to her—that even though she's always been there for me no matter what, I didn't trust her with this.

"Wait!" I cry, and turn after the cops as they head upstairs. "You can't—that's my bedroom. And even if . . . He didn't do anything!"

Hendricks glares at me as she grabs the knob on my door and turns. It's not like I was under oath or anything, and cops lie to people all the time. I'll be damned if I'm going to stand by and let them drag my boyfriend off to jail. It could *kill him.*

I step forward as she pushes into my room, messy and private and . . . it's empty. I try to keep my relief quiet with a long, controlled breath. He's not there—of course not. Probably still in the attic, or he slipped out the window or—

George steps out of the shadows, hair tousled, still wearing sweats and a T-shirt. He blinks as he looks between me and his phone.

My stomach drops, heart sinks.

"George Culhane?"

"Yes?" he answers.

"We'd like to take you down to the station to ask you a few questions. Do you have a parent or guardian?"

"I'm eighteen," he says, eyes lingering on me. "And I'll go with you."

"Thank you for your cooperation," Hendricks says, glancing at me with no sense of subtlety.

"I'm sure it's just a misunderstanding," George adds as he grabs for a sweater.

"You can't take him!" I interrupt. "He didn't do anything. Mrs. Wolcott is lying to you."

"Stand back, please." Costa steps between me and George.

"George, listen to me, please. Don't go with them." Just before he's in the hall, I shout, "What if they keep you overnight?" and he stops, reality sinking in. He's dealt with the police for decades. I *know* he knows they'll keep him for as long as they want. That inevitably, eventually, he'll see sunlight. And it will kill him.

"I'm with you," I say quietly but sincerely. "No matter what."

George twists away from Hendricks' guiding touch and catches my eye. In the shadows, I see the monster in him—and I am not afraid. He growls, "Stay behind me."

CHAPTER 29

GEORGE

There's a moment between accepting my fate and deciding to fight where I'm at peace. Eighty-odd years is a good, long run. Lots of people don't live that long, and most die not long after. If I were human still, I'd be nearing the end of my life. Fighting is exhausting, and look what I've done to Howard—what I'm still doing to him. I should have left the night Sue discovered me living at Howard's. It was only a matter of time before he told his mother the truth.

I can't blame Sue. I've known plenty of young people like him, desperate for their parents' acceptance. I'm sure he thought he was doing what was best for Howard. And maybe he was. I'm the one who put Howard and his oma in this position. They don't deserve it.

276

But that peace begins to simmer away at Howard's insistence, at his desperation and anguish. He's right to worry about them keeping me overnight. If they do, they'll have no idea why I'm refusing to leave the station in the morning. And they'll get the shock of their lives if they decide to drag me out the station doors. I might be ready for my life to be over, but not like that. I remind myself that now is my best chance—not only to save my own life, but also to not lose Howard. Haven't I lost enough people in my eighty years?

And to lose yet another person to *Jacqueline*? Her destruction stops now. Howard's with me. No matter what.

"Stay behind me," I say.

With the ease of a dancer, I spin and latch onto the female officer's neck. Her blood goes down as hot and satisfying as a holiday meal. I feel the other officer's hands on me, pulling and prying to no avail before he trades them for his baton. I tighten my hold on the woman, bracing against the hard, blunt pain. I remember that pain; it's a throwback, really. The thud of each impact resonates through my bones as loudly as Howard's shouts, though I don't really hear either. Can't hear anything but the woman's heart pounding in an attempt to push blood to her vital organs. I focus on it, drinking until I hear her pulse weakening and feel her knees buckling. I don't have to kill them, just get away. I let go of her neck and let her body fall limply to the ground, ticking her off like a checkbox on my to-do list. One down, one to go.

"What's going on up there?" Oma calls.

"Stay downstairs!" the cop shouts as he fumbles for his gun. I bare my fangs once more, but before I can grab his throat, he's down. Where he once stood, Howard stands, holding the antique lamp from his nightstand. He looks between its base and the fallen man, his hands shaking as he tries to maintain his grip.

"Howard!" Oma's slow shuffle is suddenly the loudest thing in the house. "Howard, are you okay? Tell me what's happening!" Her feet sound at the bottom of stairs she shouldn't climb, toward a scene she shouldn't have to witness.

"What did you . . . ?" I begin. But I trail off. It's not worth asking what he's done or why.

Howard answers anyway, still holding the lamp. "He was hurting you," he says as he tries to catch his breath.

How can I blame him? I'm the one who's killed before, not him. I'm the one who knows how to clean up messes. He did it, and he's scared, but he's committed. To me.

I should have left. I should have left, I should have left, I should have—

"And I love you," Howard says suddenly.

We lock eyes.

"Did I kill him?" he whispers, and this time he doesn't look.

I ignore the question. "I love you too."

I take his hand and lead him away one more time. Because one of us knows what it means to fight the law—and survive. "That won't be the end of them," I tell my strong, brave, stunning mortal boyfriend. He's never looked more ruffled, more scared, more out of breath. But he can do this; I know it. "Say goodbye to Oma. We have to go."

CHAPTER 30

HOWARD

I don't realize how cold it is until we're north of Cross Street. Not with the adrenaline rushing through my veins. Not with George's blood-warm hand in mine as we run through alleyways and between shops, sticking to the shadows.

The dull thud of the lamp hitting Costa's head plays over and over in mine. The realization of how soft flesh is and how hard skull is—that I could have killed him with more strength and the right angle. He didn't die, right? George would have known; he would have said something. I can't have killed someone.

"This way." George takes my hand and pulls me off Charles Street, away from the drunks flitting between bars. I trust him—I have to. George was born here; he knows these streets and this part of the city maybe better than I do.

I squeeze my eyes shut for a moment as I follow, trying to block out Oma's confusion as she watched George and me race down the stairs. The look on her face flashes before me: relief that it wasn't me hurt, fear at the implications of what might have happened upstairs. I'd ignored the questions she'd frantically thrown in my direction, saying only, "Stay down here," with a comforting hand on her shoulder, and "I love you." George had glanced up at the sound of Hendricks moaning, and then looked to me with a silent, *We need to go.* So we did. I didn't even really say goodbye.

To think I was worried about meeting with my principal tomorrow.

I know where we're going—knew as soon as that first cop fell. I'm not sure who's leading whom, though, or who decided that this would be our destination; we both just know like our minds are linked, and maybe that's because he's a vampire or we're in love or both. I do believe the world would be a better place without some people. And there's one person specifically who has made my life— George's life, Sue's life, James' life, the lives of my classmates—hell.

George slows to a stop, lagging behind on the curb as I reach Sue's front door. "Howard, wait," he says, not even out of breath while I am panting. He glances at the door, at me. At my cuts and bruises.

I wait, because it's George asking and I love him, but I wait too for whatever he's going to ask of me after that.

"You don't have to do this—it's not too late for . . ." He grabs my hand and tugs me close. Both of us have blood on our hands. "I just mean, you're not a killer." The "yet" hangs between us. Because he's right—I haven't killed anyone with my own hands. But I've wanted to, have encouraged George, have celebrated their deaths and wished for more. "You can still get out of this. Still have a life, go to college, keep your friends and family."

What life, though? Not the one I spent eighteen years building. Not the friends who will inevitably fall away, and not in the least because they think I'm going rabid. Not Oma, horrified by what I did and by how I betrayed her trust—or so I imagine. "How?"

"I'll turn myself in."

"Then what? Burn alive in your jail cell when the sun rises? Absolutely not—I'm not letting you die for me. Besides, even if you did, I just attacked a police offer. What kind of life would I have without you? I'd have no friends, no future. I'd be the queer freak who dated a vampire. Who lost everything and everyone he ever cared for. You can't."

I don't think George needs to breathe, but he draws a long, slow breath and takes my hands back into his. He kisses my fingers like I'm a king wearing jeweled rings. "You're right. But you can still have a *life*. Or a type of life . . ."

I look at him closely, at his mouth. His fangs. "The type of life that isn't one," I say with complete understanding. There are ways we can be together that others can't. "Let's begin now."

I knock quietly on Sue's door, not wanting to alert his mom—not yet. He opens it, red-faced and worried.

"Oh, thank god you're okay. When you didn't respond to my text, I—"

Sue gasps. George's footsteps are barely audible, but I can feel him beside me. He takes a step forward. Blood still stains his lips, like he snuck into his mom's makeup.

Sue tries to slam the door shut, but George catches it and then throws it open so hard, Sue goes flying back. And my boyfriend holds the door open for me like a gentleman as I step inside. He follows and closes it quietly behind us, turning the dead bolt.

I sigh as I bend down to Sue's level. I never wanted this. He was always the stronger and more confident of us, but the second I found that same strength to stand up for myself—that same conviction in my aims—he couldn't handle it. My only real friend. Grief floods my chest as I say, "I told you not to tell your mom."

Sue crawls backward, struggling to find purchase before finally turning and scrambling to his feet. Terror stretches across his face as he looks between me and George and shouts, "Mom! Run!"

And what luck—she appears, holding a basket of laundry. Dirty, I hope. Though bloodstains are hard to get out regardless. Her eyes widen as she sees the blood-covered boys in her living room. As she recognizes us.

She drops it and runs, but George is a blur in her wake. Sue catches my eye only for an instant, then takes off after them—and I'm not far behind. I don't know his house well, because we never wanted to spend time here after school and on weekends. Because his mom fucking hates people like us.

We catch up to them in the kitchen. Mrs. Wolcott frantically grabs her phone from its charger, but George swats it from her hands with such force that it slams into the dishwasher and then falls to the floor, the screen black and broken like a spiderweb.

As he reaches for the old landline and rips it from the wall, she fumbles for something, anything. For one of the dozen hilts in a wooden knife block.

She pulls out a knife and thrusts it into George's chest. Sue gasps—and then screams as he watches George grab his mother by the neck and hoist her straight into the air. When she gasps for breath, when she struggles, he holds her tighter.

"Howard!" Sue cries. "Do something!"

But neither of us moves. Him because he's scared. Me because I know my boyfriend can handle himself. He's earned his strength over the past few months the same way I have: through facing those who would wipe us out.

George glances down at the knife sticking out of his chest and drops Mrs. Wolcott almost as an afterthought. Like she's an annoyance rather than a threat. *A type of life.* This is what we could be together, do together. Pick off those who would pick us off, like we said. One by one. I can't help but wonder what his grace and strength would feel like in my own body after I've felt helpless for so long. What fresh blood would do for me. What I could achieve. What *we* could achieve.

Her leg cracks when it hits the floor, and she yelps in pain, gasping for breath. George is still examining his knife wound when Sue rushes toward his mother. But a pale hand shoots out between them, stopping Sue.

George's voice is calm, almost unbothered, when he says, "No, Sue," and slides the blade free from his chest. He holds it, bloody, at his side. "Your mother and I need to talk."

CHAPTER 31

GEORGE

Howard washes the knife in the sink as if Jacqueline used it to chop vegetables rather than stick it in my chest cavity. He fits it into the dishwasher—already full of dirty dishes. How convenient. We'll run it after we leave. Courteous of us, really.

I considered putting down a tarp or some trash bags on the floor, but what's the point when we already left behind a mess at Howard's house? Reckless then, reckless now. A fitting start to our increasingly inevitable new life together. Sue and his mom sit tied to kitchen chairs. Silently, because I told Jacqueline I'd tear her throat out if she made a sound. And told Sue I'd tear his mother's throat out if *he* made a sound. I don't want to hurt the boy. He'll grow up all right. He'll go to college, bring his experience as president of the QSA with him, win hearts and change minds. He's thoughtful and passionate and vibrant, and I won't take that from our community. But his mother has a lot to answer for—and Sue is better off without her.

"What do you want from us?" Jacqueline's strained voice grounds me.

"Well, that's what I'm considering, isn't it?" Not that she could know. I don't give a shit about making her feel good, though. "I thought I wanted to kill you, Jacqueline—just you, not Sue. I came here specifically to kill you. . . . But I think I've changed my mind."

It hurts, if I'm being honest. I have Jacqueline right where I want her, and now I'm not sure what I want. Her death is almost too simple an end for how she has tormented the people who were, and should have been, her family. How she's tormented class after class of queer high schoolers. But if death is too simple, then an apology isn't close to enough—and I'm only one person. It's too late for James, too late for those who've graduated. Probably too late for me as well, but I'm going to see this through, and maybe . . . maybe it's not too late for Sue.

"Wait, wh-what are you . . . ?" Sue's voice trembles as his eyes land on Howard's, desperate for help.

But none comes. Howard's with me now. He understands.

"It'll be easier to show you," I respond. And show him I do. With one hand, I tilt Jacqueline's head back, expose her neck. With the other, I brace myself for the bite. My fangs sink easily into her flesh, her throat jostling between my jaws as she screams. It's jarring, I know. Probably more so than if I'd taken out a gun and shot her in the leg; drinking someone's blood is so personal and yet so inhuman. Jacqueline *will* remember this.

I drink until Sue's screams are so loud—"Mom! Please don't kill her, please. *Mom!*"—that I can't ignore them anymore. I'm not too concerned about the neighbors; it might be a historic home, but Jacqueline has clearly spent a lot of money upgrading it; I'm sure it's soundproof. I let a final gulp of her blood coat my mouth, then turn my head and spit. Dark red splatters the kitchen tile.

I continue quietly, "I'd always wanted to meet you, you know. Georgia—that's your middle name, right? My namesake."

Jackie's head lolls side to side. She's barely conscious, but I know she can hear me.

"When I learned James had named his only child after me—I'm incapable of having my own children and doing the same—I thought . . . this is what immortality feels like. To raise someone, to impart your love and experience. To watch them grow into their own person with hopes and dreams.

"I had hoped that since your father was queer, you might be sympathetic. Actually, that you might be more like Sue here. Enthusiastic, caring, bright." I catch his eye; there's empathy in them. I don't linger on it. "Instead, you plagued your father's life and ruined mine. And then started in on your son's."

At this, Jacqueline gives me a *fuck you* look, but it's weak. Pathetic.

"I thought maybe I wanted an apology for all that you did to your father, and through him, to me. But what would that achieve?

And your approval or recognition of my love for James is meaningless. James and I have been part of each other's lives, despite time and distance, since we were teenagers—since before I became what I am now. Nothing you can say will make that any more real than it always has been."

I squat in front of her, resting my arms in her lap and examining her face. There's fear there.

"So what do I want? I want you to know that *now*, for the time being, you have your son's love. But one day—and I hope it's soon—he will recognize that you're the real monster and cut you from his life. Then you'll be all alone."

Sue sniffles in the chair beside his mother, unable to wipe the tear that slides down his face. I'm only sorry he isn't standing beside me and Howard. I walk over to him and squeeze his shoulder in solidarity, then glance at Howard, my confidant and partner. I know I'm lucky to have him, because I'm not sure I deserve this. Unlike Jacqueline, though, I love my family. My real family.

I kneel before Sue's chair and look into his eyes. I didn't come here to hurt him. He's family, too. And someday he'll learn what real love feels like. Not *whatever* his mother is masquerading as love. "You're going to do great things," I say to Sue. "I believe that, and I believe in you."

Howard crosses over to us and rests a hand, warm and comforting, on my shoulder. His words are equally so. "We should go."

Neither of us wanted this to happen, but sometimes you give up your ride home for your friends' safety, and then a monster attacks you and changes the course of your life. Or sometimes you meet a monster and he kisses you, dooming you to death, love, and immortality.

Sounds so romantic when I put it like that, but . . . there's nothing romantic about what we've done in this kitchen. Howard knows what's waiting for him once we leave this place. He wouldn't be with me still if he didn't want it. I reassure myself with his presence. That I am not the same to him as the thing that bit me under a grimy bridge. I'm still going to be the death of him.

I turn back to Sue and cut the zip tie holding his left arm. His phone I place in a cabinet across the room, showing him where it is. Giving me and Howard enough time for a head start while not leaving the boy totally helpless. I don't want anything bad happening to *him*.

"Don't ever come looking for us," I tell Sue before stepping back and giving Howard his final moment. Leaving a friend isn't easy, just like leaving your mom isn't easy.

He throws his arms around Sue, almost knocking his chair over. I watch tears stream down Sue's face as he clutches Howard's back with his free hand, and I wonder if Howard is crying too. I never knew my last moment. Never got to say goodbye to my friends Donna and Franklin. Never got to say goodbye to James—the first time.

His "Goodbye, Sue," is muffled against his friend's shoulder. It's a long, lingering hug, the kind that acknowledges there's so much more to say and they'll never get to say it.

Something tickles my cheek. When I reach up to swipe at it, a wet pink drop coats my fingertip. I wipe the tear away, not wanting to draw any further attention. This is their moment. That James' grandson will live on—and his terrible daughter, if her son decides so—is my final gift to him.

"Howard, please don't go, please," Sue cries unabashedly on his shoulder. "I'm so sorry; I never meant for all this to—"

"I know," he says, finally pulling back. Stepping back. Joining me.

I take Howard's hand—

"But it did."

—and lead him out the back door.

CHAPTER 32

HOWARD

I t's cold—so fucking cold again that the heat of the moment has fled my body and we're alone in the dark beneath an overpass. Cars rumble overhead infrequently. George looks around the place as if it's familiar. He rubs his hand across my back before drawing me against him. He's not shivering like I am. He's warm, actually. I can only imagine from the fresh blood coursing through his veins.

I let it warm me now before I go cold forever.

"This is where it happened, isn't it?" I ask.

He nods against the side of my neck. "Used to be a bridge here, but, well . . . you can't stop whatever the government decides is progress."

"We can try."

I feel George's little *hmm* vibrate against my skin.

Sixty years between one monster attack and the next. Not that I really consider George a monster. If I did, I'd have to consider myself one. . . . I suppose queers have long been considered threats. We aren't, in that we'd generally just like to live our lives in peace. But also we are, because we threaten the precious status quo. And like George said, we have to get their attention if we want change. We have to threaten what exists.

"I'm cold, George," I say. "I don't want to be cold anymore." He pulls me closer and tilts his head back so we can press our cheeks together. Slides his warm hands up the back of my shirt and rubs them over my spine.

"That better?"

I nod. We rock slowly in each other's arms for a minute against the distant sound of train horns and bar patrons. I don't usually feel this alone in the city. That's why I like it: the vibrancy of living alongside others, seeing the same neighbors on their stoops, walking to get snowballs at the corner shop, knowing that even though the party bros are a loud nuisance, someone's always around.

Then it hits me. "I didn't get to say goodbye to Oma. . . ." I don't finish, because I don't want to think of the mess I've left her in. I want to imagine it will be okay. That she'll be okay. Oma is resilient; I have to have faith. "I just don't want her to worry about me."

"I'm sorry." George squeezes me, kneads his fingers into my muscles like dough, and I melt in his arms. "You should have had more of a choice."

I don't indulge that comment, because every choice that led

me to this point was mine. I could have ignored the hot boy in the grandpa sweater at the vending machines after he slammed the door in my face. What if I had? Who would I be? Still quiet, scared, banking on the next phase of my life for the opportunity to blossom. No George.

"You promise we'll be together forever?" That last word is no longer an abstraction or metaphor. Feels so real, standing on the edge of it.

"I promise."

"And we can use our powers for good, or whatever." I can't help but smile at the phrase. Like we're superheroes, when we're very much not. Antiheroes at best, villains at worst. But, like, in the way villains have often been queer-coded: hot, flashy, and fun as hell. "Make the world better for those who're tired of waiting or can't afford to."

"We can. We will."

After a moment I add, "Just so you know, I'm still going to want a college education."

George's laugh echoes with what I imagine is his own loss, but he's no less sincere when he says, "Okay." That's when I feel his body shift against mine. Feel his hair tickle my eyes and his nose nudge at my jaw, urging me to tilt my head.

That's when I know it's going to happen. When I choose. "I love you, George."

He doesn't have to say it back. When George sinks his teeth into my throat, I know he loves me too. And as he drinks and drinks, I'm reminded of our first time. How I was inside him in every way possible. Of the ecstasy.

CHAPTER 33

GEORGE

There's a strange pleasure in walking past row houses at street level and glancing at their insides. Little dioramas of humanity, decked out with plants to remind them the world is alive or with art to inspire them. Clutter, because keeping up with everything is hard when you have a full-time job or more and are beholden to the sun. Christmas trees and menorahs alight with holiday warmth. I lean against the corner shop, just beyond the glow of its stoop lights, and look through a window where a black cat lounges.

It ignores me while I listen carefully to the television beyond it. To the clink of glasses and evening pleasantries and a woman shushing someone so she can hear the evening news.

"In a week marked by death, eighteen-year-old Howard Kuiper

has been reported missing. Two nights ago, he was questioned by two Baltimore City police officers—"

"Fucking cops," Howard huffs beside me.

"—who were found unconscious at Kuiper's residence later that evening. One of them had suffered a blow to the head, while the other victim had two small puncture wounds in her neck, resulting in severe blood loss. The high school senior has not been seen since. This comes less than a week after the death of prominent local businessman Harold Percy. His body, too, was found drained of blood. Leaves you to wonder whether whatever monster attacked the police officers didn't also claim an earlier victim."

"Whatever *monster,* indeed," I say, holding out my hand. "Wonder what could have happened to Howard Kuiper's body . . ."

Howard takes it and catches my eye, flashing a mischievous grin. Then he flinches. "Oh shit. I did it again, didn't I . . . ?" His lip is bleeding, one of his fangs tinted red.

I lean in close and run the tip of my tongue over the puncture wound. Not really kissing him, *tasting* him. Loving him for all he is and has become. "You'll get used to them," I reassure him.

A *ping* from his pocket turns both our heads. Howard pulls out his cell phone and checks the message. Really, he needs to get rid of it. These things collect too much data and are too connected to the people who know him. But it's hard, I know. Almost another death—a cutting off from the world. It was easier for me, getting turned during an era when phones were most commonly attached to the wall. Nothing to disconnect from, really.

"Who is it?" I ask.

Howard's brow creases. "Sue."

He tilts the screen so I can read the message.

Sue: Howard please respond to my texts. Everyone thinks you're dead, even I'm starting to wonder if . . . please don't be dead. Please come home. I need you. I miss you.

The latest plea in a long string of heartfelt begging. I wouldn't minimize his pain; Sue hasn't had it easy. His grief is real; wanting his friend is real. But he made his choice, and so did Howard. No going back.

I watch as Howard positions his thumbs over the screen. "What are you doing? You're not—"

"No," he reassures me. "I'm not replying to him. I'm . . . well, you can tell me it's stupid, but I'm saying goodbye to Oma. And then I'm done with this, I swear."

He's right; it's not smart. But I never got to say goodbye. Maybe it will be good for Howard—help him move on. Put his mortal life behind him so that he can begin anew. "Do what you need."

He does, and I don't look. Instead, I turn my attention back to the cat on the windowsill and give Howard his last moments of privacy.

"There," he says. "Sent."

Okay, I do glance down at the glowing screen and catch the words, *I love you so much,* and *Thank you for everything you gave me when my parents couldn't.* And *I want you to know I'm okay. And I'm sorry.* I turn slightly and wipe at the corners of my eyes so that Howard won't see.

He stares at the screen for a moment longer before swiping

the app closed and turning the phone all the way off. "And done." With that, he drops it to the asphalt and smashes his heel into the screen. The phone splinters and cracks. "Done," he says again, as if out of breath.

I lean over and kiss the cool plane of his cheek. "How do you feel?"

A smile curls across his lips. "Hungry."

When I look into his eyes, they're alight like the full moon. "Then let's go find something to eat."

ACKNOWLEDGMENTS

Till Death would not exist, first and foremost, without Christian Trimmer, who trusted me with a story both vicious and tender. And I would not be a functioning author without the constant championing and support of my agent, Seth Fishman.

Many thanks to Kara Sargent for adopting this novel and helping me see it through, faithfully, to publication. The teams at MTV and Simon Teen have been so wonderful to work with. This story would not be a book without the many of them who've contributed: Art Morgan, Nicole Tai, Jasmine Ye, Heather Palisi, Mike Rosamilia, Alex Kelleher-Nagorski, Caitlin Sweeny, Amy Lavigne, Shannon Pender, Sara Berko, Valerie Garfield, Anna Jarzab, and Nina Diaz. Furthermore, this book would be far less beautiful without the incredible skill and talent of Elena Masci. Thank you all.

Lastly—though certainly not least—I want to thank my friends and communities who keep me going, keep me writing. To my family, who unconditionally loves and supports me, even when it means skipping Sunday dinners because I'm on a tight deadline. To my niblings, who might one day read this when they can, you know, *read*. (Or not! Maybe it's uncool to read your uncle's books.) To Faith, Allie, and Tiana for their unending love and support. To the friends who imagined worlds with me, from the Shallows to Rêve and Hallowhome. To those I will continue to explore and create with—who inspire me to *more, new, different, weird*.

And to you, reader. This book—the *specific* book—you are reading is yours. Yes, even if it's a library book (because we do love libraries). There is no One Story because there is no One Reader and no one else can bring what you do to this experience. Thank you for being part of the narrative.